*A Sickening Storm - A Gripping Mystery Thriller*

*A Dora Ellison Mystery*

*Book 3*

*A Sickening Storm*

A Dora Ellison Mystery - A Gripping Mystery Thriller

Book 3

First Edition

By David E. Feldman

Copyright © 2022 David E. Feldman

All Rights Reserved

*For my family*

# CONTENTS

## Acknowledgments

Thank you to my long-time friend, Maddy Killigrew Mos, whose help with medical information has been invaluable.

Thank you to the CDC, the Centers for Disease Control and Prevention, whose website https://www.cdc.gov/ contains much information related to infectious diseases.

Thank you also to the many infectious disease laboratories—too numerous to name—along with several major media outlets, whose websites supplied me with helpful technical information.

Thank you also to the "Cops and Writers" group on Facebook for help with police-related information.

Whatever factual mistakes I've made, whether medical-related, police-related, law-related, or otherwise, have been my own.

And thanks, as always, to my wonderful readers!

## Prologue

The ride to the cemetery after work is uneventful, and so you sigh and look at the scenery. The weather has turned colder just in time for Halloween; maybe some of the little monsters would be kept inside by their parents this year. You sniffle and notice you have a bit of a cold, or, perhaps it's allergies. The foliage along the Southern State Parkway flashes by in orange and red blurs. Time was when the subtext was beauty and the art of nature, of God. Today the more accurate subtext is death. When leaves died they changed color. Was there beauty in that? Perhaps.

Once through the cemetery's stone and wrought iron gates, it's a quick ride via narrow lanes, between headstones and graves to the two graves that mattered. Once the car is parked a short distance away, you clean the area around the graves and find some smooth, small rocks to place on the headstones to mark the visit. Then you sit and talk, much the way you had before, only the conversation is essentially one way now. Still, you speak about the system's brutal unfairness and how something has to be done. The conversation is cathartic but falls far short of relief. Such injustice is intolerable and cannot be allowed to continue.

Looking at their graves, you know that Mom and Dad understand— they always have. But relief? There is none, and that cannot be allowed. So one day, it comes to you: *why not create your own?*

And so you have. Of course, you have to explain, as you do on each visit, the why of it—the justification. Innocent people, Mom protests. No one is innocent, you respond. But you've devoted your life to the good, to helping people, Dad insists. True, you agree. And your relief is doing exactly that. Medical injustices are common—very much the norm nowadays—and nothing is done. Nobody pays. Ever.

How could anyone breach the walls of lawyers, the ramparts of judges, the moats of legalese, and the mountains of administrators that the medical industry brings to bear?

Such horrific wrongs are laid bare daily, if you know where to look —all demanding redress. Who would speak for the multitudes of innocent victims, for the agony of their children?

And as the sage said, if not you—who?

So, you do the research at work, and you find the tools, the implements. You collect allies, friends—and you find the perfect source. Microbes, germs, viruses and their keepers. You give them appropriate, temporary homes. Airborne, blood-borne, food-borne, fluid-borne. Containment and transmission are very much within your scope of understanding, and what you don't know, you learn. And what you don't learn, you leave undone.

*Oh, well...*

How appropriate that during a worldwide pandemic, you are spreading your own brand of pandemic in the name of justice, in the name of redress.

In the name of love.

• • •

Afterward you check your research. This is the way it's supposed to be. Righting so many wrongs. Delivering microscopic warriors for justice. And with delivery, relief.

And then…the vials of blood are ready to visit so many potential helpers. The inhalers are prepared. The delivery systems armed. So many beds, all filled, all ready to help. So much potential justice.

Time to go to the healing place. Healing? How could such a misnomer be allowed? At least add a caveat, a qualifier—we heal, *now and then;* we cure, *though we also kill.*

But now is not the time to complain; now is the time to take action. Now is the time for business. And a good business plan must be executed.

*Now is the time for execution.*

## Chapter 1

Beach City was a small city of about 35,000 residents on a barrier island along the south shore of Nassau County, Long Island. On late summer days the beach and boardwalk were crowded with happy residents, visitors, families, lovers, and friends. Restaurants did brisk business, and nowhere more than the west end, where the young and young-at-heart flocked to bars, open air restaurants, and venues to party and enjoy live music and each other's company. Beach City's biggest challenge on summer days and nights like these was the availability of parking.

Despite the COVID pandemic, the city was doing business very nearly as usual—this city where only two years earlier, a female sanitation worker named Dora Ellison had solved the murder of a very special police lieutenant, and six months earlier, that same woman, who had briefly been a police cadet, had, with the help of a local librarian, solved the murder of the twin brother of a city council member. In so many ways, this late summer day was indeed like many others.

One place where it was not was the local hospital, the Beach City Medical Center, which had been temporarily disabled during Superstorm Sandy in 2012, but after a year of repairs and public debate that focused on the challenges of sending patients to the nearest hospital on the other side of a draw bridge, the BCMC reopened to the public amid much acclaim and fanfare.

Like hospitals all over the country, BCMC was a locus of medical industry players—from pharmaceutical companies, whose research uncovered new treatments for dire ailments and extended the lives and comfort of those with the right insurance, to lobbyists, who helped to keep such companies afloat by cozying up to politicians, to multiple levels of administrators, who often found themselves caught between drug company reps, local politicians, the insurance industry, and to the doctors, many of whom had mortgaged their lives and futures for careers that had not panned out to support the lifestyles they had expected.

And, of course, at the bottom of the pyramid were the patients who, if they had insurance, and as long as the insurance companies behaved as expected, enjoyed a reasonable standard of care, and who, if they did not have insurance or their insurance was wanting, suffered with substandard care and sometimes with no care at all.

To this complex and often unmanageable stew was added the COVID virus in early 2020, and its variants. The virus waxed and waned as people wore masks or did not, were vaccinated or were not. Life changed, activities changed. Many restricted their activities and stayed away from crowds and public gathering places including malls, restaurants, movie theaters, and concerts. Others continued to participate in these activities and some of those contracted COVID, while others did not. Some people who barely went out at all contracted it.

Life became ever more tenuous and precious.

• • •

Despite his doctor's and his wife's assurances, Marvin Josephs was anxious about his trigger finger surgery. He was in one of six beds in a medical suite that was a pre-surgery holding area. What with the low temperature in the suite and the nurses and PAs bustling around, what with his being naked under this thin, faded chartreuse gown, he was finding it hard to distract himself from picturing his hand and the little sheath in his ring finger being sliced open. He thought of his passengers—of old Mrs. Evans, who sat in the seat opposite him every day and talked about her cat Meoma, who had just had kittens. He'd told her about his own cat, Mrs. Baggins, who was so like a tidy little person. He thought about the Jameson twins, little girls from a broken home who somehow managed to be "A" students, and who both planned to be doctors. He had no doubt they would succeed.

He had been a bus driver for seventeen years, and loved every minute of it—well, except for that first week, when he had struggled with the routes, and day two, when he had driven on a state parkway where buses were not allowed. Or the moments when others on the road were less than courteous. But he took such moments in stride, and had come to love the passengers—his people—and they loved him. They were part of one another's days, sharing to whatever degree they were comfortable their trials and tribulations, their health, job, and family challenges and triumphs. Their lives.

When his right ring finger began sticking open whenever he tried to close his hand, he had ignored the problem at first. For several weeks he had been able to make a fist, but that finger had required a little extra effort. Then he had taken to shaking his hand out, which allowed him to make a fist, but eventually he had only been able to close his hand with assistance from his other hand, and for a bus driver, that was a problem. It was what led to the appearance of surgery on his horizon—in the distance at first, as he had been able to forestall the cutting with a series of cortisone shots. But eventually, the shots had stopped working, and his orthopedist explained that more shots were not recommended, as they would begin to degenerate the joint.

So, he had reluctantly gone along with the doctor's suggestion and scheduled the surgery. Thankfully, the procedure was ambulatory, and he would be home in a few hours, briefly on pain meds, then back to work and the resumption of his normal life. Back to his bus, and his people. He missed them already.

He signed the necessary paperwork and was wheeled into the operating theatre, where, from his point of view, far too many people were milling about.

And then he woke up. He had not been unconscious for very long. The surgery, he was told, had been a success. He had no pain...yet.

Alison was by his side, wearing her mask as required by COVID protocols, and telling him that the worst was over.

Alison was wrong.

• • •

Two days later, Marvin came down with what he first assumed was COVID, but a test quickly proved it was not. Then he thought it was the flu. He had a low-grade fever and chills, a headache, some nausea, difficulty swallowing. Perhaps it was strep throat, Alison suggested. But then he began experiencing anxiety connected to normal activities—fear of drinking water, fear of people, fear of food. He had never been an anxious person; both he and Alison were happy and easygoing.

A telehealth session with Dr. Ronelli shed little light on his symptoms, except to say that patients sometimes had strange reactions to anesthesia and to keep track of any changes in his symptoms and to call him back if necessary.

Two days later, the anxiety subsided and both Marvin and Alison were relieved. He had stopped taking pain medication a day earlier, so they hoped that his symptoms were a medication-related aberration.

But that night he was up all night, his thoughts running wild and, toward morning, he began hallucinating.

"Alison! There's a horse! Oh, my God—get it out! It's up on its hind legs! Alison! Call the police! Oh, my God! Oh, my God! Helllllp!"

Alison had been in the kitchen preparing soup, which she had planned to bring in and spoon feed him, since his right hand—his spoon hand—was still bandaged. She dropped the ladle into the pot, splashing herself with hot soup, cursed, and rushed into the den, where Marvin had been convalescing in a cot.

She found him, eyes bulging white, mouth turned down at the sides in a rigid grimace, legs drawn up beneath him, his back pressed hard against the wall behind the cot. He had no idea who she was.

The following day Marvin vomited until his stomach was empty, then had dry heaves, and then vomited blood. He began moving about the room, first in a crouch, and then leaping, his arms shooting out to the sides. He growled like a bear, screeched like some giant bird, and finally went into convulsions.

Dr. Ronelli, who never made house calls, made an exception, but took one look at Marvin and called 911. Marvin was rushed to Beach City Medical Center, where he lay in the emergency ward for an hour and a half, and then was admitted to a private room. Soon after, the alarms connected to his monitors went off, and after a flurry of futile activity, Marvin was pronounced dead.

• • •

Alison Josephs sat before a social worker and a nurse, who did their best to explain that Marvin appeared to have been suffering from an infection that, they were certain was unrelated to his surgery.

"I find that hard to believe," Alison said, clutching her rosary beads, pressing a thumbnail into them one at a time. "He was fine when he went in for the surgery, except for the finger."

"Well…as far as we know," said the social worker, whose name was Lola Edelstein.

"He was!" Alison insisted. "And I'm fine. How could he have had an infection? He had no symptoms and I had no symptoms."

"Still, it does appear that he may have been infected." The social worker's phone rang. She pushed the button for that line and picked it up. "Lola Edelstein," she said, then listened and sat back, stunned. She hung up the phone. "That was the lab. We had them fast track Marvin's blood work and the two tissue samples from Marvin's brain that were required once we had a preliminary diagnosis."

"Tissue … from his brain? What diagnosis? I don't understand." Alison was clutching her beads with both hands now.

"Your husband died from…rabies."

• • •

The following day, Marvin's cat, Mrs. Baggins, was euthanized, as was required upon a positive rabies test, despite Mrs. Baggins's lack of symptoms. Alison also received a call from Lola Edelstein confirming the hospital's findings that the disease could not possibly have originated from any of their staff, representatives, equipment, facilities, or processes.

Alison sat for hours at her kitchen table, staring at their cat's food dish and Marvin's empty chair, unable even to cry.

## Chapter 2

Ricardo Morales was exhausted. He had tried to get out of bed to shower, and then to feed and walk ChaCha, his bulldog. He had planned to head to his job as senior line cook at The Elegant Lagoon—a job he enjoyed, and where he was allowed more creativity and autonomy within his position and his little area of the kitchen than many of the line cooks he knew at other restaurants.

He had been tired, then exhausted, for days, but the Lagoon had been host to two weddings, a bar mitzvah, and a *quinceañera* in the last three weeks and he had known he would be drained in the days following these events. He'd been prepared.

But this was more than work-related exhaustion. He barely managed to crawl out of bed and give ChaCha her breakfast, then take her out to walk in front of the house, where she peed and clamored to come back inside. ChaCha was asking for food—nothing new for his beloved eating machine—but she hadn't touched her breakfast, which was odd. He took a closer look and shook his head, disgusted by his own lack of attentiveness. He had given her tuna out of a can rather than her food. He called his sister Margarita to see if she was available to help out with ChaCha and pick up a few things at the store. If he was going to stay home from work, he knew he would never make it to the supermarket.

Margarita arrived forty minutes later, having stopped at the post office to return a pair of shoes she had purchased from Amazon. She knocked, and when Ricardo did not answer, she used her key to let herself in.

"Ricardo?" She stood just inside the door, listening for his answer. Nothing. "Ricardo? Dónde estás?"

She heard his groan and followed the sound to the bathroom, where she found her brother kneeling in front of the toilet, his black bangs flopping over his eyes and saliva dripping from his lips.

"What can I do?" Margarita asked, concerned. "How can I help?"

Ricardo's head lolled forward and from side to side, like some animal in the throes of pain or sickness. She knelt beside her brother and took him by the shoulders. "Let me help you stand up and we'll get you to bed."

He turned his head to look at her, and Margarita was startled by his blank expression. Her brother seemed not to know her. She quickly found that he could no longer speak or walk, and his body shuddered with tremors. Once she got him into bed, she called 911, who sent an EMT team with a stretcher that was fitted with sprockets and tracks, like a tank, for traveling down stairways. Margarita waited several hours with Ricardo at Beach City Medical's ER, filling out forms and verifying insurance information, while explaining to the triage nurse and admitting authorities that Ricardo was neither mentally ill nor on drugs. He was sick and needed medical attention, ASAP.

The hospital personnel disagreed. They strongly advised that Ricardo be admitted not to a room upstairs in the medical wing, but to a floor in the combination detox and mental health unit, so that whatever drugs he might be on could be allowed to leave his system, and the status of his mental health could be properly evaluated. Margarita insisted that their family doctor be consulted and, once found, Dr. Stevenson agreed with the hospital staff's decision. Margarita reluctantly approved Ricardo's admission to the detox and mental health ward. Later that night, she received a call that Ricardo had passed away. She rushed to the hospital to try to learn more.

"We believe it was a stroke, or perhaps food poisoning," said a resident named Orville who had seen Ricardo the previous day. Orville wore a pair of impossibly thick glasses on his forehead. He glanced at Ricardo's chart, without the aid of the glasses, then back at Margarita. "We'll run some tests and get back to you," he promised.

Margarita felt bereft—at sea. Their parents were gone, and while they both dated, neither had been in a serious relationship for many years. They had each other, and ChaCha. They were one another's family.

She went back to Ricardo's apartment and found a shoebox of old family photos in his closet, made herself a cup of hibiscus tea, and began thumbing through them. In one she saw herself and Ricardo on a neighbor's lawn, with the little gang of kids from their block, with whom they had played red-light-green-light, giant steps, and hopscotch.

She sat for an hour next to the window in Ricardo's kitchen in the dying afternoon light, her memories sparked by the images before her. Finally, she put the photos back in their protective plastic bag, lay the bag gently in the shoebox, covered the box, returned it to the closet, and went back home to wait for the hospital's call.

Three days later, as she was boxing Ricardo's belongings, which she had planned to either throw out or give away, Margarita finally received a call from a neurologist named Graverman who was affiliated with Beach City Medical Center, who explained that Ricardo had contracted something called granulomatous amebic encephalitis (GAE), a condition that is nearly always fatal.

"I've never heard of it," Margarita responded. "I've heard of encephalitis; that's a brain infection, yes?"

"That's right," said Dr. Graverman. "This particular brand of encephalitis is caused by something called a Balamuthia infection, which is exceedingly rare, but does happen."

"How?" Margarita wanted to know. "How did this happen?"

But Dr. Graverman had no answer for that.

• • •

Suzanne Chaikin loved to run. She was fifty-five years old, in terrific shape, and had been running for just over thirty years. Early on, running had been an escape from a painful breakup with her boyfriend at the time, a breakup she was now grateful for, because that pain was what introduced her to her favorite pastime. She felt free when she was running—the only time she truly did. She was a bird, a gazelle, a feather in the wind—aloft and gliding—emotionally, physically, and spiritually. She was soaring!

Running was such a positive in so many areas of her life, but ultimately, the greatest benefit she gleaned from this, her favorite exercise, her hobby, her meditation, and her prayer, was spiritual.

Suzanne had been aware of the pain in her hip for several months, and at first she had tried herbal and so-called natural remedies, and she had thought that had worked. Now, though, months later, she believed that her perception may have been wishful thinking or a placebo effect.

Within a month of trying the natural remedies she cast them aside in favor of a cortisone shot—which had worked for nearly a year. Then she had another, which worked for a few months. Ultimately, once the pain was a steady six on a scale of ten—nine when she tried to run—she had decided to have hip replacement surgery.

She had laid on the table in the operating theatre, naked except for a flimsy puke-green gown. The doctors, nurses, and their assistants were helpful and comforting. When she mentioned how cold she was, a blanket was immediately brought to cover her.

That was the last thing she remembered before waking up in recovery in a lot of pain. She was given ten milligrams of a painkiller, which helped, though some pain remained. An hour and a half later, she was in a room with another patient whom she could not see, as a curtain bisected the room. Almost immediately, a physical therapist arrived and got her on her feet and walking a few steps. Once she managed that, Suzanne was encouraged to walk into the hallway as far as she could, which was perhaps fifty feet, then back again. She was certain her running practice helped, since she was accustomed to pushing herself to go further and faster, and that competitive spirit served her in this initial healing phase following her surgery.

The pain on the second day was much worse. The remnants of the surgery anesthetic had worn off and the pain pills barely dented the searing agony that spread up and down her right side. She could do little but moan, beg for pain medication, and wait.

Albert was with her once she was in her room. He hadn't shaved in two days and was a handsome, loving presence in his stubble and ugly green turtleneck sweater. He held her hand while she cried from the pain, and gently reminded her that her discomfort would soon subside. And when she cursed in response, Albert remained steady and patient and there for her.

She would soon be home, selling and maintaining website and SEO services for their clients, many of whom were lawyers who relied on their web presence and search engine rankings as sources of business. While her mother did not visit, Albert reminded Suzanne that Muriel was asking for her and sending hugs and kisses.

Once she was able to walk up and down three steps she was sent home, where another physical therapist and a nurse visited her, and she was taught to care for herself. She learned new ways to put on socks, and to use a grabbing implement to reach for ingredients in the kitchen.

She was progressing just fine until the fifth day, when everything changed. She awoke with a terrible headache and stiffness in her neck, which progressed quickly and brutally until her neck and head pain overtook her hip pain, which had by that time diminished significantly. She suddenly lost the ability to walk. Her ability to balance on her feet was gone, which puzzled her physical therapist.

Her headache, a new, horrific pressure pushing outward from the inside of her forehead, had become intolerable. She grew nauseous and threw up in the hospital bed. The following day, Suzanne lapsed into a coma and three days later, she died.

Albert was on the phone nearly all day for several days, trying to find out what had happened. While he and Suzanne were aware that all surgeries, including hip replacement, carried with them some element of risk, the fact that she had sickened so quickly and died with no diagnosis or treatment was bizarre and unacceptable.

Three days later, Albert received a call from an out-of-state lab. A Dr. Samuel O'Neill explained that Suzanne had died of Naegleria fowleri, also known as brain-eating amoeba, a disease that was all but unknown in the United States, where only a handful of cases were reported annually.

"How could she have caught this thing in the hospital?" Albert demanded to know.

"I'm not in a position to comment on how she caught the disease," said Dr. O'Neill, "but it usually enters the body through the nose, and is most often found in infected warm water. I'm so sorry for your loss."

## Chapter 3

Alison Josephs had a vial of Xanax in the medicine cabinet. The prescription had been Marvin's, prescribed by a psychiatrist he had seen for all of fifteen minutes. After his only appointment and what he had termed the "wacky" experience following his taking of the pill, he had wanted nothing to do with Xanax or the psychiatrist who had prescribed it, so the pills had languished in their shared medicine cabinet, first on his side and then, once he realized they were still there, on hers. She hated to waste medicine, whose cost was one of the great scourges of modern times, in her opinion.

After two days on Xanax, her to-do list had grown long and daunting, so she stopped taking the pills, put them back in the medicine chest, and went to work. She had to arrange for Marvin's funeral, contact the bus company, three banks, four credit card companies, two insurance agents, and their family lawyer. She left the relatives for last because they would be the most painful, and indeed she cried with his sister, her brother, and three of their cousins before finding herself with her patience spent, her sanity tottering, and one last number to call.

The hospital.

She put the call off by bringing up the hospital's "contact us" page and filling out a form, but five minutes later found herself again looking at that number, which, she quickly learned, was the facility's main switchboard. She clicked to the orthopedic surgery department, but found no contact information—just an information-only internet brochure. The department did not seem to have doctors, nurses, or assistants with available email addresses. Next, she returned to the "contact us" section and looked for a place to lodge complaints, but found none. So she called Dr. Ronelli's office, but was told by a recording that the office was closed, though he had so-called convenient hours on Tuesdays, Thursdays, and Fridays. Today was Wednesday.

She then called the hospital's main number and found the switchboard operator polite and receptive, but busy. After several minutes on hold, the operator returned to the line and suggested Alison reach out to the hospital's Patient and Family Advisory Council, whose function was to promote a harmonious relationship between Beach City Medical Center's patients, administration, staff, medical personnel, and the community at large. The office was closed for the day.

Alison took another Xanax.

• • •

Margarita found a listing on the Beach City Medical Center's website for Patient Advocate, along with a phone number. She called and, when prompted, left a message summarizing what had happened to Ricardo and asked that she be called back as soon as possible.

A different number was listed for bilingual Patient Relations, so she called and left the same message in Spanish. A third number was listed for the Performance Improvement Department, so Margarita repeated the process with a call to that number.

She suspected that the people at the other ends of these numbers communicated with one another, because she received a call back an hour later from Patient Relations, but never one from the Performance Improvement Department. The woman, whose name was Rose, was compassionate and polite and assured Margarita that the Beach City Medical community shared her family's grief and was there to support her in any way they could. Margarita explained that support was nice, but she wanted answers. Was it really possible that Ricardo had died from encephalitis caused by a Balamuthia infection, which was so rare that only several hundred cases had ever been reported in all of human history? Rose explained that medicine is an inexact science and that everyone walks around vulnerable to disease every day. In fact, Rose said, Balamuthia typically takes weeks or months to appear, and so it was certain that Ricardo had come into contact with the disease well before his hospital stay, an unfortunate circumstance the hospital's personnel could not possibly have foreseen, prevented, or avoided. Margarita asked Rose the same question she had asked Dr. Graverman. "How could this have happened?"

"While we cannot know for sure how your brother contracted Balamuthia," Rose explained, after putting Margarita on hold for fifteen minutes, "it typically enters the body when soil contaminated with the Balamuthia amoeba comes in contact with a break in the skin or when infected airborne dirt particles are inhaled. Ultimately, we cannot know for sure, but please know that we are *always* here for you."

Rose gave Margarita the web address of a grief support network that was affiliated with the hospital. Margarita did not take down the information. She had her own grief network—a family that included two sisters, another brother, and seventeen cousins.

"There is always the possibility," Rose noted, "that Ricardo may have infected others at the hospital." Margarita quickly hung up the phone.

• • •

Albert Chaikin had hoped to bury his beloved Suzanne quickly, as is Jewish custom, but the medical center wanted to perform forensic tests to learn whatever they could about her death. Albert sat *shiva* for a week, but did not refrain from all activity during that period. He had been a corporate lawyer for twenty-five years, and while malpractice was not his expertise, he was acquainted with several malpractice attorneys, so he reached out to Benjamin Schwartzberg, an on-again-off-again golf partner whose specialty was medical malpractice. After a twenty-minute conversation, Albert hung up, disappointed. Ben had listened to the facts of Suzanne's case, then asked a few questions, then hesitated.

"This isn't going to be what you want to hear, but I'm your friend and I'm going to tell you the truth."

"That's all I can ask," Albert said.

"Malpractice is a tricky thing. Absent a smoking gun, it is difficult to prove. I'm not saying I won't look further into this. I'm your friend, and I will, if that's what you want. But malpractice—I honestly don't see it as a legal course of action."

"What about forensics? Can't we have an expert investigate how this could have happened?"

"We could try, but again, and I'm not saying this is a hundred percent, but I don't think we'll get anywhere."

"And why is that?"

"Because forensics is about determining cause of death, time of death, and so forth."

"Exactly!"

"In this case, we have that information. She was killed by a brain eating amoeba—forgive me if I don't have the technical name."

"I do—Naegleria fowleri. I've been seeing it in my sleep."

"Well, what we would want to know is how that amoeba got into her body. What were the circumstances, where did it occur, and how? That's not really what forensics does. That's honestly a much harder thing to track down."

Albert thanked Benjamin and called the New York State Department of Health, by whom he eventually was given similar information. He then called two criminal lawyers, both of whom referred him to medical malpractice attorneys. Both also told him he was free to go to the police, but that their answers would likely be the same. People get sick. People get rare diseases—tragedies, certainly, but not crimes.

He was tempted to go to social media and rant about the hospital, but was smart enough to know that he would end up on the wrong side of *their* lawyers if he did. But he did have one ace up his sleeve.

• • •

George S. Campbell received the intercom call telling him that his cousin Albert was on the line. "Put him through," he said.

George was in his mid-fifties, a shade over six feet tall, and perhaps thirty-five pounds overweight. His face had a grayish cast, he wore brown rimmed glasses, and his thinning hair was dyed a deep brown and punctuated by red highlights. His speaking voice had the deep timbre of a radio announcer. He listened carefully and politely, and he radiated an aura of power that had taken him far in business because it was combined with his baritone eloquence to lend an air of gravitas and resonance to his words.

"I'm glad to hear, Albert, that you've gone through the channels we make available."

"My wife is dead. She stayed in your hospital, and now she's dead of a practically nonexistent disease!"

"I'm so sorry for your loss, Albert. I know Suzanne meant the world to you. We all loved her."

"Even in her fifties, she was an athlete. She took care of herself. She's had both doses of the COVID vaccine and the booster. She did nothing risky."

"Sometimes even the most careful of people have the most terribly unfair situations show up, and that seems to be what's happened here."

"Can you look into this, George?"

"I already have. When something of this nature occurs, it's always brought to my attention. What took Suzanne's life is something that is exceedingly rare and difficult to diagnose."

"But you're sure that was the cause—"

"We are, Albert. I'm *so* sorry, but yes, we are. We will handle the necessary arrangements here, as well as transportation to a resting place or funeral home of your choosing."

Albert sighed. "Thank you, George."

• • •

After ending the call, George made two more calls. He was aware of the three bizarre deaths that had occurred within a few weeks of one another, and their exceedingly rare yet nearly always deadly causes. He had spoken with the personal physicians and specialists who had seen all three patients, as well as with every resident, nurse, and other staff that had cared for them.

His first call was to Dr. Madison Laghari, a medical examiner for an upstate county whom George had met two years prior at a conference in Atlanta, Georgia. Dr. Laghari had impressed him because she was not only an ME but also a forensic pathologist. He was pleased that she was available. Once the preliminaries were out of the way, he got to the point and told her about the circumstances surrounding the fatalities.

"As saddened as we are about these deaths, which I can only assume are unrelated, I have to consider the hospital's well-being."

She finished his thought. "And you want to track down the source of these diseases to keep the hospital out of any liability cross hairs."

"Well, I wouldn't put it that way," he huffed. "We have to make sure that our medical investigations leave no stone unturned in getting to the root of each of these untimely deaths. We pride ourselves in being state-of-the-art, and it's my job, as the desk where the buck stops—"

"To see to it that there's no hospital vulnerability."

He laughed. "Ever the charmer, Madison. I had forgotten how blunt you can be."

"I strive for accuracy—and truth."

"Perhaps one day you will work directly with the public and acquire a bit more nuance in your communication."

George could hear the impatience in her voice.

"Here's what I've acquired, and what my job entails. As I'm sure you know, we are trained to look for cause of death, which you have explained has been done by your own ME in these three cases. We look at toxicology, serology, which is the analysis of blood, and the sanctity of evidence collection, including DNA. We also occasionally, but rarely, examine living patients—usually in connection with sex crimes. What I can say without driving down there is that there seems to be nothing that leads one to believe these are anything but tragic accidents of circumstance that happened to occur within a short period of time. We look at crime scenes, but in this case, there are none because these are not crimes, and I see no evidence from where I sit that the hospital bears any responsibility. There is, in fact, nothing to say where any of these unfortunate individuals caught the diseases that killed them, except perhaps, in one case."

"In which case?"

"The encephalitis that killed..." She paused, reading. "Mr. Morales, whose cause of death typically requires at least a few weeks, even months, to reach the toxic level, which would mean that he certainly would not have contracted the disease at Beach Medical."

George could feel all of the muscles in his chest relax at once. "Is that something to which you'd be willing to testify?"

She hesitated. "I would testify, yes. But what I would say would sound very much like what I just said."

"Thank you, Madison. I know your time is valuable."

"It is. But before I go, there's something else you should know—in fact, you probably already know it, but it really should be top of mind.

These cases need to be reported to the Department of Health. Your ME and medical director must do this; it's inherent in their jobs. But I'm sure you know this. Have a nice day, George."

George then called Dr. Roger Ravell, BCMC's medical examiner and explained that he wanted to delay the reporting of these cases to the DOH. Ravell argued that he was obligated to make his report as soon as was feasible. George explained that the survival and imminent growth of the hospital relied on the medical examiner's delicate handling of his report. He went on to explain that he was only requesting a brief delay, easily chalked up to bureaucratic miscommunication. Dr. Ravell reluctantly agreed.

George then made a similar call to Dr. Akira Matsumoto, Senior Medical Director and Patient Safety Administrator of Medical Affairs, and made the same request.

"I can't do that, George. We are obligated by law to—"

"This is a special request by Dr. Ravell, who is still working on his final, detailed analysis of these cases. We want to be absolutely certain of the contents of our reports."

"Well…if Dr. Ravell needs a little more time, I don't see the harm in a brief delay. The accuracy of our reports is paramount."

George's next call was to another long-time acquaintance he rarely had occasion to speak with, only this one was a lawyer who was kept on retainer by the hospital.

"Sandra."

"Mr. Campbell. I was wondering when this call would come."

"You've heard."

"Everyone's heard."

"That's not good."

"Whether it's good or not doesn't much matter, from a legal standpoint. What matters are the circumstances of these deaths and whether or not the hospital is legally liable."

"And…?"

"One never knows what might happen in a courtroom, but in my opinion, there is negligible, if any, legal liability. Have you spoken with a forensic—?"

"Pathologist. Just now."

"And?"

"She says the same."

"Well, then."

"And yet, neither of you says there's zero vulnerability."

"There rarely ever is."

## Chapter 4

Adam Geller was sitting in the office of his private investigator business with his feet on his desk and his back to the entrance. He was not-so-subtly conveying the message that he did not want to see anyone. He was watching a TV comedy on his iPad, something he did often. Why not? He was the boss, and he had needed constant cheering up since his wife, Abigail, passed away six months earlier. His business specialized in divorces, specifically, catching cheating husbands—well, spouses; wives, he found, cheated too, though for some reason husbands rarely sought his expertise in proving their cases. Perhaps shame that their wives needed satisfaction elsewhere was the reason. His job was not proving their, or anyone's, case. His job was pursuing the truth.

Adam was sixty-four years old and five foot eight, with hair that had been gray for twenty years and was finally getting around to thinning. He also sported a gray mustache and goatee, and the remnants of what had once been a muscular physique. He had been a bit of a gym nut in his day. Unfortunately, it was no longer his day. He walked, stooped slightly forward, unless he remembered to stretch, which was perhaps once a month. He had a slight limp from his so-called good hip, which was letting him know it wanted to be freed from his body in favor of a new titanium replacement, perhaps so that it might go off and see the world or do whatever liberated hips do.

Adam was irritable and impatient and was fine with that, though now and then he got too wound up and had to remind himself to take it easy.

If, somehow, he forgot to tell himself to take it easy, Thelma, his crabby, fifty-seven-year-old office manager, would be sure to remind him, and do so with her trademark withering glare and a car horn voice that would give anyone pause.

He noticed with satisfaction that his office was the usual mess. Thelma had given up trying to convince him to organize his case work. Somewhere under all these papers was a desk. According to Thelma, somewhere under this mess was also his late wife; she had said that once and only once. It was the only time he had ever truly lost his temper with her. Since then he had maintained a studied, cantankerous distance, sending her vibes that warned her against daring to invade his preoccupations. They coexisted warily, each needing the other and, on the surface, not happy about it.

His coat was on the floor in a closet that was devoid of hangers. He had long eschewed a landline in favor of his cellphone. He used apps. His office wasn't really his office; it was a room with a lot of paper strewn about. What made the room his office was his knowledge of which paper was which, where it was, and what relevance each had to any work that may or may not be at hand.

His office was him; he was his office, and he was always on the move. This—this was a rented space filled with papers, a bit of furniture, and somebody's nasty old aunt. It was also a four-alarm fire waiting to happen.

His home was similar to his office, except that it included an equally messy bed and something that passed for a kitchen circa 1972.

His cellphone rang, then rang a second time.

"You gonna get that?" Thelma honked. His cellphone was his business line, and also rang on a second phone that Thelma kept on her desk, which was as neat and orderly as Adam's was messy.

He pretended not to hear. "I asked you a question!" she demanded.

Adam smiled to himself. Annoying Thelma was one of his few happy diversions.

"Hey, Mister! I'm talking to you."

He made his voice as dainty and pseudo-polite as he could. "Thelma? I'm sorry, I can't hear you. The phone is ringing. Would you mind answering it, please?"

"Would I mind," she muttered. "Rhetorical question, if you ask me." But she did answer. "Geller Investigations. Hold on a second." The foghorn voice again. "Mister Geller? You here to take a call from Detective Gerald Mallard?"

"Of course, Thelma. Thank you *so* much."

He took out his phone, removed his feet from his desk, and sat up, hoping that the change of posture was conveyed in his tone of voice. "How can I help you, Detective?"

Mallard's brassy tone was nearly as annoying as Thelma's honk, even through a cellphone. "I got a call from someone who's looking for a private eye. You available?"

"Who is it? What's the case about?"

"He's the CEO of Beach City Hospital."

"George Campbell?"

"Look at you, all up on current events."

"Current events? My Abi died at that facility, and you joke?"

He could almost hear Mallard's sigh.

"So, what's the case?"

"I have no idea."

"You have no idea?"

"Is there an echo on this phone? He won't tell me. He says he'll only talk to his lawyer and a highly recommended PI. That would be you."

"You highly recommended me? So now I'll have to get you a Christmas gift, right?"

"Don't get too excited. You're the only PI I know who isn't either an idiot or a barely reformed asshole."

"You have his cell?"

"I do, but he wants me to give him yours if you say you're interested. So…you're interested?"

"Just give him my number. We'll see if I'm interested."

Three minutes later, the phone rang again.

"The phone's ringing!" Thelma brayed.

"Is that what that is? I knew I'd heard that sound before, I just couldn't place it. I thought it was tinnitus."

"You gonna answer it, Mr. Smartass?"

"Actually, yes, Thelma. I think I'll take this one."

"I think I'll take this one," she mocked. "After that, turn up the heat!" she yelled.

"Turn up the heat?"

"Hell just froze over."

Adam sighed and pushed the answer button on his phone. "Geller Investigations. This is Adam."

"Thank you for taking my call, Mr. Geller."

"Please, call me Adam."

"Thank you, Adam. This is George Campbell, CEO over at Beach City Medical. Gerry Mallard told you I would call?"

"How can I help you, Mr. Campbell. Or, should I call you George?"

George's tone went from hopeful to frantic. "We have a situation here. Our patients have been coming down with terrible and rare diseases."

Adam didn't answer right away. "I don't understand. You're a hospital. You're exactly the place for them to be."

"No, no, no. These are patients who are here for other things. A trigger finger—a nothing operation. And the patient suddenly has rabies. A hernia patient—here to have a hernia repaired. And he comes down with a Balamuthia infection that is so rare as to be virtually impossible, and then goes on to die of GAE."

"GAE?"

"A rare and deadly form of encephalitis—brain infection. And most recently, a hip-replacement patient suddenly is killed by brain eating amoeba."

Adam raised his eyebrows. "Well, while these are undoubtedly tragic, aren't such possibilities part of the risk that goes along with being a patient in a hospital?"

"Our conversation is confidential, right? Like attorney-client privilege? I should have asked that first thing."

While Adam knew that the answer to this question was "no," he was intrigued. "Of course."

"Good. So, yes—technically. We are always at some risk of contracting illnesses. I suppose that would be what would come out in court—not that anyone's talking about court."

"So, no one's raised the possibility or threat of malpractice?"

"Adam," George's vocal timbre had deepened and taken on the austere gravitas of a principal scolding an obstreperous child. "We never, ever use that word."

"I'm glad to hear that. But you haven't answered my question."

"Which one? You asked two."

"Aren't these tragic deaths a possibility at a hospital that sees as many patients as Beach City Medical?"

"Technically, legally, yes. But in a more practical sense, all three of these cases are impossible. It would be like, like, like suddenly coming down with rinderpest!"

"Rinderpest? Never heard of it."

"Of course you haven't. It's been eradicated since 2011."

"Ahh."

"Look, the reason for my call is that I think someone is infecting people with these diseases on purpose."

"You think this is criminal? As in, murder?"

"Exactly. Although in one case, it seems the patient had to have been infected months prior to having been here."

"See? There you go. A logical explanation, however unlikely and tragic."

"I've brought the subject up with some colleagues and our ad agency, and everyone thinks the idea is crazy. Well, it may be crazy, but I want to hire you to prove me wrong. We have our holiday gala coming up in less than two months, and this could be a PR nightmare."

Adam was silent for a moment, thinking about the families of the victims. His own recent loss had left him with a heart that lay vulnerable to others' losses.

"Did Detective Mallard tell you that we primarily handle divorce cases?"

"He did, but he also said he trusts you. Said he worked with you on numerous cases when you were on the force."

"True."

"And he has faith in your skills, and in your discretion, so I'm hoping you'll make an exception."

"Mmm."

"So, you'll take my case? I would be happy to pay your fee in advance."

"Can you give me an hour or two, maybe a day?"

"Of course. Take some time. Think about it. But please, don't wait too long. God knows who will come down with what next!"

Adam hung up and dialed Gerry Mallard's private line.

"Adam?"

"Gerry, why would you steer a case like this to me? You know I don't handle much besides divorces and anyway, this George Campbell sounds like he's a few bananas short of a bunch!"

"I don't know what you mean by 'a case like this,' when I don't have any idea what the case consists of, except if George Campbell is desperate for a PI, you're the man I'm calling."

"Well, I don't take criminal cases, if that's what this is, and I certainly don't take medical cases. I'm set up for a particular niche, and I do a good job with that niche, and it pays and I don't have to run all over hell and creation, risking my Medicare-ready body on some crazy client's idea of a crime."

"Hey, it's his dime."

"I don't want to waste anyone's money."

"Er, ah. You know…" Mallard began.

"What? Spit it out." Adam rolled his eyes. "What do you have up your sleeve, Gerry, and has it been there all along?"

"I'm wearing a short-sleeved shirt, Adam. I think I may have an answer to your problem, and possibly George's—despite not knowing exactly what his problem is."

"Oh, really?" Adam tried to sound as doubtful as he could.

"Let me make a call, and if it goes the way I hope it will, I'll call you back with a possible introduction."

"To what? To who?"

"To whom, Adam."

"I just said that."

"You said…just give me a little time. Someone—two someones, actually—have just recently been talking to me about a problem that you may just have solved."

"Well, I don't know what you're talking about, but I'll wait a little while before I call Campbell back and tell him I'm not interested. I just feel bad for the guy. He's not in a good place."

• • •

"Dora? Gerry Mallard."

"Hello, Detective. What can I do for you?"

"It's not so much what you can do for me, as what I can do for you."

"Well, you've got my attention."

"After you left the academy, you and Missy talked a bit about becoming private investigators."

"Well, yeah, but we realized that even if we went through the process of getting the license, we don't have the experience. While I have a bit of training from my time at the academy, you really need more—much more, when it comes to running the business and getting clients. It's a catch-22. To become a private investigator, you need experience. But how do you get that experience, unless you're a private investigator?"

"There's another way."

"Sure, have a career as a cop first."

"Something just dropped into my lap. What if you could work for a private investigator, under his license? I happen to know one who might be in the market for an apprentice—maybe two, seeing as how he has work he's reluctant to turn down, and won't do himself."

"As in a live case?"

"That's right. Are you interested?"

"Let me talk to Missy. You think he might take on both of us?"

"Talk to her. Then, if you want, I'll set up a meeting and you can ask him yourself."

• • •

After a two-sentence conversation during which Missy's response was "Yes, of course!" Dora called Detective Mallard, who set the appointment up for first thing the following morning, prior to Missy's shift at the library.

Upon entering the office of Geller Investigations, which was in a strip mall several blocks from the library, Dora and Missy found themselves face to face with an unsmiling woman with suspicious eyes and a 1950s hairdo. She leaned forward, elbows on her desk.

"And this is about…?"

"We have an appointment," Dora explained. "Set up by Detective Gerry Mallard."

"I don't know about any appointment." The woman clenched her lips and hardened her glare.

"It's okay, Thelma. They have an appointment," called a voice from the back of the office.

Thelma swiveled her chair. "Nice of you to tell me." She turned back to Dora and Missy. "Well, don't look at me! Go on back."

"Lovely woman," Dora said as they headed toward the rear of the office, where they found the owner of the voice facing away from them, watching an old rerun of *The Odd Couple* on an iPad. They waited, and, after a few moments, he paused the video and looked at them. He didn't say anything at first, just appraised the two women.

Dora was five feet, eight inches tall and one hundred fifty five pounds, all of it muscle. She walked lightly, on the balls of her feet, like the athlete she was. She wore her dark brown hair short—just over her collar. He skin was slightly tanned from walks on the beach. Missy was shorter, rounder and softer than Dora, with a paler complexion, and features that spoke of her South Asian heritage.

"So you're the famous Dora Ellison," he said finally.

"Not sure how famous I am—but I am Dora Ellison."

"Excuse me for not shaking hands. Ever since COVID…"

"We feel the same," Missy volunteered. "I'm Missy Winters."

"The librarian. I know. Detective Mallard speaks well of you both. Says you're a couple of pretty decent amateur detectives, if"—he looked at Dora—"occasionally too enthusiastic."

"Yeah, well. Some people ask for it."

"If you're working for me, you can't go off and make those decisions for yourselves, as it can blow back on me…and my license."

"Working for you?"

"Well, you want to be private detectives, don't you? I might just give you the opportunity. I have a case—medically related—that's come to my attention."

"We have no medical background," Dora said.

"But your partner's a research professional."

Missy nodded. "I do have access to medical databases."

"Well," Adam sat back in his chair, swiveling slightly from side to side, watching the two women over steepled fingers. "Like you, I have no particular medical knowledge, but a good detective can look into just about anything—ballistics, causes of death, trace evidence. There are always experts to find and consult with. I don't typically take on cases like this one, but I'll bring you up to speed, if you're interested, and if we come to an agreement, I'll train you, explain what you can and cannot do, and you'll work the case and answer to me."

"Seriously?" Dora breathed.

"Extremely seriously. You'll get one day of training. The rest will be on-the-job and via printed material I have around here somewhere." He waved at the garbage dump on his desk.

"You'd hire both of us?" Missy wanted to know.

"Better to have a partner—work as a team. Keep an eye on each other. I will need to sign off on everything—to be informed about whatever you learn and whatever you're going to do. In the beginning, you'll be trainees and you'll be literally investigating—looking into things—and that's all. You'd start with that. Not actually doing. Just looking into. You don't know enough yet to be taking actions that might be wrong, might endanger people, particularly clients or their cases. Is that clear?"

"Abundantly," Missy said. "One question. What about my job at the library?"

"Initially," Adam explained, "you'll be learning part-time. We'll work around your library hours. Maybe your partner here will fill in the hours when you have to be at work. Just let me know when your shifts are, and we'll figure it out. Sound good?"

Missy looked at Dora and nodded, then looked back at Adam. "Sure!"

"When do we start?" Dora asked.

"There's no time like the present," Adam said, and he nodded toward two office chairs. "Pull up a chair."

• • •

Once out of the car and through the lot and into the building, your fear returns, but it's vague, thanks to your scripts. The leather packet of full syringes and spare vials digs into your waist from under your lab coat—the pressure a faint reminder of tonight's purpose.

The two RNs on overnight whom you've befriended wave and call friendly "hellos" from the nurses' station, and then go back to their monitors and paperwork.

The corridor turns just past their station, and the hall becomes a maze of IV stands and beds. The ward is so full that patients have been temporarily situated in the hallway. Such is modern medicine during the era of COVID-19. Everyone is tested and/or vaccinated and boosted, and everyone wears masks.

Coughing and labored breathing echo through the ward; heart monitors beep and hum. So many patients have been displaced by the virus. Someone cries out. Pain moans through tired lips. An old woman groans.

You stop for a moment in the hallway. You hear music, but not the empty, sterile, generic brand one hears so often in elevators, malls, hospitals, or other public venues. No, this was music played on a real piano and sung with a very real, very human voice—a voice imbued with feeling, with heart. With love. The music stops you in your tracks, and you are irresistibly drawn to it—a siren song.

But the song ends, the magic ends, the spell is broken, and you continue on your way.

The first patient, in PICU—the pulmonary intensive care unit—is propped up on three pillows. Her dyed black hair falls about her shoulders, and her prominent cheek bones, large eyes, and thick lashes suggest that as regally beautiful as she is today, she had once been more so. She reminds you of your mother, who died of a broken heart after your father's horrific mad cow death. Her tanned, lined face suggests that she is or was well-to-do and had, perhaps, lived in Florida or some similar climate. An endotracheal tube is connected from the base of her throat to a respirator. A sphygmomanometer checks her blood pressure at regular intervals. The ICD-9 number on her chart is meaningless without appropriate decoding paperwork; the same could be said for the CPT code. Thoracentesis, the removal of fluid from around her lungs, had been performed, and tumor cells had been detected. High levels of CEA in her blood indicate cancer—in her case, lung cancer. She had been prescribed an antiemetic for nausea, and cyclophosphamide, the prescribed chemotherapy.

The woman's prognosis is not good. A moment bent over her, and the syringe comes quickly out of its holster. The woman sighs in her drugged sleep. The syringe is returned to the far chamber of the carrying case.

On to the next patient, the next messenger.

• • •

The first of Dora and Missy's lessons with Adam Geller focused on finding people who did not want to be found. Skip tracing relied on first having accurate information—starting with a name, even a partial name, and date of birth. If the date of birth was unavailable, look for anyone who might know the individual and ask them. The person you were searching for or their known associates might have social media accounts. If they did, those accounts might provide a line of communication. Their Facebook feed might show their location or movements. Their friends' Facebook accounts might also provide clues or reachable associates. An attorney might be able to subpoena cell phone records, and the numbers found in those records could be called for information.

If no friends or family were available, a drive through their last known neighborhood, along with knocking on a few doors, might yield useful information.

Publicly available or membership databases and county courthouses could provide official records about property ownership and marriages, as well as civil and criminal files. The folks at the courthouse would probably be happy to help you find the information you needed.

After about an hour, Dora felt as though the insides of her head were turning to cotton. "What about our case?"

Adam looked steadily back at Dora for a long moment. She was beginning to wonder if he had heard the question when he answered.

"Before I say anything, what's your take?"

Dora glanced at Missy. "Well, since our client wants to know if these illnesses were given to the patients on purpose, I'd learn what I could about the illnesses in general and about the patients, to see if that's even feasible."

Missy looked dubious. "What about HIPPA laws? No doctor or hospital is going to give us access to patients' private medical information."

Adam gave a half-smile, raised an eyebrow, and pointed at Missy. "Good point, but don't worry about it. They will. You'll see."

Missy looked surprised, then thoughtful. "I guess we'd look at who had motive and means, right?"

Adam nodded. "You would."

Thelma's voice called from the front of the room. "Any idea how many people are pissed off at their hospital, doctors, or insurance companies? Try the immediate world. Good luck!"

Adam rolled his eyes and answered. "Ever the optimist. Thank you, Thelma. That'll be all," He turned his attention back to Dora and Missy. "I'm going to arrange for you to meet with George Campbell, our client, the hospital's CEO, along with Dr. Akira Matsumoto, BCMC's Senior Medical Director."

"Already?" Missy asked. "But we don't have very much information. Shouldn't we be better prepared?"

"I think we're ready," Dora said, with an encouraging nod to Missy. "We're not expected to know very much. We just ask questions and make note of the answers, maybe record them."

"Right. Just make sure to ask permission if you're going to record," Adam reminded them. "Mr. Campbell is expecting to be interviewed sometime today, and he is making Dr. Matsumoto available as well, so I suggest that you get yourselves over to the hospital, then call me before you split up and interview each of them separately. By the time you're there, I'll have information as to where to find them."

## Chapter 5

Dora and Missy had driven to Adam Geller's office in Dora's turbo, so they continued on to the hospital together.

"I know that, as a librarian, you're used to looking up your answers," Dora began, intending to reassure Missy. "But here, the conversation is the research. This isn't like school, where you study, memorize, and get tested. This is on-the-ground learning. We just ask about the patient and the disease. Why was the patient at the hospital, how is the disease that killed them typically transmitted?"

"I guess I could research that too, on my own," Missy suggested. "And we'd need to know what precautions were taken, who their attending physicians, nurses, and other personnel were. Yikes, this sounds like a lot!"

"One thing at a time," Dora said. "We can do this."

True to his word, Adam had arranged for Dora to meet with George Campbell in his office and for Missy to meet with Dr. Matsumoto in the hospital cafeteria in the basement. Fresh N95 masks, which were a requirement for all visitors in the facility, were available for them both at the hospital's front desk.

As they entered the main interior hallway, they heard the music. Piano, beautifully played, along with vocals, beautifully sung. The two women stopped, glancing at one another, and listened.

"I know that voice," Dora commented, and began walking toward the music.

The song ended and there came the sound of faint applause as another song began. The first had been an American Songbook standard, sung by Frank Sinatra or Tony Bennett. The next song was a famous Motown hit.

They arrived outside a large room with double doors and floor-to-ceiling windows that faced the hallway. Dora and Missy stood at the windows, watching and listening.

"Kelvin Franklin," Dora observed, and when Missy looked confused, she explained. "He's part of the crowd I know from Rudy's. Friends of Rudy and Agatha, and of Vanessa."

Vanessa Burrell was Agatha and Rudy Raines's sister-in-law, whose brother, Jesse, had been murdered six months earlier. Rudy's was a bar owned by the six-foot-four-inch husband of Agatha Raines, one of Beach City's City Council members.

They and a large group of close friends congregated by night at Rudy's Bar, where some of the men participated in a not-so-secret poker game, and by day at Mae's Diner. Several of the friends worked at Beach City Medical Center, where Kelvin Franklin often entertained elderly, infirm, or memory-challenged patients, to their nearly unanimous delight and appreciation. Clinicians agreed that their enjoyment of Kelvin's music brought them healing and, in fact, restored some of their lost memories—bringing them back to the days when they had first enjoyed many of the songs.

Kelvin was ruggedly handsome, with high, sharp cheekbones and quiet, watchful eyes. He was married to Martine, the love of his life—a woman beloved by everyone with whom she came in contact. A large, motherly woman with luscious, creamy, coffee-colored skin that was the envy of all her friends, and either scarlet- or lavender-colored lipstick.

She loved to quote psalms, but her favorite quote was "it's not about having what you want; it's about wanting what you have."

Dora and Missy listened to two more songs, at which point Kelvin noticed them, gave a bright smile, then turned back to his audience.

"We should get going," Missy suggested.

"Meet here in an hour, or text me," Dora suggested, and Missy nodded her agreement. Dora thought she saw a diffident look on Missy's face. "You okay?"

"I guess." Missy sounded hesitant.

Dora took her hand reassuringly. "You can do this." She pointed confidently at her friend. "Hey, you're a *librarian*."

Missy giggled. "Yeah. I am."

"Okay, then."

When Dora reached Campbell's office, the door was open and the hospital CEO was seated behind an enormous wooden desk.

Dora knocked.

"Miss Ellison?"

Dora nodded and Campbell beckoned her in. His desk took up nearly half of the room. A computer and small stack of papers sat on top, next to a picture of a red-headed young woman. Behind him stood two large wooden cabinets that matched the desk. The walls were filled with framed photos of Campbell at hospital events, dinners, banquets, and meet-and-greets with officials at every level of the medical community and government, along with several sports and entertainment celebrities.

Campbell stood and indicated one of the chairs arrayed opposite his desk. "Have a seat. Please excuse me if I don't shake your hand."

"I understand and feel the same," Dora agreed and sat where she'd been directed.

Campbell looked surprised, as though he had not expected that response. He rubbed his face with his left hand and began. "So, my lawyers have advised me that if I am shown to have impeded an investigation, I can be charged with obstruction."

Dora nodded. "I'm no lawyer, but that makes sense."

"And yet," he held up a finger, "I don't want to cause unnecessary public panic."

"'Course not."

"As I'm sure Geller has told you, I have my suspicions that these illnesses were intentionally transmitted."

"So I'm told, yes."

He shook his finger at her. "I want you to understand that my—that our—top priority is containment."

"Of course. Do these diseases spread easily?"

Campbell shrugged. "You'd have to ask the medical people that, but I suspect that each one is unique."

"But to ensure containment—"

"I didn't mean medical containment, though of course we want that as well. We have experts for that, and they'd better do their jobs, if they want to keep working here. No, I meant containment of awareness, of knowledge of what's occurred. After all," he shrugged again, "what's really happened here? Some folks got sick and died. A shame, certainly, but part of life and, particularly, life in a hospital."

"I'm a little confused, Mr. Campbell, as to what it is exactly you'd like me to do."

He gave her a hard look. "Do you expect me to tell you how to do your job?"

She held his gaze. "I expect to have clarity as to the parameters of my work for you."

George stared at her, unblinking. Then he smiled, and waved his finger in the air. "I like that! You've got spunk. I like spunk." He sat down, his expression still serious but less antagonistic. "This is an unofficial investigation—a fact-finding excursion, let's say. And if or when you uncover anything 'police-worthy,' we will of course call in the police or the CDC or the Feds."

Dora digested this. "What about HIPPA issues?"

"Mmm. I'm glad you asked. You're a civilian and a non-hospital employee and, on the face of it, cannot have access to patients' personal records."

"Exactly."

"However," he held his finger up again. "Every patient signs a release, as part of their admissions or pre-surgery packet, that grants law enforcement, including hospital security, the police and," he waved his hand, "multiple other authorities access to patient records in case of an emergency. I am temporarily hiring you as part of our hospital security team." He pointed a finger at Dora. "You are hereby deputized. I will put that in writing and fax it to that intransigent woman who works for Geller."

"Thelma."

"Why in God's name does he keep her on? Anyway, if we need it, I know a judge or two at just about every level of government who ought to be willing to procure warrants. Oh, and one other thing."

Dora waited.

"No PR. The hospital gala is in, let's see, six and a half weeks, and we need to raise at least five million plus to pay for state-of-the-art diagnostic equipment we've already had installed in oncology and pediatric cardiology, and a new, specialty wing that is already in the planning stages and just about ready to move forward. We're already promised much of what we need and we cannot jeopardize that funding. If this is all just bad luck, there'll be nothing to say about it publicly; it will be over and done with. But if this is criminal and, worse, ongoing, which I'm sure it isn't—we'll have a shitshow on our hands."

• • •

Dora waited about twenty minutes in the hospital lobby until Missy found her and they were back in the car, heading toward Geller's office.

"So I learned why Campbell really wants to hire us," Dora said, glancing at Missy. "He's terrified of the effect bad press will have on fundraising. There's a gala in a month and a half and the money is funding a new wing."

"Money," replied Missy. "Doesn't surprise me."

"What'd you learn?" Dora asked.

"That Dr. Matsumoto is deeply concerned about these cases," Missy explained. "Not so much about PR. I get the impression that he's a doctor who, while he might be aware of hospital politics and money, doesn't care about those things nearly as much as he does about the health of patients."

"I'm glad you heard something positive. This guy—" Dora shook her head. "Just glad we're contractors and we don't work for him permanently."

"Well, I liked Dr. M—he said to call him that. Says everybody does. He explained that the protocols and processes at the hospital, which were state-of-the-art before COVID, have been strengthened and tightened since the pandemic."

"So he says. Yet, even if that's true—"

"I think it is."

"Even if it is, we've seen a few years now of some disease making mincemeat of everyone's medical protocols. So why not here and now?"

"Good question. But this isn't multiple cases of one disease—one of the definitive aspects of a pandemic. It's single cases of different diseases. Extremely unlikely, given the rarity of these diseases—which are all pretty much off the charts."

"Wasn't one of these people supposedly infected well before he stayed here?"

Missy nodded. "That's confirmed. Seems to take the possibility of people getting the diseases here off the table, which will be a relief all around—though not to the families, of course. As unlikely as this situation is, bizarre coincidences do happen."

"Mmm." Dora thought about this. "Did Dr. M say anything specific about protocol?"

"He did. With his permission I recorded what he said on my phone, but I'll paraphrase, and we can write it up later for Adam. He said that first, the patient's doctor would identify that the patient has an infectious disease and treat it as best he or she could."

"Yeah, I get that."

Missy continued. "And it would probably stop there unless the disease is a particularly unusual or infectious disease as these are, or if multiple patients contract the disease, or if it's an infection that must be reported to the Department of Health."

"What happens then?"

"Depends on what's decided at that level. Infectious disease specialists might get involved. Dr. M said that before that happens they'd want to contact trace and learn about the patients' travel patterns and other aspects of their lives to see how they might have contracted their disease."

"I guess that makes sense."

"And for patients who have died, the medical examiner gets involved."

"Right."

"There's something else." Missy paused. "The most pernicious diseases are kept at secure biohazard containment facilities. There are a limited number of people with access, and if someone with access were to be engaged in the criminal spread of one of these diseases, they'd probably want to be able to keep from getting the disease themselves."

"Interesting. Do the diseases that killed the patients in these cases qualify as biohazard diseases?"

Missy shook her head. "No idea."

"Hey, look at that." They were stopped at a light, and Dora was pointing to the street corner diagonally opposite them. A man was screaming at a large beige dog that was barking, its teeth bared. The man had a metal leash in his hand, and it appeared to Dora that the dog had slipped its collar and was turning on him. He needed help before he got hurt, and before his dog hurt someone else. The animal looked ferocious. Part Rottweiler, part Doberman. She grabbed the pepper spray she'd kept from her stint at the academy, threw the car into neutral, then jumped out of the car and ran across the street, leaving her car door open.

Missy was aghast. "What are you…aw, come on! Don't get involved. You might get hurt. Oh, for God's—" She gasped as the man whipped the leash—which was a length of metal chain—around, clipping the animal's side. The dog yelped and Missy could hear the man screaming at the dog as he wound the chain around his hand, leaving a short piece hanging free.

"You're coming with me, you stupid fucking mutt!" He reached for the dog's collar, but the dog leaped away and crouched on its front paws, growling and snapping at him, yet leery of the chain, which the man swung, striking the dog on its left ear and eye. The dog cringed away, and the man lurched toward the animal, but was stopped in his tracks when Dora tackled him at the knees—his right knee, specifically— which gave. The man crumpled to the ground, screaming and clutching at his knee, which had made a popping sound as he fell, and flipping onto his side to see what, or who, had hit him.

"Ahhh, sh—who the hell are you?"

Dora pried the chain from his hand, twisting his fingers with joint locks, which left the man crying out, not knowing which body part to protect.

"You have no right! That's my fucking dog!"

"Your dog? Your dog!" Dora wrapped the chain around her fist and pounded the man's nose, which broke and spouted a small fountain of blood. "Your dog? I don't think so. Not anymore!"

The dog was whining several feet away, bleeding from the left side of her head. Dora approached her and held out her left hand while slowly and gently reaching for the side of the dog's head with her right, so she could better see the injury. The dog continued to whine, obviously in pain, but allowed Dora to approach.

"How 'bout you come home with me, girl? Would you like that? Would you, huh, sweet baby?" She knelt next to the dog, clasped the leash to her collar, and led her across the street.

The man had been moaning and struggling to get up, but now he watched Dora lead his dog away in agonized astonishment. "Hey. Hey! You can't do that. You're taking—she's taking my dog! Somebody stop her!"

A woman jogger who was standing several feet away and had been filming on her phone held the device up. "You really want people to see this?"

"Fuck you!" he snarled in her direction, but the woman shook her head and jogged away, leaving him clutching his leg and looking around for help as Dora opened the turbo's back door and led the dog in.

"Look what I found," she said to Missy, still breathing heavily. "I've got a new dog—a buddy for Comfort. What should we call her?" Comfort was Missy's chocolate-colored Yorkshire Terrier. Dora was back in the front seat, had started the car and was driving again.

"You can't just take a person's dog, hon."

Dora glanced at Missy. "A guy hits an animal like that, giving up ownership of the animal should be the least of his problems. Ooh, I know. I'm going to name her Freedom. We're going back to my place. We'll fill Adam in later."

## Chapter 6

As soon as they arrived at Dora's apartment, they took Freedom out for a walk; the dog seemed content and accepting of their new arrangement. Once they had her safely back inside the apartment, Dora left her with Missy and went out for supplies.

An hour later, Dora returned with four kinds of dog food, a dog bed, a second leash and collar, various sizes of pee pads—just in case—poop bags, and a combination food and water dish. She had also come down with what seemed to be a sinus headache, and stopped at a drug store for cold medicine.

She found Missy sitting cross-legged on the floor next to Freedom, who was lying on her side. She was rubbing the dog's belly and Freedom's eyes were nearly closed. As soon as Dora came in, the dog jumped up and began barking, and Missy had to calm her down, stroking her head and neck and reintroducing her to Dora.

Missy suggested they call the local veterinarian to make an appointment to have her checked for shots. Dora made the call.

"What did the vet say?" Missy asked once Dora was off the phone. Freedom was again on her side on the floor as Missy continued to rub her belly.

Dora had taken a tissue from a box on the coffee table and was blowing her nose. "I can bring her in first thing tomorrow and they'll look at her. The tag on her collar says her name is, or was, Lady."

"Does your building allow dogs?"

Dora smiled. "Long as they're potty trained and not too loud. Way ahead of you." She sat down on the couch. She preferred her apartment to Missy's because it was more comfortable—shaggier, was the way she thought of her place. Her chairs and couch had thicker padding and extra pillows. Her walls were painted a deep shade of purple that was Dora's favorite color and sported posters of female athletes that Dora admired.

"Do you think she'll get along with Comfort?" Dora asked.

Missy scooted over to the couch, folded her arms over Dora's legs, and leaned toward her face. "Maybe we show her how our two households can get along."

"Mmm," said Dora, and she leaned toward Missy, meeting her halfway, and kissing her slowly, gently. Missy's kiss back was soft, warm, and wet, and grew ever so slightly more urgent. And Dora responded. She was a little worried about Freedom's response to their lovemaking and had not planned for it to happen so soon, but…*c'est la vie.* Freedom left the women to each other, preferring her own daydreams and Dora's floral print carpet.

• • •

Afterward, they lay naked on the floor next to one another, and Freedom came over and lay next to them. Missy was doing a Sudoku on her phone; Dora was thinking.

Missy laughed. "She knows."

"She knows what?"

Missy turned onto her side to face Dora. "What's going on."

Dora gave a hint of a smile. "And what's that?"

Missy touched the tip of her finger to a spot just below Dora's chin. "Love."

They kissed.

"Why wouldn't she? Dogs know about love."

"Or lack of it." Missy was rubbing Freedom's head, and Freedom walked several steps away, then turned back toward them. "She wants to be fed," Missy suggested.

"So do I." Dora was looking at a pattern of light brown water stains on the ceiling. "If you wanted to get hold of some rare infectious diseases, where would you go?"

"Other than to find an infected person, I have no idea. To some particular part of the world where they occur naturally—or however they occur. Maybe bring back an infected bat or a fly or something." She paused. "Or, to a lab that deals with them."

Missy got up, slipped her underpants and shirt on, and went into the kitchen, which was an extension off of the living room. "I don't think Campbell has much to be worried about."

"Why not?"

Missy opened one of the bags of dried dog food and poured a bit in a dish, then put some water in the other side of the dish and lay the dish on the floor. Freedom immediately came over and sniffed the food. "Because there doesn't seem to be any way for the hospital to be liable. How do you prove someone got a rare disease in a particular place?"

"By finding someone else whose got it and gave it to them?" Dora got up and dressed, then went to the kitchen door to see what Freedom would do.

"Would that hold up in court?"

"You never know with lawyers and judges." She smiled as Freedom took a few bites; her smile faded as Freedom stepped away and stared at them.

"Finicky girl," Missy mused.

"I'd say Campbell ought to be worried, liability or no, for the patients' sakes, don't you think?"

Missy had opened the refrigerator, taken out a container with some leftover cooked chicken breast, and mixed it in with the dog food. Now Freedom ate heartily. Missy turned to Dora. "I suspect that in public, on the news, and at press conferences, Campbell will be the very picture of concern."

Dora agreed. "But what if these were crimes?"

Missy looked at her, thinking. "It's still only mid-afternoon. Let's make a few calls and learn what we can." She went over to the dining room table, to Dora's computer.

Dora nodded toward Freedom, who was looking at them expectantly. "I'm going to take her out. Probably about that time."

"I'll look up any labs that might be in the area—see if they deal with rare diseases."

The temperature was in the high sixties, somewhat warm for mid-October, so Dora wore the sweatpants and T-shirt she'd worn all day. She'd been right about it being Freedom's time to go out. The dog intuitively understood what Dora hoped would become their schedule and did her thing right away, at the curb, two buildings away from Dora's. Because Freedom was a good sized, youthful-looking dog, Dora took her for a run around the block, and Freedom took to it, happy to bound ahead of Dora, only to look back mournfully, as if to say, "Come on! Can't you keep up?"

Both she and Freedom were panting when they returned to find Missy at the dining room table. "I found four labs in the vicinity. Two were definitely not what we want, but I did find two infectious disease labs east of the city. I called one—both seem to be named for the scientist or doctor who runs the place."

"What did they say?" Dora asked as she removed the leash from Freedom's collar and watched the dog make for her water dish and lap greedily.

"I called the Ramesh Babu lab."

"Ramesh Babu being...the scientist?"

"An infectious disease specialist. That's what they're called."

"What did he—Ramesh is a he—?"

"I think so. I don't know. I never got him on the phone. The person who answered asked what this was in reference to, and when I told him, he said that Dr. Babu was too busy to discuss it."

"Huh. I wonder how we get past that?" Dora was looking at Missy's features, which glowed white in the light of the computer screen. She couldn't help but think of Franny. Her mind drifted back to the lovemaking with Missy that was so recent that the scent of her was still fresh in her consciousness. Missy was sweet and kind. But Missy wasn't Franny, who had taken Dora's heart when Dora had been barely old enough to give it. Missy wasn't Franny, whose body excited Dora as no one's ever had. Perhaps expecting Missy to be Franny, or to be her equal, was unrealistic. Missy was Missy—kind, gentle, sweet, supportive, and logical.

"What?" Missy was looking at her with concern. "You're looking at me funny."

"Oh. I was just thinking about what you said, about the labs and Ramesh," Dora responded hastily. "Let's call the other lab, but do it on speaker."

Missy nodded, adding, "I made some notes, created a 'George Campbell' directory, and saved them there." Missy nodded toward her laptop screen.

Dora leaned over Missy's shoulder toward the computer. "Good idea."

Missy dialed and clicked the speakerphone.

"Traxle Labs at NYSUNC," a woman said. Missy pointed to the lab name on the computer screen, which was named for its specialist, Dr. Yvonne Traxle, and was affiliated with the New York State University at Nassau County—NYSUNC.

"Is Dr. Traxle in?"

"This is she."

"Oh, yes, um. Hi, this is..." Missy froze, and Dora leaned in and spoke. "My name is Dora Ellison and I'm working with Beach City Medical Center."

"Yes. Hi, Dr. Ellison. How can I help you?"

"I'm not a doctor. I've been hired by the administration to look into some incidents of apparently rare illnesses we've had, to see if we can learn more about where they are prevalent, how they're transmitted, and so forth."

"And so forth." Dr. Traxle repeated in a patronizing tone.

Dora didn't answer.

"What are the diseases?" Dr. Traxle asked.

"Rabies, Balamuthia encephalitis, and—"

"Did you say Balamuthia?"

"I did."

"Well, first of all, you're probably wrong, since there have been maybe two hundred and fifty cases diagnosed—as in, in the world, as in, ever. And second of all, if you do have a case of Balamuthia encephalitis, someone's got a problem because it's nearly always fatal."

Dora paused. "Yes. I believe the case has been confirmed, and the patient died. I'm calling to try to learn more about where it's found, how it's transmitted and so—" She stopped herself before saying "so forth" again.

"It's found in dirt, just about everywhere. And it's transmitted when infected dirt gets into a cut or open wound."

"I see. And how long does it take for a person to get sick after exposure?"

"Normally a while. Weeks—months."

Dora and Missy looked at each other.

"And rabies?"

"Pretty big variable there. Could be days. Could be a year. Did you say you had a third disease?"

"Brain-eating amoeba?"

"Naegleria fowleri—really?"

"It would seem so."

"All three of these diseases are among the most fatal in existence. In the latter case, we're talking about a bacteria-eating microorganism that isn't technically an amoeba, though it is commonly referred to as one, but which does indeed cause a deadly brain infection. You say you've had cases of all three of these at your hospital?"

"Apparently."

"Goodness! The odds of that, except perhaps in the case of rabies, are astronomical."

"Hence my call."

There was a brief silence. "What else did you want to know?"

Dora and Missy looked at one another; Dora nodded encouragingly, as if to say "Well, go ahead."

"Um, what do these three illnesses have in common?" Missy asked.

"Other than their mortality rate?"

"Well, yes. For instance, could they originate in the same place?"

"Ahh. Hard to say, but yes, I suppose it's possible. The latter would tend to come from bodies of warm fresh water—ponds, perhaps, or poorly maintained pools. More likely in the south than here. Rabies of course could come from infected animals just about anywhere. And Balamuthia is found in soil in many places."

"So they could potentially be found in the same location."

"Potentially. Yes."

"What about transmission?"

"Well, you know about rabies. Balamuthia occurs when contaminated soil comes into contact with a cut or an open wound or when airborne infected dirt particles are inhaled. But it's just so rare. The time frame from exposure to infection would be anywhere from a few days to a few weeks, and for Naegleria fowleri, a few days to say, two weeks."

"I see, and what about—"

"Check that. With Balamuthia, it would depend on the source of the infection. Typically you'd see symptoms quite some time after exposure, unless exposure came from organ transplant. Then—"

"Would it be possible for all of these to be given to people on purpose?" Missy interrupted.

There was a long silence. Then, "Excuse me?"

"Could these diseases be purposely given to the victims...I mean, patients?"

The woman on the other end of the phone sounded flustered. "Well, goodness. There would be issues of containment, and somehow ensuring that the individual responsible isn't infected, but...I suppose so. You're talking about murder? Do tell me more."

After obtaining Dr. Traxle's guarantee of discretion, Missy was able to learn that the three deadly diseases could indeed potentially be transmitted intentionally.

Dr. Traxle asked why the hospital suspected criminal intent as opposed to natural transmission. She was particularly interested in motive, at which point Dora interjected with a brief explanation of all the reasons individuals might be upset with doctors, insurance carriers, and hospitals.

As Dr. Traxle was asking a follow-up question, Dora made a polite excuse and pressed a button on Missy's phone to end the call, then sat back and took a deep breath.

"Do you agree that her interest in this as a criminal situation was a little strange?"

Missy nodded. "Maybe so. I hope you didn't offend her with the abrupt end to the call."

Dora shrugged. "She's probably already back at her microscope."

**Chapter 7**

"I said I would hear you all out, and I will, but I can't do it if you're all talking at once!" Craig Balboni waited for the crowd that had filled the four tables at the back of Rudy's Bar to quiet down. He was dark-eyed, balding, and on the heavy side; he was also determined to wait until the crowd quieted down before he said anything more. After a long minute, he was rewarded with something resembling silence.

"Okay then. If you raise your hands, I will call on you, but let me tell you first that my experience as the president of our city's construction union may or may not translate into anything of value should you decide to form a hospital workers union. Now, who wants to speak?"

Seven hands shot up, and the owners of four of those hands began speaking at once.

"One at a time. One at a time!" He pointed. "Yes?"

Hakeem Woods looked around, realized he had been called upon, and stood up, nervously clearing his throat. "I think I can speak for most of us when I say that for years, our hours have been too long and there have been too few of us to properly care for patients at the hospital, but with COVID—Mm mm." Hakeem wore a violet cap and dark, rounded sunglasses, even indoors. He shook his head.

Aliyah, his wife, shook her head along with him and echoed him. "Mm mm!"

"For years?" someone repeated. "You mean, forever!"

Keisha Williams was called on next. "I'm not even doing this for better working conditions. I'm doing this for the patients." She tossed her head of light brown hair. Her cinnamon-colored features were tensed with stress and doubt. "I'm doing this for people like my mother."

Next to her, Tansy Willard, a perpetually frowning blonde woman in her early sixties, looked as if she'd taken a bite of a lemon. She muttered to herself, shaking her head. "You don't want to know about my mother, or my aunts, or my father."

"Okay, okay!" The union leader held both hands in front of him, palms down, patting the air. "Okay, settle down. So, tell me. What's the hourly wage for hospital workers here?"

Several people answered at once. Tansy's voice rose above the rest. "Anywhere from $12.50 to $15.50 an hour, depending on the job and seniority."

"You expect me to save someone's life for thirteen dollars an hour?" Stella Malone had climbed up on her chair, hands on hips, her dyed, jet-black hair whirling about her face as she shook her head. She had, until just a year before, sold marijuana to many in Beach City, including some of those present, but the semi-legality and near-ubiquitousness of the drug had forced a career change. Now she was learning medical billing at Beach City Medical.

"Patient conditions are terrible," agreed Nia Paulson, who was married to Big Ru and had, until two months prior, been a stay-at-home-mom, caring for Baby Ru. "Wounds aren't cleaned, bathrooms aren't cleaned, folks goin' without pain meds. And the smell—woo hoo!" She waved a palm in front of her face. Several around her nodded in agreement.

"I'm not going to kid you," Balboni responded. "Starting a union is hard. You'll need to get signatures, and once the facility starts with resistance—and they will—you're going to lose some of those people. And the hospital will deny that the conditions are what you say they are."

"Maybe they need to walk around their own hospital," Nia responded.

"Just telling you how it's gonna be." Balboni waited until the chatter quieted. "You're going to need signatures from thirty percent of your workers to give to the National Labor Relations Board. Then there'll be an election—and I've got to tell you. Unions rarely win."

"So, what we supposed to do?" someone yelled.

"We can ask the facility to recognize the union voluntarily," Balboni answered.

"Hah! Good luck with that!" Stella sat down again and folded her arms across her chest.

"Legally," Balboni continued, "employers are not allowed to retaliate, bribe, or threaten you for organizing."

"Keyword," emphasized Keisha. "Legally."

"Exactly right," agreed Balboni. "They'll do everything they can to stop you. It's on you to stick with this and to get folks to sign up and stay signed up. For now, your job is to get those signatures. You all have my card. I'm available any time you want to talk. I suggest we meet at Rudy's at this time every week, long as Rudy's okay with it." He glanced at Rudy, an imposing, 6'4" presence behind the bar.

Rudy nodded. "Always," he said quietly.

The room had grown silent. Seated at the bar, three hefty young men in similarly tailored light blue collared shirts and jeans had closely followed the conversation and, now and then, given one another knowing looks. They were union busters, newly hired by George Campbell.

. . .

You walk through the hospital lobby, wearing your mask and your badge. You look around with disgust at the slogans on the shiny wall posters promising the best care modern medicine has to offer.

But you say nothing.

You again hear the music as you pass the large room with the tall windows near the main entrance. And again, the music stops you in your tracks because it is played and sung with such joy, such love, such warmth. For an instant you are transported to your earliest youth, when your mother sang to you, and you sigh inside.

Then the song ends and your insides go hard again. The memory door in your mind slams shut, and you continue on your way.

You take the elevator, making sure to sanitize your hands before and after, and to use your elbow to punch the button for the third floor.

But you say nothing.

You walk the floor, peeking into rooms, smiling at the patients, but your mind is filled with disgust at the empty hypocrisy that is every-where in this awful place.

But you say nothing.

You glance at the nurses and doctors you pass in the halls and your breathing grows shallow, and your chest tightens with hatred for them all, for the system that produced them and purports to hold them up as wonderful examples of healing.

But you say nothing.

You arrive at the patient's room, double check to make sure you've got the details right, then walk in.

And then, you take the action that will sacrifice this one life in the name of truth and clarity.

· · ·

Once Dora and Missy were provided access to the three cases, they tentatively confirmed what George Campbell, Dr. Matsumoto, and just about everyone else at BCMC had already concluded—that these were tragic, even bizarre happenstances, and that other than having been at Beach City Medical Center at about the same time, none of the deceased patients were connected in any discernible way. Their diagnoses were unrelated. They did not see the same physicians. Their rooms were not in close proximity to one another; they seemed to have had no friends or family in common. Their employment histories and those of their family members did not overlap.

The only new and relevant piece of information that came to light was that Ricardo Morales had briefly been a patient at the Beach City ER two months prior to his most recent stay, which left open the possibility, however remote, that he had in fact been infected at the facility after all. He had sliced one of his fingers open while cutting vegetables in his kitchen and required stitches.

While infection at BCMC was a possibility, Dora and Missy's conclusions and, therefore, Geller Investigations' official finding, was that no evidence directly supported the theory that infection had occurred at BCMC, much less that it had been intentional.

The two investigators emailed their official report and explained their process of investigation and their conclusions to George Campbell via video chat.

"Mr. Campbell," Dora paraphrased from the report, a physical copy of which she held in her hand, "we see no connection between the cases of these three patients, other than their having recently been patients at your facility. We see no evidence that anyone on the BCMC medical staff or anyone else, for that matter, negatively impacted the health of these individuals. We find no connection between their cases, a finding supported by Dr. Matsumoto and the BCMC medical team."

Campbell, who had appeared tense at the start of the session, visibly relaxed. "Good. What about a motive? Did you find any reason anyone might want to harm these patients?"

"We did not," Dora confirmed.

"Nor are we aware of any threats against the facility on social media," Missy added, looking at Dora, who agreed. "Nor any mentions that rise above the grief or frustration one would usually find when a patient's stay does not go as planned or does not end well."

The hospital CEO sat back and folded his arms. "Just because you didn't find a motive or connection doesn't mean one doesn't exist. It may be that the individual is smart enough to hide their activity well."

Dora breathed a small sigh. "What do you see as a possible motive? Why do you think these were intentional?"

"Your medical director doesn't see anything beyond unfortunate, tragic illnesses," Missy added.

George answered quickly, as though he'd been expecting the question. "Infections such as these, at least two of them anyway, are so rare as to be nonexistent. The fact that they occurred at about the same time in the same place is a red flag."

"Well," Dora said, thinking through her response as she spoke. "Is the possibility of these diseases being transmitted intentionally more or less likely than their occurring naturally?"

George looked baffled yet spoke with intensity. "I wish I could tell you. It's awfully strange and of course these are tragedies we wish we could have prevented, for the sake of the patients and their families. Our reputation is that we stand alone at the pinnacle of healing on Long Island. Having multiple rare, fatal diseases occurring in our facility is all but impossible, and absolutely unacceptable."

Neither Dora nor Missy stated the obvious—that the "impossible" had, in fact, occurred.

• • •

For a weeknight, Rudy's was packed. As COVID and its ubiquitous Omicron variant waned, Rudy's business grew, until he took out the tall, clear plastic dividers he had installed between every two seats at the bar. He also added tables in a few of the spots where he had removed them to allow for the required six feet of space between them.

Craig Balboni's construction union crowd took up three tables and Rudy and Agatha's personal friends and regular bar patrons took up another three, which left two tables for whomever was able to get to them first. Balboni's crowd was sixty percent blue-collar and white, while Rudy and Agatha's crowd was about eighty percent Black, ten percent Latinx, and ten percent white.

Dora and Missy were part of the latter ten percent.

The two groups had found themselves on opposite sides of a conflict a few years earlier, a conflict that led to a chair-throwing, window-busting, police-calling brawl. Since then, they had, with Balboni's and Agatha Raines's influence, learned to focus on their mutual, shared interests rather than their differences.

Everyone was reasonably happy, and peace reigned.

Hakeem Woods wore his trademark violet beret and dark, round sunglasses that would not have been out of place in the 1970s. Now and then someone told him this, but he just laughed and said that was fine. His arm stroked Aliyah's back. His bride of seventeen years wore her black hair in long, beautiful box braids that were streaked with gold. He was talking to the Ru brothers, Big Ru and Little Ru, but everyone at all three tables, and many at the union tables, were listening, as this information concerned them all.

"That's just it," Hakeem was saying. "We are serious as a heart attack. We have a lot of volunteers, and we're determined to get it done!"

Little Ru scratched his head and rubbed the sides of his bearded face. "Keem. Listen to me. It's been tried before. And it's failed. I don't see how you can succeed, what with Campbell and his crowd set against any union of any kind. What's changed?"

Keisha Williams, who was a medical coder at BCMC, answered for Hakeem. "We got God on our side."

"Mm hmm," Little Ru said. "Well, 'scuse me, but did the union organizers have God on their side last time? I guess not."

Several people started arguing at once, but Hakeem held out a hand for quiet. "One difference is, we're much more organized. Can I prove it this minute? No, but wait and see."

"Let's talk about something else," said Eunice Paulson, who was married to Little Ru. Together they owned a successful construction company that worked with Craig Balboni's union. "Hey, Ags!"

From two tables away, Agatha Raines heard her name called. "Hey Eu!" she called back, and the two friends laughed.

"How's the little prophet?" Eunice yelled.

The little prophet was the nickname everyone had given to Samuel, Agatha and Rudy's adopted little boy, now eighteen months old. They had tried and failed for years to get pregnant and remained over the moon about the adoption.

Agatha shrugged and held both palms in their air, close to her sides. "Doin' the best I can."

The men at Rudy and Agatha's friends' tables argued passionately about sports and even more passionately about sports betting, which was newly legal. Most of them also participated in a constantly-moving poker game, usually sponsored one way or another by Rudy himself.

"C'mon, man," Big Ru was saying. "They made the playoffs last year and they'll make a run this year. Trust me."

"I do trust you," LaChance Williams, who was married to Keisha, said. "But the Knicks are done. They won't make the playoffs, and you can take that to the bank." The hubbub around the table had quieted as he spoke. LaChance was a successful banker and investor who was known for only making predictions when he was certain of the outcome.

Several men immediately reached into their pockets for their phones and opened their betting apps.

At another table, some of the women were cooing over the new hairstyle of Shanice James, a hair colorist and West African beauty, with satin black skin and confident, sedate features. She was the queen of all she saw, and the queen now sported a daring faux-hawk that was universally examined and approved.

A sweet voice began to sing a familiar song and the entire bar hushed as Kelvin Franklin began his performance. The few in attendance who had never heard the beloved local performer and friend to many were momentarily startled into believing that the late Marvin Gaye himself was in attendance or was somehow performing from beyond the grave.

As everyone agreed that things truly were not "what they used to be," Twirly McTeague, a white woman known as a "hippy chick," despite being in her late forties, began to dance—spinning gracefully between tables, her red and yellow dress whirling around her as she moved, her arms undulating like independent ethereal beings.

Martine Franklin, Kelvin's wife, joined her, dancing in place with a sweet, placid smile. While her day job was senior project scientist at a well-respected engineering firm, her nights saw her as the unofficial, beloved centerpiece of the crowd at Rudy's Bar.

• • •

You had given a lot of thought to your next visit to the hospital. You had to choose the diseases, which would have to be virulent and deadly.

You had to acquire and contain the pathogens and determine a means of transmission. Your work would be the contributing, determining factor in multiple patients' outcomes and the fallout would be felt far beyond the patients and their families. Justice.

Your work was shifting the paradigm of the facility, of the local health care system itself. Changes would be made, cover-ups would be initiated, public relations and advertising campaigns would be affected, and major donations would be reconsidered.

And one of the vicinity's most ambitious health care initiatives of the modern era would, of necessity, grind to a halt.

What a shame that people had to give their lives for this.

• • •

Dora and Missy sat beside Adam Geller's desk; each held a small glass of red wine in a dainty plastic chalice.

"Here's to the successful first case of my two new detectives," Adam said, holding his glass aloft and leaning toward his guests. They all touched glasses and sipped.

"George Campbell expressed his appreciation to me over the phone just an hour ago and if he's happy, I'm happy."

"To happy clients." Dora held her glass aloft, and they again toasted and sipped.

"Thelma will provide you with your checks on your way out and, in about a week, your business cards."

Dora and Missy exchanged an excited glance.

"I'm not going to stay," Dora said. "I don't want to drink more than these couple of sips, since I'm driving. I have a babysitting job I'll be working part-time, for at least a while—until our work here ramps up. And I also now have a very hungry dog who demands food, attention, and walks." She rose to her feet.

"We need to get the dogs together," Missy suggested. "Maybe tomorrow?"

"If we don't land another case," Dora agreed. "Okay to leave my glass here?" She set her chalice on Adam's desk.

"Thelma will get them. I'd shake your hands, ladies, but...well, you know how things are now."

"We get it," Dora said as she and Missy headed for the front of the office.

"I hope Freedom and Comfort get along," Missy remarked.

Thelma was holding up twin envelopes as the two nascent investigators arrived at her desk. She was working a mouse on her computer and didn't look up. Dora and Missy each took an envelope and headed for the door.

• • •

The street corner was the usual mix of bundled up, chattering children, moms, a few dads and grandparents, strollers and idling cars, all waiting for the school buses. Dora waited a short way from the primary cluster, Freedom's leash in hand with Freedom at the other end, sniffing everything and everywhere. Now that she'd had her shots, Dora could drive to the bus stop nearest Vanessa's apartment with Freedom beside her, pick up Drew and Buster, and head back to Vanessa's apartment to watch and care for her children. Both Vanessa and her apartment building were fine with the presence of well-behaved dogs.

For the moment, Dora needed the babysitting job, and Missy would keep her library job, since their contributions to Geller Investigations would not be profitable until Adam had more cases than his usual divorce load.

She had brought Freedom to Missy's earlier to take Comfort for his afternoon walk. When he saw Dora, Comfort had bounded toward her with his usual joyful welcome, but stopped short when he saw Freedom, who, being part Doberman part Rottweiler, was literally eight times his size. The tiny terrier growled, gave one authoritative bark, and Freedom responded by kneeling submissively at the door. Dora had laughed for a full minute at the sight.

Since then, anytime Freedom moved, Comfort barked, and Freedom sat or knelt. Realizing that Freedom was likely traumatized by her owner, Dora stopped laughing and hugged Freedom while explaining the situation to Comfort and leading the two dogs toward one another until they were face to face. For the moment, Freedom remained terrified of Comfort, who seemed satisfied with the arrangement.

The yellow bus arrived, screeching to a halt, its blinking red stop signs extending like ears from either side of the front, its door folding open as children spilled out and onto the sidewalk.

Seven-year-old Drew led his younger brother out of the vehicle, taking him by the hand, as Buster descended the steps by stepping down with his left foot, bringing his right foot down to meet it, and continuing in that fashion. The boys wore matching fall outfits: brown and white plaid button-down shirts, dark brown corduroy pants, and puffy blue down vests.

Dora could see that Buster had been crying. She knelt next to him, with Freedom crowding in to get a look at the boys. Buster was still shaken by whatever had caused him to cry, and he lurched away from the big dog, but Dora pulled his brother Drew and Freedom together, so little Buster could see that the dog was friendly.

"Do you want to tell me what happened, Buster?"

Buster picked his nose and shook his head.

His brother answered for him. "Big boys were picking on Buster. He came and sat with me."

She stroked the side of Buster's face. "Oh, no! Are you okay, Buster?" She looked him in the eyes, doing her best to radiate compassion and a sense of safety, but Buster would not look at her, and examined a booger on his finger instead. "Well, we can talk about it later. For now, meet Freedom, my new dog."

"Really?" Drew was exuberant. While dogs were allowed in Vanessa's building, the boys had never experienced life with a dog at home. It was a subject they raised to their mother now and then.

Buster had been looking at the ground, but now cautiously looked up. "Really?" he repeated.

"Mm hmm, and Mommy says he can stay with us sometimes in the afternoon."

"What's for dinner?" Buster asked, at once forgetting the dog, the bully, and his nose.

"Macaroni and cheese with Brussels sprouts."

"Brussels sprouts…with *salt*," Buster corrected.

"With salt," Drew agreed.

As they walked, Dora allowed each boy to briefly hold Freedom's leash while she kept the excess leash close at her side. The boys readily took to her new pet, and she to them.

Once home, the boys played together in their room for an hour while Dora made their dinner and looked in on them every so often, and Freedom trotted after her. Both boys loved science, and planned to be astronomers or astronauts when they grew up. They played separately yet in close proximity to one another with age-appropriate introductory science toys.

After dinner, Dora brought both boys into the living room and explained the rudiments of fighting and keeping themselves safe. She began by standing in a classic boxing stance. "You stand like this, with one hand next to your face so if someone tries to hit you, you can block his punch with your arm. Your other arm stays lower and protects your chest and ribs. Keep your elbows close to your body." She modified each boy's stance.

"Good. Now, what will you do if another boy tries to punch you like this?" She extended a jab toward Drew's chin, and Drew moved his arm somewhat awkwardly to block. "There you go! Now you, Buster. What will you do if someone tries to punch you this way?" She aimed a slow right cross towards Buster's midsection.

"Tell my brudder," Buster said, and Dora laughed.

"Well, okay. Yes, you can tell Drew, but you can also block his punch with your arm." She moved his arm into position while Buster watched, not understanding. "Again, if someone punches you like this, what will you do?"

"Run away!" Buster cried.

"That's good, too! Now, listen, boys. If someone tries to hurt you, you don't have to let him...or her. If someone tries to punch you, it's okay to punch them back, okay? But only if they hit you first. If they just say mean things or they're not nice, no hitting, okay?"

The boys nodded solemnly. "And Drew," she said, looking the older child in the eye, "if someone tries to hurt Buster, it's okay to make them stop."

Drew nodded. "I take care of him."

"Exactly. You take care of Buster. Now, do you know what time it is?"

Drew shook his head. Buster's face lit with joy.

"Pastrami!" Buster cried.

"Astronomy! That's right!"

She sat on the floor, her back against the couch, and the boys sat on the couch, one behind each of her shoulders, as she read from their favorite astronomy book.

"Today, we're reading about Pegasus, who was a horse with wings." She pointed to a picture of the white, winged horse.

"Like a bird," Drew observed.

"Like a bawd," Buster echoed.

"His mother was a bad monster lady, who had snakes instead of hair." She pointed to a picture of the Medusa.

When they were finished looking at the book, Dora sat with the boys at the window and showed them the Pegasus constellation in the clear, November sky. The boys looked from the book, which included thin, white lines between the stars, to the sky, to the iPad program Dora held up and through which the boys could look at the constellations and see their defining lines superimposed against the sky. Whenever they did astronomy, the boys made sure to be on their best behavior.

• • •

Tilda Tolleson tried to think of her students, who were so much of her life's focus and who brought her joy that transcended just about any challenge. But her health was mysteriously deteriorating every day. Every part of her body hurt and she was too exhausted to move, too exhausted to lift her legs, to get out of her hospital bed, even to go to the bathroom. She was too weak to eat.

The man in the bed on the other side of her hospital room was moaning pitifully and constantly. She barely noticed the nurses who changed her IVs and took her vitals, or the residents who made their rounds early in the day and spoke quietly among themselves after looking her over.

Still, until now she had managed to picture her students, their earnest little third-grade faces, as they raised their hands and gave such serious answers to her questions in class. The pain in her head was becoming unbearable, and with it came piercing white lights that flashed behind her eyes, searing a place deep within her skull. She was beginning to find that she could no longer think, no longer will her mind to focus on anything, including her students. Her mind knew only pain and exhaustion and clung to the faint hope it would soon end.

## Chapter 8

Charlie Bernelli Jr. was seated on the caramel-colored semi-circular sofa in the living room of the apartment he shared with Christine Pearsall. The apartment had been Christine's, but he had moved in a month prior to their wedding, six months before. The room was three steps down from the rest of the apartment and featured an open layout. Polished dark oak floors led first to a dinette and then to floor-to-ceiling windows that looked out over the seven floors below and the Atlantic Ocean beyond. The penthouse apartment was in one of the nicest build-ings on the ocean strip, as befitting the mayor of Beach City.

"Alexa," Charlie said, "play Frank Sinatra." He sat down on the couch with his second scotch, cut himself a thin slice of brie, and ate it on a pre-cut quarter slice of rye bread.

"Playing Frank Sinatra," Alexa answered.

As soon as Frank began singing "I've Got You Under My Skin," Christine hurried in as best she could in her light blue, off-the-shoulder sheath dress. She fiddled with a pearl earring as she corrected Charlie.

"Alexa, play Grateful Dead."

"Playing Grateful Dead."

"They're not even here yet," Charlie complained.

"You want to get along with our soon-to-be daughter-in-law and grandchild?"

"She's only four months pregnant and she's not even here, for God's sake."

Christine gave him a harsh look. "She's had morning sickness for weeks; she gets to choose." She gave a disapproving look in the direction of his glass. "How many of those have you had?" She half closed her eyes as she felt the sneeze coming. After sneezing three times in quick succession, she pressed her fingers to her eyes and wondered if this pain was from a migraine, a sinus infection, or allergies.

Charlie held up the bit of rye bread in his hand, then looked at his glass as though seeing it for the first time. "The bread's soaking it up. And relax, we don't have to drive, and this is family. Like C3's going to give me a hard time for having a drink or two. Migraine?"

Christine's hands went to her hips. "You need to start setting a good example. How long has he been clean now, two months?"

"Six, and he needs to stand on his own feet—to survive around alcohol." He smiled and changed the subject. "Dress still looks great on you."

"Nice try, and yes—migraine." Christine gave a disapproving sigh and shuffled back to the bathroom to finish her makeup.

A loud buzzer sounded. "Shit, they're here," Christine called, "and my makeup's not half done! Let them in and get them settled?"

"On it," Charlie said. He waited for the apartment bell, then went to the door, drink in hand, and stepped forward to hug his future daughter-in-law, who was dressed in her usual black, though this time her ensemble consisted of an argyle sweater and matching slacks. Sarah had never been one for dresses, Charlie mused, though at least, he noticed, the slacks were pressed.

"Hello, Charlie!" Sarah threw her arms around him. Charlie adored his son's girlfriend and the feeling was mutual. He wished his son shared his own gregarious conviviality, a quality that had helped him build relationships with so many of his ad agency's clients. He had hoped to bring

C3, the family nickname for Charlie Bernelli III, into The Bernelli Group, but the young man showed little aptitude for wining and dining clients, none for the creative side of the business, and even less interest in either. He also had an addictive nature so strong as to rule out any possibility of business-related drinking. Besides, C3 wanted his counseling job back, and seemed determined to drive for Uber until then.

Sarah handed Charlie a bakery box tied with string. "Butter brownies that'll make you cry."

"Can't wait." Charlie looked like he meant it. "How are you, C?" He gave his son a quick man hug and back slap. C3 was a younger version of his father, in more ways than one. His lionesque blond hair was swept back and extended over his collar, while his father's was streaked with gray. He wore a diamond stud in his left ear.

"Okay, Dad. You?"

"Can't complain." Charlie couldn't help but notice his son's long look at his scotch as he stood aside to allow the young couple to enter the apartment. He closed the door behind them and watched his son as he and Sarah sat down next to one another on the couch. C3 wore a navy blue, long-sleeved wool shirt and blue jeans.

Sarah looked at Charlie. "I didn't know you like the Grateful Dead."

Charlie smiled back. "I don't."

C3 winced. "Nice, Dad."

Charlie gave his son a pointed look. "You want me to lie?"

"It's how you make your living."

Charlie walked over to the bar, filled two glasses with ice. "We have flavored seltzer, ginger ale, diet and regular soda, ice water—?" He looked at Sarah.

"Ginger ale, please."

Charlie turned to his son. "Diet coke?"

C3 nodded. "Sure."

Charlie poured the drinks and brought them to the glass coffee table, whose metal base was an intricately sculpted cypress tree. He set the drinks on coasters. "Advertising isn't lying."

"Okay, Dad. Everything you say about every product is true."

Charlie took a long sip of his drink and exhaled noisily. He walked to the window and looked down at the people on the beach.

He turned back toward the room and grinned at Sarah. "You look wonderful. Has the morning sickness stopped?"

Sarah looked rueful. "Not entirely. But it's not as bad now."

"Did you decide to find out what you're having?"

Sarah looked at C3, who shook his head. "We want to be surprised."

"People tell me it's a boy because I'm carrying low and in the front."

"Long as you feel okay," Charlie observed. "Your people can handle the paper while you're out?"

Sarah laughed. "Oh, yeah. Lemieux and Esther are chomping at the bit."

"Are they really?" Christine had entered the room. C3 and Sarah rose to greet her, and they exchanged hugs and air kisses, as was Christine's habit. Despite the ongoing pandemic and the Omicron variant that remained rampant, the family maintained vigilance and up-to-date vaccine protocols and, when with one another, eschewed masks.

Christine's eyes swept the drinks and she exchanged a glance with her husband; they approved of C3's choice of beverage.

Sarah waited while Christine poured herself a single malt, then said, "They want to be involved in the news and reportage part of the job. Lemieux can't wait to be on the air."

"So, he'll be reading the news?" Christine asked.

"When we have special reports, yes. Which is once or twice a week, depending on what's going on. The rest of the time they'll be collecting info from sources and putting together stories, which will be posted."

Charlie looked impressed. "You do all that now?"

Sarah looked equivocal, twisting her mouth to one side. "Most of it. They pitch in, but they don't direct."

"Ahh," Christine mused. "Everyone wants to direct and produce."

C3 gave a wave of his hand. "Well, aren't you happier being mayor than when you were city clerk?"

Before Christine could answer, Charlie interrupted. "Don't let her kid you. This girl loves running the show downtown, and right here."

"Not true," Christine disagreed; she suddenly pinched the bridge of her nose between two fingers. "Have some bread and cheese." She indicated the brie and rye bread. "Oh, and I have dip!" She got up, went to the kitchen, and returned with a round, hollowed out bread filled with cheese and vegetable dip and surrounded by crackers.

C3 and Sarah looked at one another, concerned.

Charlie grinned. "Chris's selling herself short."

Sarah changed the subject. "Is Vanessa still working for you?"

Charlie nodded. "Smart woman. Picked up proofreading fast, and apparently has an English background. She even does some copy editing, and I wouldn't be surprised if she ends up writing, too."

Christine shook her head. "Woman's been through so much."

Sarah agreed. "I've heard her refer to Jesse as having been her other half."

C3 nodded. "Agatha's hurting, too. Losing a sibling's gotta be brutal—and a twin."

Charlie looked into his glass, swirling his drink. "Vanessa was well on her way toward a real estate career, but I wouldn't be surprised if she sticks with us. I hope she does."

"Dora still watching her kids?" Sarah asked.

"I think so," Charlie answered.

Christine looked wistful. "There's another one who's been through a lot. She adored Franny."

"I see Dora around town with that librarian," C3 observed. "Are they a thing, now?"

"I think they are," Charlie said.

"Good for her," Christine affirmed with a loving smile at her husband. "Nothing wrong with love."

C3 glanced toward the dining room. "What are we having?"

Christine glanced upward, thinking. "Let's see. Caesar salad, shrimp oreganata, pasta with olive oil and basil, artichokes, and cheesecake."

"And Sarah's brownies," Charlie added.

"Oooh," said C3 eagerly. "I've always found Dora a little scary. Angry, even."

His father turned to him. "She lost the love of her life."

Christine corrected her husband. "I'm pretty sure she was angry before that."

Charlie nodded in acquiescence. "You're right." He shrugged. "Seems to work for her."

Christine agreed. "I used to see her around City Hall. She was—I don't know if angry's the word—fierce, maybe. But it was a kind of cheerful fierceness, like 'Hey you, over there. Shut the fuck up and sit down.' There was a bit of a smile in it, though."

"Losing Franny had to have—" Sarah swallowed, tearing up. She had been close to Franny too; they had shared a love of classical music and literature. C3 took her hand, squeezing it. He knew her pregnancy left her frequently emotional.

Charlie broke the silence. "So, son, you going to keep your sobriety this time?"

C3 turned to his father. "So, Dad, you going to break my balls in front of the world this time?"

Charlie laughed. "Probably."

C3 didn't laugh.

"Want to hear something fucked up?" Christine lowered her voice conspiratorially. "Beach City Medical is honoring Jeremy Anderson at their gala this year." Everyone looked at Charlie, who nodded stoically. Jeremy Anderson owned the only other ad agency in Beach City.

Charlie groused, "He's donating $3.5 million toward a new infectious disease wing."

"And Antoine Julienne's matching that donation," Christine added, still looking at Charlie, who had picked up his drink and drained its contents. He got up and went to the bar to pour himself another.

"Easy, Dad," C3 said.

"Shut up, son."

Christine raised her eyebrows, looked at Sarah and C3, and nodded toward Charlie, who returned to his seat.

"What?" C3 asked.

"Guess who has to give them the award and make a kiss-their-ass speech at the gala?" Christine said.

"You?" Sarah covered her mouth with her hand.

"The hospital's still your client, right?" C3 looked at his father, who didn't answer. "So…guess you'll be making a lot of pre-dinner ads."

"Are they naming the wing after Anderson?"

Charlie didn't answer.

"We don't know," Christine answered for him. She grimaced and pinched her nose between her fingers.

"You okay?" C3 asked. Christine waved him away.

Sarah looked briefly at Christine, then at Charlie, then shrugged sympathetically. "Well, I have to run those ads."

Charlie gave her a grateful look and raised his glass. "To Jeremy Anderson, who *is* an infectious disease." He drank while everyone watched. Eventually they followed suit.

Christine gave him a stern look "Put on your big boy pants, honey. I have to hand him that award."

"Trust me," said Sarah, "our article will sound like an obit."

"So, C," his father began. "When do you see yourself getting your counseling job back?"

After a quiet pause, Christine stood up. "Let's move over to the dining room, and be sure to stop and watch the surfers." She nodded toward the floor-to-ceiling windows. "They're having some kind of fall tournament, I think. Lots of tricks."

C3 hid his hurt expression as he stood up. "So, Dad," he said quietly, leaning close to his father, "are you and Christine expecting yet?"

Charlie stopped, turned, and glared at his son.

Later that night, Charlie was sitting up in bed, reading *The Chronicle* on his iPad, as Christine slid under the covers next to him.

"Well, that was a success," he mused without looking up.

Christine looked at him, then undid her robe and let it slip from her shoulders. "I call it a success anytime we get together with your son and his fiancé."

"I guess your migraine's better."

"Mm hmm." She lay down next to him and slid her hand down beneath the blanket. "And one success deserves another."

Charlie closed the iPad and laid it on the floor next to his side of the bed. "I can't disagree with that."

Afterward, Christine donned her robe and went into the bathroom, making sure to hide the full vial of birth control pills before she returned to her husband.

• • •

George Campbell looked at the blinking light on his phone and tried to will the ringing to stop. He knew who was calling and why. Matsumoto, who lived in his cloistered little world of medicine, was calling to tell him to take drastic action because of the new cases. Challenging medical cases, patients with hard-to-treat symptoms, happened every day. Many times a day. Disruption of the rest of the hospital's function was absolutely not the answer! He knew just as well as Matsumoto did about their responsibility to the public, not to mention to the Department of Health. He shared Matsumoto's deep concern for the well-being of every patient at the BCMC. But he also had a bigger picture to consider. One patient or two, or even five could not determine the healthcare policy of an entire community. They would deal with these problems, these cases, just as an army general deals with an enemy attack. Together, the BCMC team would strategize, marshal their forces, and counterattack. Their pathologists, epidemiologists, phlebotomists, and specialists in every field of medicine were the best in the New York metro vicinity. They would not surrender. They would not shut down any aspect of hospital function. No. As far as he was concerned, it was that sort of weak thinking that had led to the bottom falling out of the COVID pandemic.

What was needed was courage. What was needed was staying the course. What was needed was inspired leadership—of the sort that was at the very core of his, George Campbell's, character.

## Chapter 9

Andy Schwartz struggled to breathe. It was a struggle with which he was familiar, since he had lived with asthma and frequent pneumonia much of his life. He was also diabetic and morbidly obese. It was the diabetes that had led to his hospitalization this go round.

His breathing came in shallow gasps, and within each gasp was a little involuntary vocal cry that was the result of the extreme constriction of his airways. His symptoms seemed to confuse his nurses and doctor, which terrified him far more than did his symptoms. He was here for his diabetes, but his caregivers were talking about meningitis and encephalitis. How could that be? What was going on? Did anybody in this place know what they were doing?

He felt the ripple in his neck and had no time to consider its cause. As he tried to swallow, he began to choke, but the ripple had become a convulsion that moved outward from his neck to his face and chest. He thought faintly of the call button and then, strangely, of his brother, Jack, and a treehouse they had built together decades before. Andy had loved that treehouse and slept there often during the summer when Andy was ten and Jack was twelve. A family of cardinals had made their home on a branch not far from that treehouse.

Andy's last thought was a memory of that family of cardinals, chittering away, and waking the two brothers up on summer mornings after their campouts in their beloved treehouse.

• • •

Dora was showering after returning from a visit to Shay's MMA. She loved mixed martial arts and had begun training at Shay's several years earlier, once she discovered her natural aptitude for the sport and for self-defense in general. The sport was an effective outlet for her seemingly bottomless pool of anger—a rage which had taken root in her childhood when she had often witnessed her mother begging her father to stop beating her. While he had been physically rough with Dora a number of times, he had regularly and violently taken out his frustrations, guilt, and self-loathing on Dora's mother.

Dora had little interest in therapy, which had been forced on her as a child; the experience had been, to her mind, an exercise in blaming the victim. Mixed martial arts was much more effective at dispelling whatever it was she was feeling; that she might be displacing those feelings was, for the moment, of little concern to her.

She was showering and thinking about the session that had just ended when she heard Freedom barking. "Be right there, Freedom!" she called, but the dog continued to bark. "Okay, I'm coming!"

She stepped out of the shower, wrapped a towel around herself and took one step into the hallway. She barely missed the large, fresh, fetid gift her new best friend had left in the hallway just outside the bathroom.

"Freedom! Your name doesn't mean you have the freedom to poop just anywhere!" She went back into the bathroom, slipped into a robe and slippers, and began cleaning up the mess, making sure to tie the garbage bags closed. She saw with satisfaction that Freedom had retreated to her bed, a round, soft cushion with low fuzzy sides that would keep her warm and cozy as she slept. The Doberman Rottweiler mix watched her new owner clean with what Dora imagined was guilty silence.

A buzzing distracted her; Dora's cellphone was ringing from her bedroom night table. The I.D. said Geller Investigations.

"Hello?"

"It's happening again. Can you call Missy and get down here right away?"

"I'll have to see if she's working. Either way, I'll be right over."

Fifteen minutes later, she walked into Adam Geller's office, was ignored by Thelma as she walked past the office manager, and sat down in one of the chairs adjacent to her new boss's desk. For once, Adam was not watching TV on his iPad, but was typing into a computer.

"I'm making notes based on the call I just received from George Campbell. They have another two cases. Where's Missy?"

"Working for two more hours. I'll fill her in, unless you want her to come by later."

"No need. I'll print this out and go over it with you and you can do the same with her. If you have any questions, just call me, or better yet, ask Campbell or Matsumoto. Hang on." He finished typing and printed out three identical sheets of paper, two of which he handed to Dora.

"Tilda Tolleson was in the hospital last week for an abdominal resection. She has Crohn's disease, which causes inflammation of the digestive tract and can lead to abdominal pain, diarrhea, fatigue, weight loss —"

"I get it," Dora said.

"She's a third-grade teacher," Adam went on, "not that that's relevant. She had to have a piece of her intestines removed and a colostomy bag attached."

"Okay. So what happened to her?"

"She came down with something called," Adam paused, glancing at his computer screen, "African trypanosomiasis, also known as African sleeping sickness."

"Whoa. Is she alive?"

Adam nodded. "For now, but she's in bad shape. The disease is usually fatal unless caught early, and Campbell said they're not sure they caught it in time."

"What are her symptoms?"

"Fever, terrible headaches, exhaustion, swollen lymph nodes, and body aches. Her mental state is affected, which indicates that the disease has progressed, perhaps too far."

"So, what's next?" Dora asked.

"There's a second case."

"Shit."

"Andy Schwartz, age twenty-seven. An obese man—and diabetic. Married to the love of his life. Came down with something called Hendra virus, which tends to come from a particular species of bats. Usually found in Australia—and no, he had never been there. Mr. Schwartz is only the eighth known human case."

"Ever?" Dora asked.

Adam nodded and pressed his lips together. "He passed away this morning." He checked his screen. "He died of pneumonia. He'd had asthma, which may have been a contributing factor to his demise, but make no mistake—it was this Hendra virus."

Dora sat back, momentarily stunned. She looked down and scanned the information Adam had given her. "We're really in the deep end of the pool here."

"Campbell is freaking out because this means the hospital might receive bad press, be forced to cancel their gala event—"

"And won't receive those big checks." She shook her head, amazed at the man's upside-down priorities.

Thelma's voice sounded from the front of the office. "You should never have taken this on. It's an impossible case! You should have stuck with divorces. The hell do you know about medical cases? I said it from the beginning—stay in your lane! I hate to say I told you so!"

Adam's answer was equal in volume but milder in tone. "I tend to agree, except for one thing. You *love* to say I told you so." He rolled his eyes and looked at Dora, his gaze fixed and focused. "I'll tell you what's next," he said. "Back to work. I'm pretty sure the hospital needs to report this to whatever medical authorities they answer to—perhaps at the county or state level, perhaps the CDC and, given the possibility of this being a crime, perhaps the FBI."

Dora considered this. "I thought you needed an interstate aspect to call in the feds."

"You can always invite them in to help, and given the threat to public health and Campbell's priorities, I think it makes sense in this case—before more people die. I'm going to call him back to discuss. Why don't you call Dr. Matsumoto to see what else you can learn, before you fill Missy in once she gets back."

Dora rose to go. "Understood. Will do."

• • •

According to the woman who answered his office phone, Dr. Matsumoto was unavailable, but as Dora was driving home a few moments later, her phone rang.

"Ms. Ellison. Akira Matsumoto. When I heard you called, I wanted to get right back to you. I know about the new case."

"Two cases, I'm told."

"I know about the teacher—African sleeping sickness, but the other—yes, I see. Mr. Schwartz. Hendra." He sighed. "I've been explaining to George about the precautions we will be taking, and changes to our operating procedures I believe are necessary."

Dora pulled into her parking lot. "Like sealing off the affected areas of the hospital?"

"Much more than that. The problem is that George wants to wait before doing anything—draconian, to use his word. He understands that we have medical protocols we need to follow, but he's concerned about the hospital's image and an event we're holding just before the holidays."

"I take it you disagree." She found a parking space and shut off her car. There was a slight pause as the call transferred from her car's audio to her phone.

"My job is caring for our patients. I've reached out to the chairman of the board and asked that they convene an emergency meeting. Until then, there's nothing I can do as far as the public's access to the hospital. As far as investigating these cases as criminal—I don't know. I've thought from the outset that the notion seems awfully far-fetched. George and I disagree on this point."

Dora let herself into her building, took the stairs to the third floor, and entered her apartment, as Freedom gave three ecstatic yips and bounded forward. "From what I've been told," she surmised, "the cases themselves are awfully far-fetched." Freedom jumped up on her hind legs, and did what looked like a little dance, her paws on Dora's chest. "Aww, good girl. Good to see you too!"

"Sorry?"

"Oh. I just got in; I'm talking to my dog."

"Yes, these cases are extremely unlikely. I don't like to say impossible, because, after all, here they are. But criminal? I find that hard to believe."

"You're a doctor, not a private detective."

"Point taken. Let me give George a call—try to reason with him, then call you back."

Dora clipped the leash onto Freedom's collar and they went together back down the stairs and out the front door. Dora's phone rang again.

"I saw you called." It was Missy.

"Yeah. Two more cases. Two more diseases."

"Oh, no!"

"I just spoke to Matsumoto. He's getting pushback from Campbell about making changes to hospital procedures. Campbell's afraid of the impact on their wallets."

"Wonder how the families of the infected patients feel about that."

"Exactly. One died, the other's hanging on. Matsumoto's trying to get the hospital board together for an emergency meeting. He's also going to try to talk some sense into George Campbell, then get back to us."

"I'm on my way over."

"Great. See you in a few."

• • •

Dora waited while Freedom sniffed along the curb, found the spot she wanted, and peed. While she waited, her phone rang again. Dr. Matsumoto.

"Spoke to George," he said. "Here's what we came up with. He insists that there is no proof that these are anything but people getting sick in a hospital setting—"

"He sees this as hospital business as usual?" Dora asked doubtfully.

"So, officially, he doesn't think it would help matters, including the prognoses of patients, to go public. I made it absolutely clear that we need to report these cases to the DOH and I'm moving forward with that. We will also need to put CDC protocols into place. We need to maintain transparency, and I suspect our insurance carriers, the board, and the public would not be happy about any delay."

"Understood, and agreed."

"In any case, I'm reaching out to the CDC, asking that they double check our data and confirm the protocols we'll need to put in place. For now, and while we wait for the board, here's what George and I came up with. No more visitors. At all. Visitation had been limited anyway because of COVID, but for now, only residents, nurses, and aides will be allowed access—anywhere there are patients. Only those with bracelets that denote that they have reason to be in that part of the hospital, on that day, during that particular shift will be allowed access. Everyone will wear bracelets, which will be of different colors, and the pattern of colors will not, I repeat—not—be the same every day, each week. They will change, and the changes will appear random."

"That all makes a lot of sense."

•  •  •

The two tables that had been pushed together at the back of Mae's Diner were filled with BCMC employees of assorted backgrounds, ages, and colors. Keisha Williams and Hakeem Woods had agreed to speak with everyone present about forming a union, while the rest of their original group did the heavy lifting of finding, informing, and convincing several physician's assistants, aides, clerks, and employees from both the hospital and its affiliated senior facility, Beach City Assisted Living. Coffee had been provided for all. Everyone was a mixture of suspicious, dubious, and hopeful.

"We all know that the working conditions at the hospital and assisted living are making it hard to do our jobs." Hakim looked at each of the nine people who had shown up. "That's tough on us, on our wives, husbands, children—and on the patients."

"Is my supervisor going to know I'm here?" asked a woman in a dark blue aide uniform that peeked out from beneath a brown corduroy coat.

Hakim shook his head. "Not from us. We're not here to get anyone in trouble. We're just looking for better working conditions and care for the patients."

Keisha lifted her chin. "And this is the only way we're going to get it."

A woman from Honduras tentatively raised her hand. "I'm still waiting for my green card. Will joining a union hurt my citizenship?"

Keisha shook her head. "We ain't gonna mess with that. But we are asking people to commit in writing to what we're doing."

"The law says we can do this," Hakeem went on. "They're not allowed to stand in our way, harass anyone, punish anyone. They can't do surveillance or fire you for advocacy."

"But it won't be easy," Keisha added. "The administration will fight back, and if you sign the union card, you're in for an uphill battle."

"But we're no strangers to uphill battles." Hakeem was feeling invigorated and excited, and he could see that some of those present were inspired too. Their eyes shone with excitement and hope.

"I'm in," said Cherise, who worked as an aide at the assisted living center.

"Not me," said Martha Robinson, a clerk at the hospital. "I can't afford to risk it. I'm barely making do as is."

Keisha looked at her. "Don't you want to do better than make do?"

"Yes, and I'd like to win the lottery and be a foot taller too. You can't promise any of those."

"I can promise you a fighting chance."

Martha bit her lip and shook her head. Her friend, Louise Tanner, who worked alongside her and was ten years her senior, put up her hand. "I'm in. If we don't try now, we may never get anywhere."

Martha turned and stared in shock at her friend. "You serious?"

"I'm dead serious."

"Well…" Martha reached out and took one of the union cards Keisha was holding out.

. . .

Missy and Dora sat on Dora's couch, coffees before them on the table. Missy spoke first.

"I'd be interested in finding out what the CDC has to say. What are the by-the-book protocols in a situation like this?"

"Not really our job to know," Dora answered.

"Well, there could be liability if the hospital does the wrong thing, and I wouldn't want to be on the wrong side of that." Missy turned toward Dora as she sipped her coffee.

"Why?" Dora wanted to know. "We're not advising them about liability or the medical side of this. We're not lawyers or doctors. We're doing a criminal investigation—or the run up to one, to see if they want to call the cops in. What about calling those infectious disease specialists again, run some of this by them to at least get a better lay of the land?"

"Why don't we start with that?" Missy had brought along her computer; the two nascent investigators shared notes via Google Drive. Missy opened a document and dialed the phone number of the first lab.

"Babu Laboratories."

"Yes, hi. Is Dr. Babu available?"

"Who is calling?"

"My name is Missy Winters. I'm a researcher looking into infectious diseases, and I have some questions about particular pathogens."

"I'm sorry, Dr. Babu is unavailable, but if you leave your number, Dr. Winters, I'll see that he gets the message."

"Sure." Missy left her phone number. "To whom am I speaking?"

"I'm Dr. Spontana. Like Dr. Babu, I'm an infectious disease special-ist, but any information given out on the part of the laboratory would have to come from Dr. Babu."

"I see. Well, thank you. I'll wait for Dr. Babu's call."

Missy looked at Dora and raised an eyebrow.

"How 'bout we try the other one?" Dora suggested.

"You want to call her? That would be, let's see, Dr. Yvonne Traxle."

Dora dialed. "Dr. Traxle? My name is Dora Ellison. I'm calling as a follow-up. We spoke recently?"

"Ah, yes. About criminal intent behind rare disease infections. Don't tell me you have more such cases?"

Dora paused. "I don't believe I said we had any cases in the first place."

"Ah. My apologies. I made the assumption. How can I help you to-day?"

"I was wondering what the protocols would be if rare, deadly, infec-tious diseases began showing up in a hospital."

"You'd go over whomever the patients had been in contact with, where they'd been, and, of course, you'd double check hospital proce-dures and make sure everyone and everything was followed to the letter. There are also guidelines that would need to be put in place, but to an extent, those would depend on the disease."

"I see, and—"

"Assuming everything was in order—and it probably was, given that we're talking about extremely rare diseases, I suppose you could look at criminal possibilities. Who might do such a thing? And why? What might motivate a person to go to such lengths? Who would want to harm innocent patients?"

"I'm sorry. Are you asking as a psychologist?"

"I'm an infectious disease specialist, but I'm also a human being with a curious nature. If someone is infecting people purposely, I have an interest as a clinician in seeing justice done, and a curiosity as a human being as to why someone would do such a thing. Are they angry with the hospital? The system? These individuals? Are the individuals somehow connected?"

"Exactly why I called. What else can you tell me about the proper protocols for dealing with infectious disease outbreaks in hospitals?"

"First of all, it is crucial that the diagnoses be correct and confirmed. Some diseases may appear, to your average internist, to be other diseases. So, to ensure proper treatment, you want to make sure of correct diagnoses, followed by correct treatment. Then, I'd suggest you visit the CDC website. That's where you'd find the appropriate protocols."

"I see. Well, thank you." Dora ended the call and looked at Missy with an expression of intrigued curiosity. "Now why do you suppose she brought up criminal possibilities?"

## Chapter 10

George Campbell stood stock still at the front of the room, his arms folded over his chest; only his eyes moved, watching the doctors, nurses, physician's assistants, technicians, department directors, and security who filed into the hospital's crowded mini auditorium. Everyone wore masks, as COVID protocols remained ongoing, though the Omicron variant was waning in the New York area.

Dr. Matsumoto joined George at the front of the room. Dora sat off to one side, phone in hand, ready to record the relevant audio into her voice memos. Missy was working at the library.

Once everyone was seated, George stepped up to a microphone and blew into it.

"Hello? Okay, everyone. Settle down." He paused as the room quieted. "Thank you all for being here. Dr. Matsumoto, the board, and I have asked everyone who isn't in surgery to attend this brief meeting so I can inform you about an extremely serious situation that is unfolding here at BCMC, and to dispel any of the rumors that may be floating around."

He paused. "First of all, I want to assure you that we are scrutinizing every process, every procedure, all equipment, the actions of all personnel, every doctor, nurse, PA, and equipment source. Everything we do, and everyone who does it, is being examined and vetted."

He looked at Dr. Matsumoto, nodded, and took a few steps back as Dr. Matsumoto stepped to the microphone.

"Hi everyone. Yes, we have had several documented cases, including four fatalities to date, from four different diseases—at least three of which we do not normally see at BCMC or any hospital. These are rare, infectious, deadly diseases and, while I do not want to cause a panic—we have procedures and guidelines in place to deal with the situation—it is our responsibility to keep everyone informed. Each department will receive specific instructions. We will summarize some of those here today. We are also reaching out to infectious disease specialists at our laboratory affiliates for additional guidance. The changes and new procedures will affect multiple areas of practice and multiple hospital departments. These include but are not limited to air filtration, for which, in addition to HEPA filters, we will conduct infection-control risk assessments and make changes as necessary. Engineering and custodial will also assist as needed."

Matsumoto paused for questions, but there were none. The room was filled with the sound of rustling and whispering as people took notes or turned in their seats to softly exclaim to their neighbors.

The senior medical director continued. "Infection control will oversee these processes and answer to both myself and Mr. Campbell, and will, in effect, become a multidisciplinary hub. Construction and renovation will be analyzed for airborne vulnerabilities, and the environment, food, and care of immunocompromised patients will be scrutinized and prioritized, with the same checklist and analyses to applied to the rest of our patients as soon as possible thereafter."

He paused again. "All medical-related department directors have been given strict instructions as to how to prevent and eliminate pathogens with procedures that go the next step beyond COVID protocols. Infection control is priority one. All protocols are to be followed to the letter and any concerns shared with staff as appropriate."

George Campbell stepped in front of Dr. Matsumoto and spoke into the microphone. "We have already begun the process of limiting the locations that will be accessible to solely those that are appropriate to your job function. Bracelets that are color coded to hospital locations are being given out and will be checked by security teams that have been bolstered to meet the increased demand."

Dr. Matsumoto stepped in front of George. "Just as we made adjustments for the pandemic, so too are we making adjustments to meet this new challenge. Please understand that Mr. Campbell, the board, and myself have faith in your ability to rise to this new challenge."

Felice Ramirez, the public relations officer, looked at George expectantly, then whispered to him. He nodded, and she stepped to the microphone. "Just a few—just a few other items. The records department will be conducting epidemiologic reviews of many medical and laboratory records as we work to trace these pathogens. The need for isolation of patients, airborne infection isolation rooms, and/or negative pressure rooms will be evaluated and made available on an as-needed basis. Amended guidelines for the handling of blood, bodily waste, and equipment have been made available to all departments. As of now, new PPE guidelines are in place; if anyone does not have these or has any questions, please see me afterward. A hospital-wide no visitors policy is in effect as of now. All procedures will be continuously monitored, evaluated, and adjusted as needed." She turned to George, who gave a barely perceptible nod.

She continued. "We expect all of you to review and implement every new process for your job description and department immediately.

Reach out to your department director, Dr. Matsumoto, Mr. Campbell, or myself for any clarification or with any issues. Thank you, everyone."

•••

Hospitals are complex institutions made up of medical professionals, their staffs, administrators, and a host of employees, all of whom are charged with caring for and protecting the public health. Because hospitals are made up of human beings, each with their own preferences, abilities, and challenges, many with substantial pride and egos, the implementation of directives may not be performed as smoothly or efficiently as expected.

Federal and state guidelines for the management and reporting of infectious diseases affected every department of the Beach City Medical Center. Many of those in charge of instituting the new policies and changes were accustomed to being in charge of their own workspaces, rather than being told what to do and how to do it.

While, on the face of it, everyone understood and accepted the need for the new guidelines and procedures, there was grumbling, pushback, and intransigence. There was complaining and foot dragging, and there was outright refusal to implement what some saw as draconian, unnecessary procedures.

The process of fitting the hospital for the management of multiple infectious and deadly diseases was a cumbersome, awkward, often frustrating process, rife with miscommunication, aggravation, and confusion. The process was long and tempers were often short. Everyone had been jittery before the pandemic. Now, everyone affiliated with BCMC was anxious and waiting to see what would happen next.

• • •

Dora was sitting cross-legged on Missy's living room floor with Freedom's head on her knee; she was looking at Missy's laptop, which sat on the floor in front of her. Missy was on the couch, working a Sudoku on her iPad, with Comfort beside her.

Missy looked up and watched Dora for a few moments. Freedom raised her head; Comfort barked once and Freedom lowered her head.

"What do you want?" Missy asked suddenly. Dora glanced up, but said nothing, so Missy repeated the question. "What do you want? With us, I mean."

Dora shrugged without meeting Missy's gaze. "I don't really know."

"When might you know?"

"Miss, I was monogamous for a long time, with someone I was deeply in love with."

"I know that."

"I do like being with you, and I do trust you."

"Well, then."

"What do *you* want?"

Missy looked away.

"What?"

Missy pressed her lips together and looked Dora in the eye. Freedom gave a warning growl.

"Shhh," Dora said to Freedom.

Missy paused, then sighed. "I want to be in a relationship. A loving, trusting relationship, and I can offer that to you, if and when you're ready."

"Sounds like you're kind of hesitant."

"Well," Missy hesitated. She bit her lip. "Your violence scares me." She exhaled through tight lips and shook her head. "That stuff in the church parking lot—oh, man. I can't be going through that stuff. I'm a librarian, not James Bond."

Dora blinked a few times. "But it's never, ever directed toward you."

"I know," Missy murmured. "But still..."

Dora nodded slowly. "I understand." She looked at Missy with gentle compassion. "So, what does that mean for us?"

"You're a special, special person. You saved my life."

Dora snorted. "After putting it in danger in the first place."

"True."

They both laughed.

Missy bit her lip. "There are also financial issues. I have bills to pay."

"So do I. My primary income right now is babysitting."

"Yeah, but you have some savings from your sanitation job. Maybe...maybe I'll work with you—at Geller Investigations—part time and keep my library job."

"If that's what works for you."

"Well, don't pout!"

"I'm not pouting," Dora protested, clearly pouting.

"All right, let's get back to this. I've been thinking."

"Well, there's a good thing."

"Yeah, well, the infectious disease doctor said, and everything I read is in line with it, that it's impossible to truly trace how these people got these diseases."

Dora nodded. "Other than interviewing them—contact tracing, which they may need to sign up for in advance."

"And even then…"

"Right. Even if you could do it, it would be hard to have fast, precise knowledge."

"So, what are you saying?"

"If these are really crimes instead of practically impossible coincidences, we need a different approach."

Missy waited.

Dora looked at her and smiled. "Bait." Her cellphone rang. "Speak of the devil. Campbell."

"Hello, Mr. Campbell. What can I—"

George sounded frantic; his voice was a half-octave higher than usual, and he was speaking too quickly. "Have you seen what they're saying on Facebook and Twitter?"

"No, I haven't. When you say 'they,'—"

"They…everybody. Local groups. Moms' groups," he sputtered. "People! They're accusing BCMC of allowing people to get sick, to catch deadly diseases—to die!"

"I'm sorry to hear that."

*"You're sorry?"*

"You've got a bad situation on your hands."

"We—*we've* got a bad situation on *our* hands."

"Right."

"So, what are *we* going to do about it?"

Dora looked at Missy as she answered. "We have an idea."

· · ·

Tanya LaRue was a curvy woman with dark blonde hair wearing a clingy, flocked-heart bodycon dress, teardrop platinum earrings with small sapphires in their centers, and a charming smile. She was the owner of the Real Women Boutique that had opened several months earlier on Beach City's retail strip. Charlie Bernelli had taken her to lunch at the Bellissima Bistro to discuss her upcoming ad campaign.

Tanya had signed on with The Bernelli Group as her ad agency, but the pandemic had kept many customers away from retail establishments and Tayna had chosen to delay the store's grand opening, which was to coincide with a branded ad campaign.

"So?" Tanya touched Charlie's wrist with her fingertips. "What do you see as our headline and can you still get your infamous detective to model for us?"

Charlie kept an eye on the bartender, who was making his old fashioned, to make sure he didn't shake the ingredients. As his drink and Tanya's tequila sunrise were delivered, he again turned to his guest.

"I haven't spoken to Dora recently, but when I first brought it up, she was thrilled. She enjoyed modeling for the city's tourism campaign and people recognize her all the time for it."

"And for helping bring some ba-a-d people to justice," she emphasized, tapping his wrist again on the words "bad people." Her fingertips remained on his wrist, sending little electric shocks through his arm and into his chest. He raised his drink with his other hand.

"Well, she's recognizable around Beach City—sort of has her own brand," Charlie noted, "and would be a good face for your brand."

"And a good body for our brand," Tanya added. The boutique owner would herself have been a good body for her brand; she was a beautiful, voluptuous woman who was obviously proud of her beauty and, from Charlie's point of view, exuded sexuality.

"Did you have a particular idea for a slogan or campaign focus?" she asked, her fingertips tapping on "slogan" and "focus."

"What do you think of 'More Love'?"

Tanya gave a little gasp and sat back just enough to convey her joy without having to release Charlie's wrist, which she squeezed in her fist. She looked into his eyes for just a second without a word, then breathed, "Peerrrrfect."

He smiled, flattered. "I'm glad."

"Why don't you put my cell number into your phone so you can call or we can meet as other ideas occur?"

Charlie took out his phone and recorded Tanya's number. "Feel free to reach out to me, anytime," he said. "Really." She was looking into his eyes again; he wondered if her intent was as erotic as her effect on him was. He thought of Christine, and suddenly his sweet bride faded in his mind to ordinary, even drab.

• • •

That evening, he and Christine had just finished getting dressed when the doorbell rang. "Ooh, they're here," Christine said, and hurried to the door. Charlie was buttoning his shirt and slipping on his loafers, which he wore around the house without socks, despite Christine's disapproval. He overheard Christine's effusive greeting, first to his son, and then to Sarah.

When he emerged into the living room, he found Christine standing with the couple at the window, admiring the crimson and violet sunset. She was wearing a gold, sleeveless chiffon maxi dress with a thin shrug dotted with tiny pearl-like sequins.

"The morning sickness is gone," Sarah was saying. "Now, all I have to deal with is this crazy craving for cured meats, which is really strange as I've been a vegetarian for years."

"You never know what a baby will want," Charlie said as he walked into the room. He gave his son a pointed look, then a slap-on-the-back man hug, and kissed his future daughter-in-law, then stepped back and appraised her. "Maybe showing…"—he caught himself—"a little." He glanced at her, unsure of the situation's proper etiquette.

Sarah giggled. "You're being polite, Charles. But it's okay, you know, to tell a pregnant woman she's showing."

"Long as she really is pregnant!" Christine added, laughing.

"I think Sarah looks absolutely radiant." C3 took Sarah's hand and led her to the couch, where they sat down. "Get you a ginger ale?" C3 asked. Sarah nodded, and C3 went to the bar.

"My new client would say that women of all sizes are gorgeous and to be celebrated," Charlie proclaimed.

"Nothing wrong with that," Christine responded. "Though I'm not sure you believe it."

Charlie's smile vanished, but he said nothing.

"All women *are* beautiful," C3 observed. Surprised, Charlie looked thoughtfully at his son.

"Who's the client?" Sarah wanted to know.

"The new boutique on the strip—Real Women."

"Owned by…?"

"A Tanya LaRue," Charlie answered. He grinned. "Sounds like a stripper name, right?"

"Nice woman," Christine said. "I met her at the chamber meeting two weeks ago. Are they getting any traffic?"

"It's slow, but that's why she hired us," Charlie said as he got up to make himself a drink. "What can I get everyone?"

Once everyone had their drinks and was relaxing in the living room, Sarah sat forward. "C and I have something to tell you guys."

Charlie looked hopeful. "The sex of the baby?"

"Um, actually, we do know the sex of the baby, but that's not what we meant." She exchanged a look with C3.

"We're having a girl," C3 announced. "Her name will be Olivia."

Charlie clapped his hands. "Olivia Bernelli—our granddaughter!" He couldn't resist standing up, going to Sarah, and giving her a kiss and an awkward hug, since she remained seated. As he returned to his seat, he touched C3's arm in a gesture of congratulations.

Sarah looked into her lap, seemed to gather herself, then spoke again with another glance at C3. "We had some tests that are a routine part of prenatal care."

Christine went still, her hands in her lap. "What tests?"

"Well, we had something called the first trimester combined test, which is a blood test that measures the levels of certain elements of the blood, followed by a thing called a nuchal translucency test, where an ultrasound is used to measure a specific area on the back of your baby's neck."

"If these are normal tests, why are you telling us about them?" Charlie wanted to know. Christine gave him a severe look, silently telling him to be quiet.

"We're having follow-up tests, but the preliminary indication is that the baby may have Down's syndrome."

"Oh, my God!" Charlie sat back, looking stricken. He gulped his drink.

"Charles!" Christine chastised.

"We're having a follow-up called an integrated screening test, and there will be other testing beyond that."

C3 was holding his fiancé's hand between both of his; they looked at one another, and both their eyes filled with tears.

Sarah swallowed, then went on. "There's also something called a CVS test, and there's amniocentesis."

Charlie was looking from Sarah to C3 and back again. "What will you do if that's the diagnosis?"

"That's none of our business," Christine said, sharply.

Charlie took a swallow of his drink. "The hell it's not. You think C's qualified to make a decision like this? No offense, Sarah, but I know my son. He can barely keep his own shit together."

C3 stood up suddenly. "Listen, Dad. I'm a grown man and I'm right here. I'm working my ass off, staying clean and sober and present for my wife and family."

Charlie ignored his son; his focus was on Sarah. "What will you do?"

Sarah looked back at him, unblinking. "We're keeping the baby no matter the diagnosis."

Charlie threw his hands in the air. "Aw, for fuck's sake!"

"Charles!" Christine glared at her husband.

C3 sat down again beside Sarah. They hugged for a long time, swaying in each other's arms.

Christine turned to watch them and smiled.

• • •

That night, as Christine was getting undressed, Charlie was in their master bath with the shower running. He'd probably had too much to drink—but with good reason, he believed. He had been obsessively considering sending the text for much of the evening, and had only just now made his decision.

He took his cell phone from his pants pocket, found Tanya's number, and sent the text.

## Chapter 11

Dora and Missy were seated opposite George Campbell in his office. George rose from his seat, went to the office door and closed it, then sat down again.

"Until now, we have refrained from reporting these cases to the state and federal authorities. While we are required to report many diseases, we do have leeway to refrain from reporting the rare solitary case, and since each of these cases is a solitary case of that disease—we only have one of each, thus far—with nothing to tie them together except for my own, perhaps paranoid, suspicions," he smiled, "we have kept knowledge of these tragedies within the walls of our hospital." He looked at the two women, as though expecting a response.

"I see," said Missy. Dora said nothing.

"These decisions have been made by four of us together, and with the approval of the board."

"The four of you?" Dora repeated.

"Myself, our senior medical director—Dr. Matsumoto—the medical examiner, and the director at our lab—which is an outside contractor."

"Which lab would that be?" Dora asked.

George gave her a long look. "I don't think that information is something you need at this time. I'd like you to pursue and hopefully eliminate the possibility I brought up at our first meeting, and the reason for your hire—that these diseases are being intentionally spread. That would have nothing to do with an outside lab that has no access to our patients. We send out to them. They do not come to us."

"Understood," Dora said, a bit stiffly.

"We recently had a meeting of all clinical personnel and went over a range of CDC recommendations as to how to deal with outbreaks such as these. All our personnel—from doctors to custodians—are making appropriate changes to procedures."

• • •

Dora went to sleep with her head on one end of the old pile of Franny's clothes she slept with every night. She imagined the clothes still smelled like Franny, and perhaps they did.

"What am I going to do, babe?" she whispered and paused, listening, then said, "I know. When in doubt, do nothing." She turned to her side, facing the clothes, her eyes closed. "Yes, I like her quite a lot. I trust her —which is saying something. But she can't replace you, babe." She smiled. "I know," she said. "She doesn't have to."

She began to softly sing a song that was also a prayer Franny had sung to her when she'd been deep in the throes of her PTSD.

*"Hashkiveinu Adonai, eloheinu l'shalom, v'ha-amideinu malkeinu l'ḥayim."* The English translation was "Lay us down, oh Lord God, in peace, and raise us up again, our King, to renewed life." The prayer helped her sleep, and helped keep away Dora's own personal nighttime monsters.

She awakened the following morning to the doorbell ringing repeatedly. She went to the door, her arms folded against the cold, and found Missy, grinning in the sunshine in a gray hooded sweatshirt and jeans.

"We're hanging out with the group in an hour. Or did you forget?"

Dora turned and headed back toward the kitchen, leaving Missy to close the door and follow. The coffee machine was set to a timer, so the brewed coffee was nearly an hour old. She poured two mugs, set them on the table, went to the refrigerator, and returned with half-and-half and a Tupperware container of muffins.

"Made these yesterday. Banana and cinnamon."

"Oooh, girl can cook." Missy took one of the muffins from the container and took a bite; she chewed slowly and stopped. "Um, Dor. You said these are banana and cinnamon?"

Dora gave her a sleepy nod. "Yup. Had two an hour after I made them. Why?"

"Would you mind if I took a look at your cinnamon?"

Dora shrugged, got up, went to the spice rack next to the sink, and returned with a small container, which she held out to Missy.

Missy took the container, sighed, and gave it back to Dora. "This isn't cinnamon."

Dora examined the container. "Paprika. Shit."

Missy giggled. "And you didn't notice?"

Dora sat down, sipped her coffee and looked at Missy. "You making fun of me?"

Missy held up both hands. "I would never!"

• • •

An hour later the two sat around the periphery of a wood-paneled conference room on the second floor of the hospital with thirty other people.

Advocates for Improved Care was to be a combination PR campaign and investigatory vehicle dreamed up by Dora and approved by Adam Geller and, later, George Campbell. Members would be encouraged to share their stories of unhappy hospital experiences and would receive free therapy and the attention of hospital staff, who would work with the hospital administration to investigate issues and challenges brought to the group's attention. The idea was to flush out anyone who might be purposely infecting hospital patients.

At the same time, new hospital procedures already in place were restricting access to hospital areas to only those who were specifically approved and who wore the appropriate ID bracelets. Suspicious individuals would have their information and the suspicions of security personnel logged into the hospital's computer system, and this information would be cross-referenced with what Dora and Missy learned at the Advocates for Improved Care group.

The group's facilitator was a social worker named Shirley Nelson, a light skinned woman with short, boyish brown hair and brown-rimmed glasses. "Welcome to Advocates for Improved Care. We are here as a source of emotional support for anyone whose experiences at BCMC have been less than satisfactory. We have no connection with law enforcement. We are a forum for the candid, unfiltered expression of views and experiences of former or current patients and their families." The social worker's expression softened, her eyes exuding kindness. "This is a safe environment," she continued. "No one need give their last names or any identifying information about their case. Those who wish to do so can be assured of the discrete availability of caring therapeutic professionals who are here to offer free support, as well as an honest investigation of any and all complaints and issues. Questions?"

A balding man in his fifties with a fringe of gray hair and a cocoa brown mustache that matched his skin color raised his hand. "Will hospital representatives be a part of these meetings?"

Shirley shook her head. "I am here as a facilitator and therapist, and will not be communicating any identifying information to the hospital."

A woman in her seventies, wearing gray-framed bifocals and a white wool sweater over a pink blouse, tentatively raised her hand. "If the hospital's not involved in the group directly, how will our complaints be investigated?"

"Good question," Shirley answered. "The hospital administration will make their communications director available to myself and my staff so that we may pass along any specific case complaints, when requested. Unless you request otherwise, you and your families will remain anonymous."

"But if we remain anonymous, how can you investigate our case?" the woman continued. "I'm confused."

Shirley nodded "To address systemic concerns that may be ongoing, we would not necessarily need identifying information. To resolve a specific complaint, having such information may of course be helpful. When the time comes, we would discuss the situation with you privately, and you would make the decision as to what information to include or not."

The woman in the gray bifocals and wool sweater raised her hand again. "I guess I'll start, as long as no one is going to hold what I say against me."

"No one will even know who you are," Shirley assured her.

"Well, then. I came in recently after a fall. I've been falling more of late, and it scares me. I've had several friends pass after falls. Osteoporosis, you know. Well, I was pretty sure I had a concussion, and since the hospital is small and it was a busy Saturday night, I was told I would have to wait a bit in triage. Okay. Well, just then a woman comes in with her husband leaning on her shoulder and says he's been having chest pains. They told her what they told me. They'd have to wait. So they sat down with me and other people in the waiting room. Well, this woman's husband died of a heart attack, right there in the waiting room. I found out afterward that the wait was because they were having a hard time with a man who was having a seizure in one of the ER beds. Hard to believe no one could help this poor fellow with the heart attack!"

Next to speak was a woman with wrinkled pecan skin and long, black hair. "Two months ago, I had a pain in my stomach, and my husband told me to come here. I took over-the-counter pain killers, but it still hurt real bad. I sat here, waiting, while they took other people. Nobody took me seriously. The pain kept getting worse, and I kept asking when they could see me, and I could tell the lady behind the counter—two ladies really, because I was here for two shifts—they were getting annoyed with me. I said to them that I thought I had a problem with my appendix, but they didn't listen. Eventually, I was in so much pain I was yelling. That's when they checked me out—I was making a disturbance, so they couldn't play with their phones or whatever. A few hours later, they took out my appendix." She shook her head. "You gotta make noise, or they don't take care of you."

Next up was a gaunt woman with short, sandy brown hair and a reddish brown complexion. She sounded exhausted. "My name is Margarita Morales. I lost my brother to a disease no one ever heard of before. A disease they say is impossible to get. If that's true, then tell me, where's my brother? I sleep two hours a night. We were babies together. We played tag in the street. We sang songs together, even though our voices were not good." She managed a small smile. "There's something evil going on at this hospital. I don't know what it is, but trust me. It's evil, and it's here." She sat down, her expression bleak, then leaned back and closed her eyes.

A young Black woman in a beige blouse and a green blazer with an infant in her arms was next to speak. "Four days after I was due to give birth to this one I came in, right after my water broke at home. My contractions were bad and they put me in one of the ER rooms, where a doctor came in and checked me. She told me my water didn't break, and I said 'yes it did,' but she didn't seem to believe me, and she left the room. A half hour later, she came back, said I was ready and dilated, and they brought me to delivery, where I had my daughter. But even there, the nurse was just messing around on a computer while I was pushing my baby out. It seemed like no one cared."

Dora and Missy looked at one another, silently sharing compassion for the people in the room as the stories continued.

• • •

Sarah Turner was dictating and pacing back and forth in the tiny waiting room that bordered the two *Chronicle* offices.

"A meeting was held by the upper tier of the medical staff and administration at BCMC about a deadly and dangerous situation that is unfolding at the hospital, and about which the public has yet to be officially advised."

She paused, and Esther looked up. "Sound okay so far?" Sarah asked, and Esther nodded.

Sarah continued. "A meeting was held on the second of this month that included all department directors, senior medical staff, and administration, along with representatives of the construction and janitorial staff of the hospital..."

• • •

George Campbell was reading out loud from his computer screen and looking up every now and then at Dora and Missy, who were seated opposite his desk. "Campbell is quoted as instructing all personnel at the meeting to scrutinize every process, every procedure, all equipment, the actions of all personnel, every doctor, nurse, PA, and equipment source —everything that is done, and everyone who does it, to whatever degree is humanly possible."

As he read, he rapped his knuckles on his desk, emphasizing his words.

"BCMC has had documented cases of four of the deadliest diseases known to humankind—including four fatalities so far—from four different pathogens—at least three of which are not normally seen at BCMC or any hospital, for that matter." He glared at the two women, who said nothing. He stopped reading and addressed his guests. "*The Chronicle* goes on to name the diseases and talks about how deadly they are."

"That's accurate, right?" Dora asked.

"Sure, but someone at our meeting leaked it to the press. In fact, I'm pretty sure someone was taping our meeting and gave the tape or digital file to the press. What they wrote is pretty much word for word."

"Undoubtedly," said Missy. "And it could have been pretty much anyone."

"Well, maybe this news story will flush someone out," Dora suggested.

"Maybe the article will damage the hospital's reputation!" George continued to glare at his guests.

"Sounds like the article does talk about how hard your people are working to address the situation," Missy pointed out.

George snorted, turned back to the screen, and began reading again. "Areas of the hospital that are undergoing change as a result of these new policies include but are not limited to air filtration, engineering, custodial, infection-control, construction and renovation, and all medical-related departments." He skimmed to a point further down in the article. "Focus is on preventing and eliminating pathogens, with infection control now priority one. The records department will be conducting epidemiologic reviews of all medical and laboratory records in an attempt to trace these pathogens. The need for isolation of patients, airborne infection isolation rooms, and/or negative pressure rooms will be evaluated and made available on an as-needed basis."

He looked up. "So, I guess the answer is yes."

"So this isn't really an unfair picture of your meeting," Dora suggested. "And I would think it would be good for your reputation."

George leaned forward. "It was a private meeting!"

Dora shook her head. "I think it's unrealistic to expect that a meeting about a life and death situation that was attended by—how many people were there?"

George threw up his hands. "I don't know. Seventy-five? Eighty?"

"A lot of people, would go unreported. People want to know about these things, and news will organically spread."

"Your job," George snarled, "is to fix this!"

Dora sighed; Missy looked anxiously into her lap.

George's desk phone buzzed and George picked it up, listened for a moment, then slammed it down again.

"And now, the meeting is all over Facebook!"

• • •

The balding man in his fifties with the gray hair and brown mustache returned for the second meeting of Advocates for Improved Care. "My little sister has all sorts of medical issues and they can't seem to figure out what's wrong with her," he explained. "She once waited six hours in the ER waiting room, despite being in *bad*—throwing up, gasping in pain. The nurse took a look at her and insulted her. Next time, they told her she had to take this pink pill. She told them she couldn't take it because she was allergic to it, but they made her take it anyway. She had a seizure and nearly died. They told her she had the cancer. She was in terrible pain. They eventually gave her morphine, but they pulled the tube out of the IV in the middle of the night. She woke up and just walked out of the hospital, driven by the pain. They found her wandering the streets three blocks from here, with that IV connector still in her arm."

A wrinkled woman of Pakistani heritage with a hint of an accent spoke next. "A month ago my husband woke up in pain and went to the bathroom for literally hours. He had stool that kept changing, from pebbles to diarrhea to bloody. I brought him here and spent too much time doing paperwork. Meanwhile, he kept going to the bathroom. They wouldn't hook him to an IV until a doctor saw him. They did an exam of his bottom and accused us of exaggerating his symptoms! They told him he had a serious bacterial infection and gave me pills—strong antibiotics, I think. Two months later, he had a CT scan and was told he had diverticulitis. Eventually, his colon was perforated. It was a nightmare, and he was treated as if he were a child."

• • •

The third meeting of Advocates for Improved Care was on a dreary, windy Tuesday afternoon. It had been raining off and on all day, the temperature in the low fifties; the streets were strewn with fallen leaves blowing in little circles.

A big man in a wheelchair pushed by a tiny, worried-looking woman raised his hand. He had skin the color of an oak tree, shoulder length brown hair, and a sleeve of black tattoos. "I came for spinal surgery almost exactly a year ago. I walked in. They gave me a needle in my spine —an epidural, and then I had surgery. Well, when the anesthesia wore off I was screaming in pain. They couldn't give me enough meds—and this was still through the epidural! The nurses kept telling me I was being too sensitive. Jesus! Four days later, I told them I still couldn't feel my legs—and this pain in my back that wasn't getting better. They ran some tests and said they found a tumor on my spine that had been aggravated by the epidural. It's been a disaster ever since. As you can see, I'm still not walking and my sister"—the worried-looking woman managed a small smile—"takes me around and nurses me. I'm done with chemo and the doctors say I have a 50-50 chance of walking." He shrugged, his mouth twisting in a grimace, and shook his head. "I'm doing my best."

A young Latinx man with tight, black curly hair and an easy smile spoke next in a gentle voice. "I have a yard work business and noticed this weird tingle in my belly. I didn't worry, and it went away. Four days later, also while working, I got these terrible pains. I had to go sit in the truck; then I had to walk around. Eventually it got a little better, but then it came back, so I came to the ER at BCMC. I was here for a while and they found nothing. I don't have insurance, so I didn't want to come, you know? I left, but the pain came back and eventually it got so bad, I did come back—three times, and the first two times I saw the same doctor and he sent me home. He said it was probably gas and reminded me that it went away each time. But the third time I saw a different doctor, who felt around and did some kind of test and said I have a double hernia, and I needed surgery. It took a while to get it done because there was no insurance. They said it would be an easy surgery. Well, it was three and a half hours. Way longer than they said. Afterward, my nurse said the first ER doctor should have figured this out. I'm okay now, but I still have to be careful at my job. There are things that are hard for me to lift."

An angry red-headed woman in her thirties wearing a nurse's uniform was next. "I've seen a lot of bad care here, I'm sorry to say, and it's frustrating because my job is to help people. I was working postpartum and had a patient who'd had a C-section. She had an ultrasound, but when they opened her up, they found her full of cancer. Imagine that?

"Another was a middle-aged man who had these terrible headaches. He came in three times and was sent home with migraine meds each time. Well, the fourth time, he also had a black eye. What they found was that he had a sinus cavity that had burst and leaked liquid into his brain and gave him meningitis. He lived—but barely.

"Another case was a woman who loved to ski. She had been having a weird muscle issue in one of her legs and after skiing one weekend, she came in—that was on a Monday last winter—and said one of her feet wasn't right. She couldn't keep her skis aligned, which is something you need to do. One of her skis kept turning outward. She was given some anti-inflammatory meds and sent home. Twice. She was treated for a sprained ankle. Well, three months and two doctors later, they found out she had Lou Gehrig's disease. Today she can't move. She's paralyzed. Gotta tell you, the crap I see here is disgusting."

## Chapter 12

Dora and Missy had agreed to dig into the notes from the hospital group after the third meeting, when they returned to Adam's office. Despite her loud, irate protests, Thelma showed them how to use the database software they would need to track down the people from the meetings, using license plate numbers they collected in the parking lot following each session. The partners had scoured the lot as group members returned to their cars and took note of the plate numbers of many of the group participants.

As they worked, Missy turned to Dora. "Notice anything these people have in common?"

"Well," Dora answered, after thinking about it. "Not many are white."

"Right," said Missy. "Maybe the white ones skip the groups and go right to lawyers."

Dora bit her lower lip. "I doubt if it's that simple, but I do agree that a lot of these are people of color. As a whole, I'll bet their care is worse."

"I suspect that, as a group, their everything is worse."

"Think most hospitals have stories like these?"

"I suspect most do," Missy said. "Caring for loved ones is emotional, and everyone expects their own care to be successful."

"I know." Dora said with a rueful smile. She was thinking of her beloved Franny, who had been intentionally killed by a hit-and-run driver.

"There's certainly no shortage of pissed off patient families."

The license plate numbers they had collected were for a half-dozen patients or their relatives who were among the angriest of the group's attendees.

The first was a license plate for a 2019 Ford Fusion, owned by the son of an elderly woman who had fallen and cracked her hip, had a pin inserted into the joint, had been moaning in her hospital room all night, from either pain or anxiety, until she'd had a heart attack the following day. The woman was Sofia Allen. Her eldest son, Brian, had lodged a complaint and come to the group. He said he didn't expect much, but wanted to follow any thread toward whatever resolution he could find. His mother would have done at least that much for him, he observed.

Another plate was for the 2017 Chevy Equinox of an angry forty-something man whose daughter had given birth to a baby with an enlarged heart. The baby had died a few days later.

A third plate belonged to a sunset-colored Kia Sportage owned by a large woman with a pixie cut of reddish blonde hair and scarlet-framed glasses, whose mother had been hospitalized for dementia and had died of edema and infection in her leg. The woman had never communicated to anyone about the condition of her leg, possibly because she didn't understand what it was. The leg was found to have a thick rubber band deeply embedded in the wound.

Another plate belonged to a black, 2020 Porsche 911 Carrera Cabriolet, owned by a quiet man in his mid-fifties with unkempt gray hair and large, dark eyes, who was attending on his own behalf. He had been diagnosed with an anxiety disorder, but he didn't talk much about medical issues. He began by briefly mentioning that he'd been in the hospital, and veered off to inform the group that his doctor and two of his nurses were members of a cabal made up of Satanic, cannibalistic pedophiles who engaged in worldwide sex trafficking.

Missy was seated at Adam Geller's desk and was working her way through the database.

"Who comes up with this stuff?" Dora wanted to know.

"It's called QAnon," Thelma's voice called from the front of the office. "Twenty percent of the country believes it!"

"Is that true?" Dora looked at Missy in astonishment.

Missy turned to face her without changing her expression. "Sixty-five million people."

"And what about that other thing he was saying?" Dora continued.

"About birds not being real?" Missy asked. Dora nodded.

"Talking about birds," Thelma's voice rumbled from the front of the office, "why don't you see dead ones everywhere? They ought to be in the streets, backyards, on the sidewalks, on everyone's lawns." She appeared in the doorway, a hand on one hip of her no-nonsense yellow and brown print dress, her hair piled high in some 1940s style. "They say there are two hundred billion birds in the world. So where are all the dead ones?" She stood for a moment, her words echoing off the office walls. Then she turned and disappeared.

"You believe that birds aren't real?" Dora called out.

"Didn't say I believed it," Thelma replied. "I just asked where all the dead ones are."

Dora and Missy looked at one another and shook their heads.

They found several former patients who had low level scientific backgrounds. One had a sister who had been a nurse at a major orthopedic hospital in New York City and whose tenure at that facility appeared to have ended with a happy retirement party, complete with photos and a short video on Facebook of her blowing out candles on a cake.

Missy turned from her computer to look at Dora, who waited. "The kid with the hernia is Carlos Rivera. He works at a hospital in the city."

"What does he do?"

"Security."

Dora paused, then shook her head. "I don't see it. He doesn't have the know-how—unless he enlisted significant help, and how would he do that?"

"Okay," said Missy. "Here's another one. The guy whose sister wandered out of the hospital while on morphine is Michael Anderson. He drives a limo. The woman who had the baby who said no one cared is Abigail King. Hmm. Seems she works at a lab that processes blood. Now, that's interesting."

"It is. Hang onto it," Dora agreed, writing the names down on a piece of paper.

They worked for another half hour. "Here's something. That nurse with the red hair? She works at BCMC, and guess who her father is?"

"Who?"

"Her name is Marilyn Campbell. Her father's George Campbell."

"Whoa." Dora sat back in her chair, tapping her mouth with the eraser end of a pencil that had been in the desk that Missy was working on. "Maybe she's twisted up somehow about her father's work?"

"Well," Missy mused, "the father sure is a piece of work. The daughter could be too, in her own way."

"Families can and will fuck you up," Dora said knowingly.

"Still," Missy continued, "I'm not sure any of these people has the knowledge to find and handle rare deadly diseases. I'm thinking that would require more than run-of-the-mill medical knowledge."

Dora was unconvinced. "Maybe. Maybe not. You get one of these people with some medical connection, and piss them off enough to make them crazy, so to speak, and you might have motive and some opportunity. When it comes to something like this, we don't know what we don't know."

"But you'll agree the nurse is worth looking into?"

Dora nodded emphatically. "Absolutely. As are," she looked at the paper in front of her, "Carlos Rivera and Abigail King."

After another hour they were finished with the list, having found no shortage of angry former patients and families of patients at BCMC, some of whom had at least a modicum of medical or scientific knowledge and ability.

Missy tipped her head to either side, equivocating. "We don't know what we don't know about the spread of deadly, infectious diseases." She looked at the computer. "All sorts of people spread disease without even knowing they're doing it. Maybe it doesn't require precision, though you'd have to be able to either keep the diseases or"—she pointed a finger—"have access to a place that does. What we need to do is to learn more about the subject." She took a breath. "We don't really know what any of these people is really capable of."

"How 'bout this," Dora began. "You research how to find and handle these diseases, and I'll check up on our list of suspects."

Missy nodded slowly. "Something else to think about. I know it's far-fetched, but you know who else has occasion to see the impact medical mistakes or failed medicine has on people and families?"

"Who?"

"Shirley Nelson—the social worker who runs the group. She has a ringside seat. And she volunteered for this position—advocated for it, in fact."

• • •

The weather turned colder as Thanksgiving approached. Crowds on the boardwalk thinned, as did the flocks of surfers in the water—though neither dwindled below the small number of avid folk who would surf, run, and enjoy the outdoors in just about any weather, year round. Walking dogs on the beach was technically against the law in Beach City, but many residents ignored the law, particularly during the colder weather, when beachgoers were rare. Most, like Missy and Dora, made sure to clean up after their dogs, keep them away from small children, and out of the roadways.

Missy and Dora took frequent walks together on the beach, often holding hands, watching the waves and letting Comfort and Freedom run free. The dogs chased after one another and bounded in and out of the surf, until Comfort decided they'd had enough and barked at Freedom to let her know it was time to go home.

## Chapter 13

Dora and Missy were sitting next to one another behind Adam Geller's desk, scrutinizing the list of aggrieved members of the AIC—Advocates for Improved Care.

Thelma stood in the doorway between the street-facing front of the office and the back room, arms folded across her chest, leaning with one hip against the doorway. "I'm sure you geniuses have thought of this, but why would a murderer come to a group designed to catch a murderer? Wouldn't a murderer stay away from a group for patients with beefs against the hospital? Besides, the murderer already has the solution to his beef with the hospital—kill people."

No one answered her.

"The silent treatment, eh?" She pushed herself away from the wall and walked into the room, stopping next to the computer at which Missy was sitting. "Adam says to show you how to track down information about the huckleberries on your list." She raised an eyebrow, waiting. Missy got up and let Thelma slide into her seat.

"Where is Adam?" asked Dora. "He's hardly here."

"He's here plenty, but right now he's chasing after some cheatin' nobody whose wife is working two jobs and raising their kids all by herself. And anyway, what I'll be showing you is the nuts and bolts of what he does." The gruff office manager slid her chair back from Adam's desk and nodded toward another chair. "Go on. The database won't look at itself."

Dora and Missy looked at one another; Dora gave a "you do it" nod to Missy, who took a seat behind the computer.

"You already scratched the surface of the database, so you know how to open it and do some basic searches."

"I do," Missy agreed, as she clicked on a program icon.

"This particular database combines information pulled from driver's licenses; book club lists; registered vehicles, including cars, trucks, motorcycles, boats and trailers; cell phone users; uniform commercial code listings; corporate officers and registered agents; certain internet search engine results; pizza delivery names, addresses, and phone numbers; public postings of liens and judgments; bankruptcies and foreclosures; names that appear in newspapers and magazines; and public professional licenses."

"Wow," Missy breathed.

As Thelma spoke, she leaned forward and pointed to menus, dropdowns, and forms on the screen, then sat back, arms folded across her chest. "You can also take the information this gives you and look up who else might have had that same address at the same time, which will give you the spouse or roommate or what have you. Then you, or maybe this one," she pointed a thumb towards Dora, "can go talk to them, if that's what you want."

"Got it," Missy said.

"But before you start following anyone around, I need to explain the way we do things around here."

"We?" Dora asked.

"Yeah, we. I have a PI license, too," the perpetually grumpy woman groused.

Thelma proceeded to show Missy how to search the county property appraiser's website, the Federal Bureau of Prisons' Prisoner Locator

Database, and the New York State Supreme Court and County Courts online access, as well as the State Criminal Courts'.

Dora would have estimated Thelma's age at anywhere from mid-forties to late sixties. She watched the woman's fingers fly over the keys, shifting from one website to another, until they had the results.

"There you go," Thelma sat back, eyes bright. The woman had reverse-aged fifteen years while she worked. Dora wondered why she was not more active in the investigatory end of the business, and whether Thelma may not have always followed the letter of the law.

Slowly, Missy took over, and began performing the searches herself. Carlos Rivera and Abigail King came up clean, but Marilyn Campbell had received a restraining order for brutality in a divorce case. The other result was even more surprising: Shirley Nelson, the social worker running the group, had two outstanding warrants for insufficient funds; the woman had a history of writing bad checks.

• • •

Keisha Williams and Nia Paulson paid for their lunches and carried their trays to the nearest table in the hospital's lunchroom. Some kind of talk was going on. Two young men in light blue collared shirts and jeans —one a white man with pudgy cheeks and wheat-colored hair that had been carefully combed and probably sprayed in place, the other a Black man with a squared off Afro, a thin mustache, and expensive eyeglasses. They were standing a few feet from where the women had taken their seats. The men looked at them and smiled. The Black man came over and put out a hand.

"Hello ladies. I'm Darius Winston and my friend is Gregory Wright. We've been asked to come by and add a little perspective to a few things."

Nia flipped back one of her plaited braids, which she wore down today. She speared a bit of barbecued chicken with her fork and took a bite. "Perspective. Really?"

Keisha had crossed her legs and tipped her head slightly back, so she was looking down at the men, though they were standing and she was not. "Huh," was all she said.

Their talk was well-prepared and rehearsed—a slickly produced show that first flattered and ingratiated, then presented a case against unionizing, and finished with compliments that further curried favor with the audience, so that the summation, which was delivered with the emotional resonance and apparent conviction of a preacher, had maximum impact. The presentation left some in the audience converted, others suspicious and dubious.

"If you go out on strike," Winston explained, "you may not be allowed to return to your jobs."

Keisha spoke without rising from her seat; her voice rose for her. "There's a health crisis happening right here under our feet. People are getting sick—out of nowhere. It's happening right here at BCMC, and nobody's talking about it."

"What are you trying to say?" someone asked.

"That's dangerous talk," came a voice from somewhere in the middle of the room.

Keisha looked hard in the direction the voice came from. "It's the truth, and knowing the truth and being able to speak the truth without fear of retribution—that right there is why we need a union. We need to know we got people behind us." She stood up, looked out over the room, then turned to look at Winston. "We have every right to organize, and management has no right to stand in our way."

"There's some truth to that," Winston agreed, his demeanor relaxed and easy. "This is America. You can do whatever you want—in or outside the workplace. We're just here to give you a clearer picture of what the future might look like. Take it or leave it. Just sayin' that if you organize, you'll see, and you just might thank me."

One of the nurses at Keisha's table leaned toward her. "By law they can't stand in our way, but that doesn't mean they won't. Before you got here, they said we can be fired for cause and replaced. Our jobs aren't regulated or looked at in any way. Hospitals, nursing homes, and assisted livings can do whatever they want—legal, illegal—it don't matter."

"She's right," Winston agreed, with a sunny smile. "Medical field's not like other industries. You have to give ten days notice if you're gonna strike, so they can hire workers to fill in."

Keisha and Nia looked at one another. Nia stood up and turned toward the people assembled. "We need to stand together. That's the only way anything will ever be done about the crazy overtime, the lack of a morning break, the—"

A man in the back stood up. "I signed up two weeks ago," he said, pointing toward the front of the room, "and the next day my tires got slashed."

Keisha had never seen the man before, and wondered if the union busters had brought him.

Gregory Wright stepped over to Nia and pulled a thick wallet out of the back pocket of his jeans. "You all should have gotten here fifteen minutes earlier, when all the food was free. But I'll tell you what. I'm going to reimburse your lunches. See, that's what we're trying to tell you. We're not bad people. C'mon. How much was that lunch—eight dollars, right?"

"Nine-fifty."

Wright held out a bill. "Here's ten." He held a bill out first to Nia, then Keisha. "And you take ten, too. And go ahead and do your thing, if that's what you think is right. Tell your friends to spend their money on a union that's here for no reason but taking it. That's all it is—a scam."

Keisha rose slowly to her feet. She pushed the money away and turned toward the lunchroom crowd. "Nobody's buying my loyalty. We're committed to seeing for ourselves, so we can take care of our families, our homes, and the patients in this hospital's facilities. We work with substandard conditions every day." She turned to Wright. "You don't work here, so you don't know."

Wright shrugged and pocketed the money. "I'm here because I was in a medical union much like the one you're trying to form. It was in New Jersey, just this side of the Pennsylvania border. I was an aide in a nursing home. Look at me, folks." He scanned the crowd. "I'm looking every one of you in the eye and I'm telling you, I was scammed by that union. We had newspaper articles in the local papers at that time. They tell the story—confirm what we're telling you. We're handing them out so you can read them for yourselves."

He took portion of a pile of papers from Winston and the two passed them out to the crowd, while Nia and Keisha looked on. Some of their friends who had signed pledge cards sat at nearby tables—Martha, Cherise, and Stella Malone, whose hair was dyed so black it was blue. All looked back at Nia and Keisha with doubt in their eyes.

• • •

"Got something," Missy said, her eyes wide with excitement. Dora was out of the office, learning what she could about Shirley Nelson, the social worker who had volunteered to supervise the AIC group.

Thelma got up from her billing work in the front of the office, came to the back, and looked over Missy's shoulder as Missy pointed at the screen, paraphrasing as she read.

"Six months ago, Marilyn Campbell was accused of striking two patients." She was looking at an online article in *The Chronicle.* "It says here that she claimed they were unruly and she was doing her best to handle them, and that both were strong, non-compliant men." She turned and looked at Thelma.

"Maybe they were strong, non-compliant men," Thelma mused, "but that doesn't mean you can whack 'em around."

"From what I can see," Missy said, "no one followed up on these accusations. At least, there's no public record of any resolution."

Thelma was squinting at the screen. "Look at the end of the article."

Missy looked and read out loud. "Prior to coming to BCMC she worked for two years as a phlebotomist at a hospital-affiliated lab."

• • •

Christine was reading but her mind kept wandering to Olivia. She was delighted that Sarah and C3 were having the baby, and was imagining herself and Charlie taking their granddaughter to the beach and some of the local playgrounds. She deeply believed that Olivia deserved a chance at life, despite the challenges she and her parents were certain to face, given her special needs. The family would need all the support they could get, and Christine was determined to give them that support.

She heard the apartment door open and close and looked up from her book. She was a big fan of Barbara Kingsolver's. The woman could make a shopping list sound brilliant. Charlie came into the bedroom and loosened his tie, his jacket over his arm.

"You're home late."

He leaned over the bed and kissed her. "Business dinner."

"Oh?" She pretended to go back to reading. "Who's the client?"

"Wally Lantanna—Lantanna Real Estate."

"How'd it go?"

He pulled off his tie, then unbuttoned his shirt and shrugged it off. "Great. He re-upped!" He stepped out of his pants and into the bathroom. She could hear him urinate, then wash his hands and brush his teeth.

He was lying. She could smell the Jean Patou 1000 Eau de Parfum— expensive perfume she had smelled on him one other time: after his initial meeting with Tanya LaRue. He wouldn't lie if all they'd done was share a business dinner. There was only one reason for him to lie. As her eyes moved across the page, Christine thought about what she might do about her cheating husband.

• • •

At 3:30 p.m. the following afternoon, Laurie, Christine's assistant, buzzed her, and said that Adam Geller was in the outer office.

"Send him in."

Adam came in smiling; they had met at various city functions and Chamber of Commerce meetings over the years and were politely fond of one another within the context of their business relationship. Geller Investigations was one of Beach City's staple white-collar businesses, along with several law firms, realtors, and insurance brokers. Adam had never failed to be an eloquent, charming, sincere gentleman—qualities Christine thought were in short supply in most men.

"So wonderful to see you." He took her hand in both of his as she leaned forward and gave him her usual double air kiss. "You look better every time I see you. That Charlie Bernelli's a lucky man."

Christine couldn't help but look unsettled. Adam was a gentleman, but also a bit of a flirt. Still, Christine couldn't deny that he appealed to her, perhaps more than usual, given the lack of any sort of gentleman in her life at the moment. "Maybe someone ought to tell him," she murmured. Seeing Adam's expression, she realized she had said this out loud, and looked down sheepishly.

Adam looked surprised. "I'd be glad to. If the man doesn't treat you like gold, just say the word and I'll make him aware."

Christine laughed, delighted by Adam's charm and show of support.

"I have a question," Adam said.

She looked at him a moment too long. "Tell you what. Can you hold the question, and we'll discuss it over drinks at The Elegant Lagoon? Would that be an imposition?"

Adam looked briefly surprised, then pleased. "Not at all. Even better!"

Once they were at the restaurant, Adam slid Christine's chair in and sat down, then signaled to the waiter, with a glance at Christine. "White wine?"

She smiled and nodded.

The waiter arrived.

"Sauvignon Blanc 2019?"

The waiter gave a polite nod of assent, then stepped away.

"So, tell me," Adam began, covering Christine's hand with his. "Is Charlie taking you for granted, and what can we do about it?"

Now that they were together, at the restaurant, Christine was less sure of herself. She waved the question away. "Charlie's—well, Charlie."

"Exactly." Adam's disconcertingly steady gaze saw right through her and she felt herself blush, though whether from her embarrassment at Adam's attention, her growing attraction to him, or their shared awareness of Charlie's obvious shortcomings, she wasn't quite sure. In fact, she wasn't sure of very much at all right now.

She took a breath and pressed her lips together. "What did you come to the office to ask me?"

"About the hospital's gala. Given this…craziness at the hospital, and the effect it may or may not have—you tell me—on the hospital's reputation, what is the city's position on participating in the gala?"

Christine looked back at Adam and, for a moment, didn't answer. Then she laughed. "Let's talk about Charlie."

Adam laughed along with her, and Christine couldn't help noticing the kindness in his eyes—their combination of admiration, respect, and good humor, and she found herself suddenly aware of his aftershave, or perhaps it was some pheromone or even a manifestation of her own feelings, though she was pretty sure it was physical. She was aware that she and Adam had come to know one another, first as passing business acquaintances, then as something more—warmly familiar colleagues whose relationship was founded on mutual respect. There was much to be said for that, and it was more than she could say for many men, particularly the one she was married to.

• • •

Earlier that day, Adam Geller had given Dora her second lesson in tracking, tracing, and surveilling. He had been out the previous day doing exactly that on one of the three divorce cases he was working, and he shared notes about his day's experience with Dora, along with tips, tricks, and advice that would build on his prior instruction and what Dora had learned in her brief time at the Beach City Police Academy six months before.

"The address we have for Shirley Nelson may or may not be correct," he explained. "You can check by calling directory assistance and asking for an operator, then saying you've got this person whose number is unpublished, which hers seems to be, but you just want to verify the address. Nine times out of ten the operator will do that—verify or deny the address as valid."

Dora discovered that the address in the hospital records for Shirley Nelson was indeed valid, and since Shirley was at work at the moment, Dora had been tasked with knocking on the doors of neighbors' homes to see what she could learn about the social worker.

. . .

Adam sipped the last of his wine without taking his eyes from Christine's. "Would you like to continue this conversation at my apartment?" He blushed. "I can't believe I asked you that. I'm sorry. That was unprofessional."

Christine didn't answer right away. "I would," she said, after making up her mind. "But I'm not going to. Whatever is going on with my husband, I'm not about to step out on him."

Adam looked at her. "Are you sure?"

She looked at Adam, then looked quickly away. "I should probably leave, because no, I'm not sure. It's not a question of what goes around comes around, but one of morals. My morals. I married him. I promised certain things—to Charlie and to God, and whatever other people may do, I do my best to be impeccable with my word."

Adam again covered her hand with his. "You're a breathtaking woman, and he's a breathtaking fool if he's cheating on you."

She smiled ruefully and pulled her hand away. "Maybe we don't have to leave quite so soon. How about we order dinner?"

They did, and after the waiter had taken their order, Adam gave Christine a sad smile. "In a way I'm glad you said no—to leaving together, I mean. My mouth sometimes writes checks my body can no longer cash." He chuckled. "Those days might be over for me. The physical stuff, I mean."

"Don't be so sure," Christine answered, smiling. "You came to me with a question about our local medical community. They might be of help with that." She nodded toward his lap.

Adam laughed. "You might be right, but truth be told, at this point in life I like the romance, kindness, and love every bit as much."

She gave him a flirting glance. "Maybe you can have both."

## Chapter 14

Emmanuel Funte lived diagonally across the street from Shirley Nelson. He was an olive-skinned man with a shock of frizzy black hair, dark, wary eyes, and heavy eyebrows. As he opened the door and leaned toward her, an Irish Setter nosed around his thigh and sniffed at Dora.

"Oooh, he's a beauty."

Funte's expression immediately changed. He grinned. "Blarney's my buddy. Has been for eleven years."

"Mmm, and hopefully quite a few more. I just rescued Freedom, a combination Rottweiler-Doberman."

"Great name! How old is he?"

"Good question. I'm not sure. The vet says that, judging by her teeth, she's probably about three."

"She—sorry."

"No worries."

"So, what can I help you with?"

Dora followed Adam's instructions: be as honest as you can be without giving much away. *Remember, people usually want to help.*

"I'm a private investigator, and I wanted to ask about one of your neighbors. Would it okay if I came in?"

Funte put on an N95 mask. "Do you mind putting on a mask? And are you vaccinated?"

Dora pulled a mask from her pants pocket. "Vaccinated and boosted."

Funte held the door for Dora, and she entered a sparse living room furnished in shiny metal and glass, with prints of beach-related paintings adorning the walls and a pair of silver candlesticks centered next to a bowl of fruit in the dining area. Blarney sniffed emphatically around Dora's middle until she rubbed behind his ears and patted his side. She pulled out her phone and opened her photo app, and held the phone up for Funte to see.

"This is my Freedom."

"She's gorgeous."

"And really smart."

"Blarney's kind of a dummy, but a sweet dummy."

"I can see that—the sweet part, not the dummy!"

They both laughed.

Funte led Dora to a blue fabric couch and invited her to sit down.

"Can I get you some coffee?"

"Only if it's already made."

"Made and fresh."

"Thank you." Dora talked as Funte retrieved two mugs from a cabinet, poured their coffees, and brought them to the table. "So, I wonder if you can tell me about Shirley Nelson. I know she works over at the hospital as a social worker. But has she been going through a particularly rough time recently that you're aware of?"

Funte sat down in an armchair that matched the couch. "How do you mean?"

"Well, she's such a compassionate person at work. I just wonder if she were going through a hard time, personally, I mean—with, say, medical or family issues, or both—would she share such things with others? What I mean is, does she have anyone who might be as understanding for her as she is for her clients or patients at the hospital?"

"Hmm." Funte thought about this, then looked up at Dora. "Cream? Sugar?"

"Oh, yes. Thanks. Cream would be great, and a sugar substitute, if you have it."

"Splenda?"

"Perfect."

They flavored their coffees, then sipped together.

"You know, between you and me, Shirley has been in some dicey relationships and perhaps has made some bad choices."

"I'm sorry to hear that."

"Well, she has a daughter who is in trouble a lot—drinks and hangs out with a crowd of kids on the beach at night in the summertime and behind some of the stores in town when it's colder. You know, behind The Elegant Lagoon and the laundromat. Sometimes they light fires in garbage cans. Mostly they drink, and they're loud. They're trouble in a sense, but nothing terrible."

"Have you spent much time talking to her?"

"A bit, yes. I have a daughter just a few years older, and she's also a handful. We've talked a little bit about what she's in for when her daughter gets to be my daughter's age. And it seems to be going in that direction."

"Has she talked about anything else? Any illnesses in the family?" Dora took another sip of her coffee and tried to look impressed. "Coffee's great."

"Thanks. I buy it wholesale at that new little coffee shop just outside of town. Now that I think of it—yes. Her mother passed—breast cancer, about a year ago. It was unexpected. She'd been sure the doctors had removed it all; she had a double mastectomy a year prior. Or, more like a year and a half ago. Her prognosis had been good. My understanding is that they botched her mother's surgery. At the very least, they didn't get it all. It was a shock. She was devastated. I know because her mother used to watch my daughter Mary."

"What was her mother's name?"

"Lucille. Lucy. Everybody loved Lucy." He gave a little laugh. "Like the TV show. But she adored, I mean adored, her mother. Lucy babysat for half the neighborhood over the years. Everyone who was anyone around here showed up at that wake. Shirley was inconsolable and really, really pissed. You know, about the unfairness of it all."

• • •

Someone in the crowd coughed and at least five heads turned to see who it was; such was the paranoia of life in the era of the pandemic.

It was after-hours on a Monday night when Rudy's Bar was typically closed. He had agreed to stay open for his friends Hakeem and Keisha, who were spearheading efforts to form the medical workers union. Since the meeting had not yet begun, Kelvin Franklin was entertaining. He had worked up a set of songs that he hoped would be popular with the crowd —a combination of Motown, 60s and 70s R&B, classic rock, disco, top 40 of the last twenty years, and old union songs he had decided to try out for the occasion, many of which had been sung by the likes of Paul Robeson and Pete Seeger, two men he and Martine greatly admired.

Wilbur, a tall, thin man in his fifties with silver framed glasses, a runny nose, and a pinched, walnut-colored face bordered by curly hair that was graying on the sides was talking to his friend Toby, an even thinner—albeit, much shorter—man with a pale, pink complexion. Both were hospital aides who brought meals to patients in their rooms and answered their calls to either see to their needs or to locate medical personnel who could.

"Well, they got to help me, Tobes. I can't eat."

Toby looked skeptically at his friend. "What you mean you can't eat, Wil? You eatin' right now."

Wilbur looked down at his slider and fries as though seeing them for the first time. Rudy had donated all of the food for everyone present for this event, the legitimacy of which was bolstered by the support and presence of his wife, Agatha, a city councilwoman.

"You heard 'bout that meetin' the suits had, right?" Wilbur asked. "Where they talked about people's getting deadly sick here."

Toby nodded. "I heard. Wasn't just the suits—was everyone in charge, of every department. What I heard is people getting crazy diseases right here at the hospital. You believe that?"

"Well, I don't know," Wilbur replied. "But I know this—crazy shit here beyond our control tells me we need a union more than ever. We sure need something."

Toby nodded vigorously. "Agreed."

"And what I said 'bout I can't eat—you know what I mean," Wilbur insisted.

"I assure you, I do not."

"I live on mac and cheese." Wilbur looked Toby in the eye, emphasizing his point.

"I love mac and cheese."

Wilbur sighed. "I also live on potatoes and gravy."

"And I love potatoes and gravy."

"And I eat beans."

"You got me there. I don't like beans so much."

"Well," said Wilbur, "we do good work that helps people—'least I believe we do. That's the truth."

"It is," Toby agreed.

"Truth is," Wilbur concluded, "we should be took care of 'way we do for others. That's fair, and that's honest, and I'm gonna keep sayin' so —polite, but sayin' so."

The two men were sitting next to each other, facing the front of the room, where Kelvin Franklin was sounding just as sweet as he always did. But now, Wilbur turned in his seat to face his friend. His head tilted slightly forward and to one side, as though bucking a strong wind, though they were indoors. "Listen here. This ain't no joke. How 'bouts you eat mac and cheese every day for a week and see how you like it. How 'bouts you eat mac and cheese because you *have to*. Look here. I care for old folks, and I sometimes steal their food when they not looking. They eat way better'n me."

Toby held up a bony pink hand. "I hear dat. I know. My Aunt Mable need to go to doctor appointments for her mac generation, and she can't get there because she got no money. She on the social. She supported by her boy, my nephew Lawrence and her daughter-in-law, Lawrence's wife, Candace. Know where they work? Hospital. They helping her out, but they barely afford to do that, because they barely making ends meet, theyselves. They want to send their daughter Larinda to college next year, and guess what, if she don't get a scholarship, she ain't goin'. Lucky for her, she's smart and she works hard."

"Mmm," said Wilbur, satisfied he'd made his point. "What she want to do?"

"I'm glad you asked. Ever since she was a little girl, she want to be a nurse, but now, seeing what life is like for her parents and their friends, she changed her mind. She wants to be a counted."

"A what?"

"A counted. Someone who count money for people at tax time."

"You mean an accountant."

"What I said."

Wilbur grunted. "Tell you who really got it bad is Ricardo Morales's sister, Margarita. Her brother was one of these people at the hospital who died—you know, one of the ones in the news."

"I know who he is."

"Yeah, well, his sister got the depress. She don't eat. She don't sleep. She cry all the time. She friends with my niece I was telling you 'bout afore, Candace."

"Mmhmm." Toby just shook his head. "You know, Hakeem's mother needs to take Uber to her doctor appointments, but she can't afford to, so Hakeem's been helping her out, which he can't. Mm mm. He can't."

The music had ended. Kelvin got up from his piano and went over to Martine, who was off to one side, and kissed her, then stood beside her with an arm around her shoulder and her head on his. They were known by their friends as having one of the happiest marriages any of them knew.

Hakeem and Keisha stood at the front of the room, the former motioning for quiet by pressing his palms downward. Keisha was motionless, her hands on her hips. Hakeem paced from one side of the room to the other and back again, a stack of papers in his hand.

"I'd like to start with some statistics about unions, so you'll be armed with facts when you talk to your coworkers. I'm going to pass sheets around with the information I'm about to give you, so you won't need to memorize it or write it down. Did you know," he stopped pacing and glanced at the top sheet, "that unions raise wages of workers by an average of twenty percent and raise compensation, which means both wages and benefits, by almost thirty percent?" He nodded, then continued. "Union workers are much more likely to have health insurance provided by their employers, and are almost fifty percent more likely to have pension plans."

Keisha picked up the thread. She did not use notes and did not move from her spot on one side of the front of the room. "Unionized workers receive more generous health benefits, not just for you, but for your dependents. You get more vacation time, more paid leave—vacations and holidays. And ladies, that includes post-natal family leave. Yes, it does!"

"I need new teeth," Hakeem said, smiling to show everyone the evidence. "But I can't afford to get them. Last time I went to the dentist was in the 1990s."

"Mm hmm," Keisha continued. "You all know my daughter Kaili. She's going to college next year, even if I have to work three jobs. And I'm already working two!"

"Now, listen," Hakeem was getting down to business. "We have enough signatures to start the union now. Fifty three percent, at last count. I know Mr. Balboni says we'll lose some, so we've got to get more and make sure to keep the ones we have. Now what we need is more volunteers to get out there and lean on people—politely, but lean on them, and remind them of what they can expect. That's what these sheets we're passing around are for."

A hand went up and was acknowledged. "Are these benefits guaranteed?"

"Nothing is guaranteed. Breathing's not guaranteed. We've got to negotiate everything, but as a union, we have more clout, and more ability to win."

• • •

Dora and Freedom waited in the late afternoon sun for the school bus that would bring Drew and Buster home. The sun slanted through breaks between the few leaves left on the pear tree that grew beside the bus stop as fathers and mothers shaded their eyes with their palms.

When the bus arrived, Buster hopped down to the sidewalk in excitement, while his older brother dragged his feet. Both boys wore tiny backpacks, but Drew carried a manila envelope with both hands, his expression as grim as his brother's was buoyant.

"Drew beat up Petey!" Buster cried, laughing and squealing.

Dora knew that Petey was a bully who had been picking on Buster. She hid a smile and lifted Drew's chin with two fingers. Drew wouldn't meet her eyes. He held out the envelope, still clutched in both hands.

"Is that for Mommy?"

Drew nodded somberly.

She took the envelope from him. "Is this true? Did you have a fight with Petey?"

Drew looked at her and shook his head. "I beat up Petey."

Dora confirmed, "Because he was picking on Buster."

Drew nodded.

"I see," Dora said. "We'll have to see what Mommy has to say about this."

Drew pressed his lips together and, sensing his sadness, Freedom came over and licked his face. After wiping the side of his face with his sleeve, Drew took his younger brother's hand, and together they walked back to Vanessa's apartment, where they found Missy waiting with her computer under her arm.

"Hey!" Dora leaned in for a kiss, but at the last second, Missy turned her head. "Okay," Dora said, trying not to let the hurt show on her face.

Missy pressed her forehead to Freedom's face. "How's my girl?" She waved to Drew and Buster. "How are you fine young men today?"

Buster beamed at her as they went into the building. "Drew's in trouble!"

"I find that hard to believe. Are you in trouble, Drew?" Missy asked, as they waited for the elevator. Drew nodded without looking at her.

"What did you do to get in trouble, Drew?"

"He hitted Petey!" Buster announced.

Missy tried not to laugh, saw Dora trying to catch her eye with a confused expression, and hastily looked at Drew. "Why did you hit Petey?"

"He was pickin' on me!" Buster pouted.

"Ohhh. Can Drew answer for himself?"

164

Buster nodded, but Drew shook his head. The elevator arrived on Vanessa's floor and the women, children, and oversized dog tramped down the hallway to the apartment. Once inside, Dora lay the manila envelope at the head of the table. On it was written "Mrs. Burrell." Dora then poured the boys their juice, and she and Missy prepared celery sticks with peanut butter, one of the boys' go-to after school snacks.

"What's up with you?" Dora muttered as they worked.

Missy didn't answer.

They brought the snacks to the table and, as the boys munched happily, Missy opened her computer.

"I learned a few things about labs that handle the deadliest diseases."

Dora pulled a chair next to Missy's and they sat with their shoulder's touching. At first, Missy edged away, but as they spoke, Dora leaned closer to her and Missy allowed their shoulders to touch.

*She's afraid of me,* Dora told herself, and willed herself to show Missy that she needn't be afraid—that, in fact, she had nothing but love for the librarian. That any violence Dora might exhibit that involved Missy would be on her behalf, to defend her—never, ever to hurt her.

"So," Missy began, slapping the table as a start to the conversation. "Hazardous diseases are handled by biosafety labs, and they range in their level of containment and protections from BSL—Biosafety Lab—two through four. The most stringent of these are BSL-4 labs run by the National Institute of Allergy and Infectious Diseases. These have astronaut-level hazmat type protection, where the technicians use robotic-type arms or gloves that are part of the machine that they reach into to work with pathogens."

"Where's the nearest one of these labs?" Dora asked.

"Nowhere near here," said Missy. "There are only four in the country, as far as I can tell, and the nearest one is in Maryland." She began reading. "There's one at the Centers for Disease Control and Prevention in Atlanta, another at the United States Army Medical Research Institute for Infectious Diseases at Fort Detrick in Frederick, Maryland. There's one at the Southwest Foundation for Biomedical Research in San Antonio, Texas, and another at the University of Texas at Galveston—not sure if that's one or two. Also, Georgia State University in Atlanta has a small one they're calling a BSL-3 and BSL-4 glove box facility. I guess it operates at two levels. Oh, and there's one more at the National Institute of Health in Bethesda, Maryland, but that one operates as a BSL-3 facility, where they research new infectious diseases."

"So, where does that leave us?" Dora sat back and looked at Missy, who closed the laptop.

"Good question. It's still pretty hard to believe these cases are occurring naturally. From everything I'm reading, that just doesn't happen. Not in clusters like we're seeing here."

Dora agreed. "You know, George Campbell struck me as kind of paranoid when we met him, but his theory that these are being spread on purpose is starting to sound reasonable—there just doesn't seem to be any other explanation."

Missy thought about this. "And yet, that doesn't seem plausible either. Someone's going to one of these labs, collecting diseases and bringing them back? I'm sure the security at these places is as tight as it gets."

"No doubt." Dora thought about this. "I don't know where that leaves us. Couldn't someone who, say, knows someone at one of these labs, just come in and steal pathogens and let them loose on people? Look at what happened last year with Jesse breaking into that drug store."

Missy pursed her lips and shook her head. "Not the same thing."

Dora lay her palm on Missy's forearm. "By the way, I got a text from Charlie Bernelli. We're invited to Thanksgiving at his and Christine's apartment."

Missy paused a beat before answering. "Oh. Okay."

Dora gently squeezed Missy's arm. "You okay, Miss?"

Missy pulled her arm away. "Why don't you tell me what you learned about the social worker."

Dora continued to look at her. "Miss—"

"I'm okay. Let's focus on this, 'K?"

"What about Thanksgiving?"

"Sure. We can go. But let's—"

"Okay. Okay." Dora switched gears and told her about her meeting with Emmanuel Funte.

When she was finished, Missy grinned. "You really convinced him you're this easy-going, sociable, neighborly—"

"'Scuse me?" Dora pretended to glare at her.

"Well…sorry. Of course you're all those things."

Dora nodded, her eyes wide, and said teasingly, "Yes, I am. And you'd best remember that, or else."

"So, what do you think?"

"About Shirley Nelson? Well, like a lot of people, she's pissed off at the hospital for messing up her mother's surgery—maybe even blames them for her mother's death. But murdering people over that? I don't know."

"I wouldn't discount the possibility. We don't know Shirley Nelson. You meet people and they seem normal, and then you learn they're crazy, or they're something other than what they seem. The fact that here she is, running this group, is kind of interesting."

Missy continued to read about BSL-4 labs while she and Dora waited for Vanessa, who arrived home at 11:15 p.m.

Once Vanessa returned, Dora showed her the manila envelope and explained about the trouble Drew was in and the reason for it. At that moment, Drew appeared in the hallway leading to the bedroom.

"I'm sorry, Mom."

Vanessa looked up from reading the letter, saw the forlorn look on her son's face, and held her arms open. Drew ran to his mother, buried his face in her breast and cried while Dora and Missy watched from the dining room table. After a few moments, Vanessa held her son at arm's length. "You know you're not allowed to hit anyone—"

Drew's face fell.

"Except," she continued, holding up a finger, "except to defend your brother."

Drew's eyes widened. "Really?"

"Yes, really. But not if anyone says bad things to Buster—only if you actually see someone hit him. Okay?"

"I saw Petey. I saw him hit Buster!"

"I know you did. You told me, and I believe you. Now, no TV for a week."

Drew began to wail. "But you just said I didn't do anything wrong. Mom!"

"That's enough, Drew. You got into trouble at school, and Mrs. Hill had to send a note home."

Drew frowned angrily.

"Now, you say goodnight to Dora and Missy, then go on to bed."

Drew looked at Dora, then Missy, his expression brooding. "Good! Night!" He turned abruptly, and stomped from the room.

Missy had a hand to her mouth and was trying not to laugh.

Dora raised her eyebrows with a deadpan look at Vanessa. "I know just how he feels."

**Chapter 15**

Marilyn Campbell lived alone in a garden apartment complex a block off the beach in the center of Beach City. She drove a 2016 Dodge Challenger, jogged about three miles every other day on the boardwalk, and did her food shopping directly north of her apartment at the Shop-Rite in the middle of town. She had no pets. As far as Dora could tell, Marilyn went to work each day, came home, jogged, did her food shopping, and little else. She probably did her laundry in her apartment, and occasionally went to one of the bars in the west end of town, and did not, during Dora's period of surveillance, bring anyone home.

Unlike the surveillance Adam did for his divorce and workman's comp clients, Dora did not have to record video or still photographs. She was simply keeping a record of the nurse's activities in the hope that something related to the case, the rash of deadly diseases at BCMC, would jump out at her.

She found nothing of note for two and a half days. She kept track of Marilyn from 8:00 a.m. through 6:00 p.m., much of which time Marilyn was at the hospital. Dora wondered how she might track Marilyn's activities within the hospital, but given the increased security and new bracelet system, she decided to let the idea go for the moment. Even without the new security protocols, she suspected that tracking a nurse's movements and activities within the hospital setting would be all but impossible.

Dora was grateful that since the onset of COVID nearly two years earlier, people did less of their day-to-day business interactions in person. Time was when people transacted business, from purchasing insurance to touring an apartment or home, in person. Nowadays nearly everything was virtual—even doctors' visits were scheduled and sometimes even attended online.

On the third day of her surveillance, Marilyn exited the hospital at 12:30 p.m., walked purposefully to her car and drove to the eastern-most bridge that led off of the barrier island. From there, she headed north for six miles, then east for just over twelve miles, and pulled into the parking lot of a large office building several hundred yards off of the highway. Tailing someone without a second driver and without being seen was challenging, and Dora was prepared to lose track of Marilyn, but her quarry drove within the speed limit and took no evasive measures.

Dora was reasonably certain that Marilyn would not recognize her, so she followed her into the building while maintaining what she thought was a reasonable distance, and arrived at the elevator as its doors were closing with only Marilyn inside. The elevator stopped at the third floor, so Dora went to the building's directory, which was just inside the outer door to the parking lot. She found what she was looking for under "T." Suite 306 was listed as Traxle Laboratories.

• • •

Several hours later, Dora had just finished showering and was drying herself off when she heard Freedom barking.

"It's okay, girl!" she called, but the dog continued to bark, so she slipped on her robe, and padded into the living room to the apartment door. "That you, Miss?" She paused, listening, but heard nothing. She had started back toward the bathroom when she heard the unmistakable whir and metallic click of the elevator door shutting, followed by footsteps echoing on the hallway tile. Her doorbell rang.

"Miss?"

"Yup."

Dora unlocked her apartment door and let Missy in. Freedom let out a joyous yip and leaped forward into Missy's arms. "How are you? You're so good! Yes, you are!"

Freedom ran back into the hallway that led to Dora's bedroom.

Missy had her laptop under one arm. She went to the dining room table, opened it and sat. Dora followed.

"I've started a case file in Google Drive. So far, I have the names that jumped out from the AIC meetings, including and especially the nurse, Marilyn Campbell, along with the facilitator, Shirley Nelson."

Just then, Freedom bounded back into the room with a bit of bird's egg blue cloth in her mouth. She whipped her head and the cloth along with it from side to side, then deposited her newfound wealth at Missy's feet.

"Great," Dora said, with a deadpan look at Missy. "My underwear."

"Yeah, Comfort runs around with mine all the time—but only when they're used."

"Good." Dora sounded relieved. "So it's not just me, or her."

"They smell like you. She loves you."

"Uh huh." Dora remained deadpan. "I think she's psychic. I was in the shower and she started barking a good two minutes before you got off the elevator."

"Probably hearing neighbors across the hall," Missy observed.

"You're too smart, and no fun." Dora nodded toward the computer screen. "So, what do you think?"

Missy took a deep breath. "I think there's nothing actionable, to quote Chief Stalwell. What we have is a chief hospital administrator who, on the face of it, might or might not be a bit paranoid and thinks someone is deliberately dosing patients in his hospital with rare deadly diseases."

"While the possibility of this occurring is pretty much nil."

"What does the girl think we should do next?" Missy asked.

Dora waggled her eyebrows.

Missy sighed. "I mean about the case."

Dora pondered this. "I think we keep working the notes—talking about it. I'll go to see Traxle and learn what I can about Marilyn's involvement with her lab. Then we try to learn more about Shirley Nelson—either by gaining access to her computer, her office, or her home."

Missy looked pained. "That will be difficult—at least the office and computer part—given the new levels of security caused by this case."

"Right."

"We could look at her social media."

Dora slowly nodded. "So…do that. I'd sure like to get a look at her computer and her email."

"I'll think about it," Missy suggested, "while you interview Traxle."

•  •  •

Traxle Labs at NYSUNC was a study in white—white walls, floors and ceiling, white tables and chairs, white pipes sealed where they entered walls, and a plethora of white machinery and brightly lit, glassed off white workspaces. Dora saw all of this through a wide window in the spartan waiting area, just inside the entrance. Two women in lab coats were working at opposite ends of the lab, one at a machine that looked like a high-tech oven, the other at a station laden with a syringe-like implement, sans needle, held in her fist with her thumb on the plunger, as she worked with clear glass vials with yellow tops that rested in a blue plastic receptacle with spaces for multiple vials. Large red biohazard disposal bins sat along each of the room's walls. The women wore green gloves and masks that appeared not so different from the N95 masks so many wore as protection against the COVID-19 virus.

"With you in a minute," came a voice over an intercom, and Dora saw that one of the women—a fair-skinned technician with thin features, high cheekbones, and dirty blonde hair which, to Dora's surprise, was not tied back—was waving at her through the window from where she stood at the oven-like machine. Dora waved back. The woman held up one finger on a gloved hand, signaling that she would be just a minute or so.

About five minutes later, Dr. Yvonne Traxle emerged through a set of heavy, sealed doors, lowered her mask and fist bumped Dora, who introduced herself.

"How can I help you?" Dr. Traxle asked.

"I work for Geller Investigations. We're private detectives who specialize in divorces and workman's comp cases."

"Okay."

Dora nodded toward the window into the lab. "That's some state-of-the-art setup you've got here. Is it BSL-4?"

Traxle laughed. "No, no. We're what's known as BSL-2 plus—meaning we're BSL-2, and handle lab work for many local physicians and some of BCMC's work, but we also have some of the containment features of BSL-3 labs. Hybrid labs like this one are on the rise, as society's needs change vis-à-vis infectious diseases. If this were BSL-4, I'd be wearing full body protective gear and I'd have had to change and shower before meeting with you. What's your interest in biosafety? Is that what this is about?" Traxle gave Dora a piercing look that was more than curious, as though she had a specific question beyond what she'd asked that she was not stating directly.

Dora kept her expression vacant. "None, really. I happened to have been reading something on the subject not long ago, and I thought it was interesting. Actually, I'm here asking about a person. Marilyn Campbell. Do you know her?"

Traxle nodded. "She's a friend. She used to work here."

"When was that?"

Traxle squinted into the distance. "Maybe two, two and a half years ago. She's at the hospital now. Nursing is what she really wanted to do, but there was a bit of a log jam in the area at that time."

"One her father helped to clear?" Dora asked.

Traxle gave Dora a searching look. "What is this about?"

Dora was prepared for the question. "Well, I can't discuss the specifics of the case, but as I said, we specialize in divorces and workman's comp. We also handle some tax-related cases. Pretty boring stuff compared to what you do."

This drew a smile, then a confused look. "She's not married and wasn't injured on the job, as far as I know." She shrugged. "So, what are your questions?"

"I'm at the fact-finding stage, gathering general information. Probably nothing there. If you could tell me a little about her, I'd appreciate that."

Traxle took a breath and again looked into the distance, thinking. "She's a lovely woman. When she worked here, she cared about her work, her patients."

"Does she get along with her father?"

Traxle looked up sharply. "Her father's a prick. If you'd ever dealt with him, you'd know that. He doesn't get along with anyone. So whatever her relationship is with him, any negative aspects have nothing to do with her, I assure you."

Dora sounded surprised. "Really? He's a man with so much public-facing responsibility. How does he get away with...being a prick?"

Traxle smoothed back her shoulder-length hair and let it fall over her shoulder. "Good question. Power is the answer. The man is accustomed to being the most powerful guy in any room, no matter what it does to the people around him."

"Really?" Dora sounded fascinated. "What's it done to the people around him?"

Traxle leaned toward her. "Well, for one thing, his wife died by suicide four years ago, and I don't think he missed a day of work. And his only son, George Jr., also died by suicide, fifteen years to the day before the wife."

"You don't think it was mental illness?"

"If it was, I'm betting it was his, not theirs." The scientist seemed to realize what she was saying. "Look, I don't know. I only know what I hear."

"From Marilyn, I assume."

"Yes, and…around."

"She blames her father?"

Traxle shrugged and stood, indicating the beginning of a dismissal. Her eyes remained on Dora. "Her father's to blame. Marilyn is a sweetheart. Sure, she's not a fan of her father, but nobody is. She became a nurse to try to undo some of the evil he's done."

"What evil—"

"I'm sorry," Traxle said, shaking her head. "That's really all the time I can give you. I've got to get back to work. Deadlines. You understand."

## Chapter 16

Dora took a gold foil-engraved envelope from a pile of mail on the middle of her dining room table. "Got this in the mail today. I think it adds a new wrinkle." She handed the envelope to Missy, who slid out its contents.

"An invite to the hospital's gala." She gave Dora a mischievous grin. "Get to bring a date?"

"I do and you're invited. Read on."

Missy's lips moved silently as she scanned the invitation. As she neared its end, she read aloud. "The evening's honorees include Jeremy Anderson of Anderson Consulting and Antoine Julienne of Julienne Inc., two of the prime forces behind the Clean Community multi-function development projects, which include Clean Seniors, Clean Living, and Clean Acres, all of which provide 'clean' living and shopping opportunities to Beach City residents and their families."

Dora nodded. "Keep reading."

An insert that went along with the invitation touted the new project the evening's honorees' "generous donations" would be funding: a new infectious disease wing of the hospital, which would be called the Anderson Julienne Infectious Disease Center, with Dr. Ramesh Babu as its director.

"Huh," said Missy. "Interesting." She gave Dora a searching look. "What do you think it means?"

"I don't know," Dora answered. "But I'll bet it's relevant to our investigation. George Campbell wants a progress report; I told him we'd be over in about a half hour."

They drove to the hospital together in Dora's car. As they walked from the parking lot toward the hospital's main entrance, they found their path all but blocked by two converging crowds of protesters with competing messages and signs. The two groups chanted and yelled, and were equally vocal and vehement, but were made up of somewhat different demographics.

One group advocated for the continued operation of the hospital and an end to mask and vaccine mandates, and was made up of working class men and women, most of whom were white, along with the occasional high school-aged student. Other than the students, the group appeared to range in age from their early thirties to mid-forties. They wore jeans, denim jackets, and other casual wear. Their signs and placards read: "Our Island Needs a Hospital," and similar messages, with a sprinkling of COVID-related signs that protested mask mandates that still remained in effect.

The opposing group was more white-collar—several men wore suits, and some of the women wore business attire; the younger of the group were more of a college-age crowd. Their signs read variations of: "Fix BCMC's Care," and "Get Your Deadly Disease Here!" and their COVID-related signs were along the lines of "Masks Save Lives," "Vaccinate!" and "You Don't Have the Right to Infect Me!"

The flashpoint at which the two groups came together was mere yards in front of the hospital's main entrance, where the two sides were at their most passionate. Dora glimpsed angry expressions on the faces of men and women on both sides and heard snippets of epithets as she and Missy hurried past, ignoring her own rather natural attraction to expressions of rage. Missy took Dora's hand and pulled her away from the group's edge.

Dora and Missy checked in at the front desk, where their appointment was confirmed and they were issued matching violet bracelets.

They had agreed that they would not discuss any suspects by name, particularly George's daughter, Marilyn. George's office door was open, and so, when Dora and Missy entered his outer office, he saw them and waved them inside.

George was in profile and arguing with someone on an office phone, facing a window that looked out over a courtyard awash in afternoon sunlight. "Be that—be—be that as it may," he was speaking over the other person, "be that as it may, my point is that someone is sabotaging our system. This simply isn't about failures within the system. Quite the contrary. We are catching the cases as they occur, so our system is not the area of—be, be, be that as it may—well, what can you expect us to do in such a circumstance? Exactly! Just what you said. Such a circumstance has likely never occurred! It *is* unprecedented!" George turned, saw his visitors, and nodded toward the seats opposite his desk. "That's all any of us can do, doctor. Well, when you know what that is, why don't you give me a call?" He hung up, closed his eyes for a long moment, then turned to Dora and Missy.

"Department of Health." His expression was a combination of sour and sullen. He saw Missy's expectant look. "Another case. Nipah virus. Common in India and Bangladesh. Comes from fruit bats." He shook his head, disgusted. "Bats…" He looked up at his guests. "I hope you have some good news."

Missy opened her laptop, handed it to Dora, and pointed to an area of the screen.

"We're here to provide the update you requested," Dora began. "We're tracking a number of the attendees of the Advocates for Improved Care group that was created."

"And?"

"We have nothing actionable at this point, other than a collection of people with grievances against the hospital about the care they or a family member received."

"Those things happen," George said, drumming his fingers on his desk. He leaned to one side, putting most of his weight on the left arm of his chair, and crossed his legs.

"We haven't found anything criminal."

"Yet," George added.

Dora nodded. "Yet." She glanced at her computer screen. "Have the new security protocols yielded any new information?"

George appeared pained. "Only that limiting access and recording one hundred percent of all visitors' names is just about impossible. Our security people are all saying the same thing—no matter what they do, some people are getting through, often while others are being questioned. They just walk past, and without hiring more security…" He threw up his hands and looked from Dora to Missy and back to Dora, his expression pleading; he suddenly looked more like a lost little boy than the CEO of a hospital complex. "Don't you have anything? Some… hope, perhaps?"

Dora remained impassive. "We do have some leads and we are following up on them, but we don't want to discuss them yet, since that's all they are—leads. Let's see how they play out."

George agreed and nodded, resigned.

"What we did learn," Missy added, and George sat forward, hanging on her every word, "is that if these were purposeful, intentional infections, not just anyone who might be angry with the hospital could carry them out. Let's talk about who *could* do this."

"Okay. Let's."

"Assuming that this…"

"Murderer," he finished for her.

"Murderer…didn't have the time or wherewithal to scour the world to find these pathogens in their naturally occurring environments, they would have to acquire them in a laboratory setting."

George brought a hand to his face, the forefinger of his closed fist lightly between his lips. He listened carefully.

Missy continued. "And the labs that handle these pathogens are not at all common. They are most likely BSL-4 labs, and there are only a handful in the country."

George frowned. "So this person would have to have access to one."

Missy nodded. "It would seem so. And that would seem unlikely."

George gave an emphatic nod. "We've got an awful lot of unlikely going on around here."

"That we do," Dora agreed. "And we are looking into that situation as we speak. Something else. I received my invitation to the hospital gala today."

George allowed himself a small smile. "I hope you'll come."

"Thank you. I couldn't help but notice that the honorees are funding a new infectious disease wing of the hospital."

"That's right. We will have greatly enhanced infectious disease capabilities." He gave a rueful snort. "I only wish we had them now."

"I also noticed," Dora continued, "that the individual in charge of this new," she paused, searching for the right word, "arena, is a Dr. Ramesh Babu."

"That's right. The foremost infectious disease authority, certainly on the east coast—perhaps in the country. Perhaps in the world."

"Mmm. But that seems an awful coincidence, given these crimes, if that's what they are. This coincidence seems at least as unlikely as some of our other unlikely circumstances. Couldn't these plans for this new facility be somehow connected to the cases we're investigating?"

George looked taken aback, as though he had never considered the idea. "I don't see how!" he sputtered.

Dora didn't answer; she could see how much the CEO wanted the event and all its accoutrements to go forward.

"You said you were talking to the Department of Health when we came in?" Missy asked.

"That's right."

"When did you say you referred this information to them?"

George looked at Missy for a long time, considering his answer. "I think it was just after the first cases. Yes, three or four days later, if I'm not mistaken. We wanted to be sure of what we had here before passing along the information as is required or, well, strongly advised, at any rate."

"Really." Missy left the word hanging.

George looked mildly confused, and Dora wondered if it was an act, to cover his actions—or lack of them. "I think so. Yes."

"And what has the Department of Health done?"

He answered promptly. "They've sent a team of investigators to do a forensic analysis."

"Consisting of what?" Missy asked.

"Contact tracing. They essentially talk to everyone these patients and their families has come in contact with, going back—depending on the illness—going back as far as is appropriate."

Missy nodded. "And how's that going?"

George threw up his hands. "Like everything else connected with this situation. It's a clusterfuck! It's like trying to keep track of who comes and goes in each area of the hospital. You get much of it right, but whatever percent slips through the cracks makes the whole thing unacceptable. You can track some of these patients' movements, but not all. And the people doing the tracking—that the government send—well, you wouldn't believe it if you saw for yourself. It's like they hired them off the street!"

• • •

"I'll tell you what I've learned here," Dora observed as they sat in the back office of Geller Investigations. "Stay away from hospitals. Lots of mistakes, lots of pissed off people and their families."

"Ask me about my family's experience with hospitals," Thelma blared from the front of the office.

"Okay," Dora answered. "Tell me about your family's experience with hospitals."

"Don't ask," came Thelma's bitter answer.

Missy waved her hand toward the front of the office, "That aside—what we're hearing is just the perspective you'd expect," she observed mildly. "We've advertised, we've asked for these people. What we really need to get a better handle on is whether someone with criminal intent—in other words, someone who doesn't play by the CDC rules—would they be able to illegally get hold of these pathogens, and handle them—dangerously, inappropriately—in one of these less than BSL-4 labs? What if they just don't care if people get infected along the way? What if they don't care about appropriate procedures? Could, say, a sociopath with some lab experience have done this?"

"In other words," Dora continued the thought, "could Marilyn Campbell have done it?"

## Chapter 17

The sun was out and the sapphire sky was clear and cloudless on the blustery Thanksgiving Day. Dora and Freedom had spent the night at Missy's apartment. Little Comfort chased Freedom around the boundary of the living room until Freedom jumped up on the couch, where Comfort could not reach her.

Missy sat cross-legged on the couch, leaning forward and stroking Comfort's throat, a half-full mug of steaming coffee in her other hand.

Dora emerged from the bedroom dressed in workout clothes.

"I'm going over to Shay's to work out for a couple of hours and try to offset the meal."

"Wait!" Missy leaned back, uncrossed her legs, and stood up. She went to the kitchen, took a last couple of gulps of coffee and put the mug in the sink. "Let me get dressed. I'm coming with you."

Dora turned. "But you hate watching me fight."

"So? I want to come. You saying I can't?"

"No, no." Dora gave a blithely indifferent wave and leaned back against the door to wait.

A half hour later they were on the sweating, smelly mat at Shay's with a half-dozen other women, all of them but Missy and one other woman dressed in sweats. Missy sat along the mat's edge. The women were Whale, Wire, Axe, Touch, Bottoms, and Shay herself, the dark-eyed, perpetually grinning instructor. Since they were seven, Shay had sat out and refereed.

Dora was paired with Bottoms, a muscular Brazilian jiu-jitsu special-ist, whose heavy brow and dark eyebrows gave her a glaring look. Dora knew her game. She easily hit her opponent, who instantly changed levels, looking for the takedown, but Dora saw it coming, took a wide stance, and pushed Bottoms's head down as a counter. Of five attempts, Bottoms only succeeded once in taking Dora to the mat, where Dora reversed and took the top position. Here too, she knew Bottoms's goal, and that she preferred the bottom position, hence her nickname. She was expert at submitting her opponents from her back.

The fighters used heavier gloves for sparring than for matches, and pulled their punches. Once someone took a mount position and began punching, Shay would step in to stop the fighters to ensure against injury. She did the same with submissions, though the submitted fighter was also required to "tap" to end the match, again ensuring against injury.

Once on the ground, Bottoms attempted but did not submit Dora, who was on top and working toward a full mount position. Meanwhile, Bottoms was attempting from the guard to isolate Dora's wrist, which Dora deftly avoided. As Dora attempted to punch down, Bottoms windmilled her arms up and around—each arm making a circle from the inside up and outward, which threw Dora off balance, causing her to briefly touch one hand to the mat to steady herself. Instantly, Bottoms grabbed hold of Dora's right wrist with her left hand and began wrapping her right arm around Dora's right arm to secure a Kimura submission.

"Shit!" Dora muttered, then slid her right leg to the side and pushed upward on Bottoms's hands, undermining her opponent's power.

Shay blew the whistle and they were done. Both women sat up in cross-legged positions.

"Everybody see what happened here?" Shay asked. Most nodded. "Dora knocked Bottoms down, where she fell into her guard and looked for mount. Bottoms forced Dora's hand to the side and, once on the mat, grabbed the wrist for the Kimura, which Dora countered by expanding her base and pressing upward on her opponent's hands."

Dora and Bottoms shared a quick hug. Both were winded and red-faced.

"You sunk that in super quick," Dora complimented.

"Yeah well, not quick enough, apparently. Where'd you learn to escape like that?"

Dora's smile was beatific. "I study up in my spare time." She tapped the side of her head. "Good memory."

Dora slid over to sit next to Missy, and together they watched the rest of the matches.

As they drove home, Dora smiled hesitantly. "You really didn't mind watching me spar? I thought you hated it."

Missy was watching the strip malls and streets through the passenger window. "It scares me to see you hurt, and I really hate the violence that comes with the job." She turned to Dora, her eyes shining. "But it also kinda turns me on."

Dora laughed. "Well, let me get showered, then we can—"

Missy emphatically shook her head. "Nope. No shower. I like you like this."

Dora laughed again, harder. "Well, all right then!"

• • •

Afterward, they showered and dressed together, Dora in cotton beige slacks and a light orange blouse with a tailored collar, Missy in red jeans and an orange turtleneck sweater.

"Won't you be cold?" Missy asked, to which Dora gave a scornful frown.

"I'm never cold—certainly not after sparring."

As they headed for the door, Dora stopped short, then jumped back. "Oh, shit!"

Just inside the door, on the center of the floor was an enormous black beetle, its antenna waving.

Dora turned away and grabbed Missy by the shoulders.

"Get it away! Kill it!"

Missy laughed as Dora slid past her, back into the living room. "I didn't know you were scared of bugs." She went to the table and took a large postcard featuring ads for women's wear, went back to the beetle, slid the postcard beneath it, and lifted the card and bug up.

Dora cringed away. "I'm not scared! I—I just don't like them. Ugh, get it away!"

"Okay. All right." Missy went to the window. "Could you open it, please?"

Dora unlocked and opened the window, and Missy held the card outside and gave it a shake; the beetle dropped out of sight. Dora exhaled, returned to the front door, and turned back toward Missy.

"You coming, or what?"

• • •

"I guess you've thought about how you'll keep *The Chronicle* going." Christine had put out two plates of toasted pita triangles covered with melted cheese and cranberries, each one topped with a pecan. She sat down at one end of the couch; at the other end, Charlie and C3 were watching a football game between the Detroit Lions and the Chicago Bears. Sarah was perched on the edge of the couch nearest Christine.

"Hire more help. Shift some of my responsibilities to Lemieux and Esther." Sarah took one of the appetizers and a napkin and took a small bite. "These are terrific."

"Thanks," Christine said. "Have you thought about working from home?"

Sarah shook her head. "How would that work?"

"Set up a virtual office so it would be seamless. Do what you can. Transfer responsibilities when you can't. Organize work flows and aspects of work into channels with software, so focus is always maintained. You can work or delegate as you see fit."

Sarah thought about this, took another bite of the appetizer, then reached for her ginger ale. "Worth thinking about. Is that what you do at city hall?"

Christine laughed. "City hall is way too dysfunctional for anything so sane, and being mayor is half an exercise in futility. Department directors don't listen to me, or if they do, they nod and smile, then do their own thing in their own little fiefdoms."

Sarah nodded. "That dress is really pretty."

"This? It's nothing special, really."

"What kind of dress is it?" Sarah asked.

Christine looked down at her dress, which was a print of red, orange, and light brown, with a V-neck and ruffled sleeves. "It's a midi wrap dress. I see you broke out your holiday look."

Sarah looked embarrassed. "Right. Dress pajamas with an orange sweater. It's all about comfort for me, right now."

Christine smiled warmly. "As it should be." Christine watched as Charlie went to the bar and poured himself another scotch. Their guests had not yet all arrived and he was on his third.

"You going to rein him in?" Sarah asked.

"Nope. He gets to dig his own hole. Me? I'm detaching."

"Really." Sarah sounded part amused, part intrigued.

"He's an adult toddler. It's the only way." She gave Sarah a pointed look. "He has to live with his own consequences. 'Scuse me. Gotta check the turkey." Christine got up and went to the kitchen.

The buzzer sounded. "Sarah," Christine called from the kitchen. "Could you buzz Dora and Missy in, please?"

Later, at the dinner table, everyone feasted on turkey, gravy, sweet potato pie topped with pineapple and melted marshmallows, green beans with almond slices, cranberry sauce, coleslaw, and cornbread. Dessert was pecan pie and ice cream.

"How is your work for the hospital going?" Charlie asked.

Dora and Missy looked at one another. "It's an ongoing investigation," Dora said.

"But some of it's public. We've read about it in *The Chronicle.*" Charlie nodded toward Sarah.

"Well," Missy answered, "that part we can talk about. As I'm sure you've read, there has been another case. Nipah virus."

"Am I right in saying that most of these cases progress to encephalitis?" Charlie continued.

Missy thought about this. "Some do, but most? I'm not sure." She paused. "Interesting point, though."

Charlie reached for his drink, finished it, then slid his chair back. "Surely they've looked at what these cases have in common."

"Surely they have," Dora said.

"Is it really possible that someone is going around giving these diseases to people?" asked C3.

"Is it possible? Yeah," said Dora.

"Is it likely?"

Dora gestured with her fork, which held a slice of turkey. "Nothing about this case is likely."

"Who would do a thing like that?" Christine wondered.

"Lot of crazy people out there," Sarah answered.

Charlie had retrieved another scotch, returned to his seat, and turned to Sarah, abruptly changing the topic. "Do you have any idea what you're getting yourself into by going through with this pregnancy? I mean, it's none of my business, but as your father-in-law—"

"You're right, Dad. It's not your business," C3 angrily interjected.

No one spoke for a long moment.

Sarah looked evenly at Charlie. "Lot of crazy people out there," she said again.

C3 put a napkin to his mouth and stifled a laugh. Dora and Missy glanced at one another, and Christine smiled.

After dinner, Charlie and C3 watched the Cowboys play the newly renamed Washington Commanders.

"I'm planning on getting my counseling job back, just so you know," C3 said to his father, who shook his head and looked hard at his son.

"You have no idea how hard it is to raise a child. And for you and," he paused, waving his hand in Sarah's direction.

"Sarah, Dad—her name's Sarah."

"Right, Sarah. For you two, it's going to be doubly hard. You'll see." Christine was clearing the table, helped by Dora and Missy. Sarah got up to help too, but Christine held up a hand.

"You just relax." She nodded toward father and son in the living room. "Go and chill with the boys. Once the table's cleared I want to talk to you about helping you shop for Olivia."

"That would be wonderful," Sarah beamed, then nodded toward Charlie and C3. "I think I'll leave them to their bonding. They've been watching football together on Thanksgiving pretty much since C was born."

She got herself a fresh ginger ale and walked to the window, where she looked at the red and violet sky above the sparkling waters of the Atlantic Ocean as the sun went down on another holiday.

**Chapter 18**

Ramon snapped pictures and suggested different poses, which Dora did her best to approximate. She felt a bit silly modeling clothing, though the clothes were gorgeous and she would be allowed to keep whatever she modeled. The problem for her was that she had always maintained a cynicism about fashion—you wore what you wore—whatever was comfortable, whatever was handy. She found the industry, the magazines, the fuss made over fashion to be silly.

And here she was modeling for a local boutique. Well, she was nothing if not adventurous, and she could use the money. The investigator work was still part-time, so much of her income came from babysitting Vanessa's two boys.

"Now turn to your left and look over your shoulder. Hand to hair. Hand to hair. You're beautiful! Gorgeous, and you know it. Show me that."

Dora stood on a little stage in front of a white screen under multidirectional lights, while Ramon walked from one side of the set to the other. Off to one side, Tanya LaRue was leaning a little too close to Charlie. They were whispering to one another and invading one another's space, and every now and then one of them whispered to Ramon, before they went back to whatever secrets they might have been sharing.

"Show me how sexy you are. Think of your lover, who just adores you—who worships you. Show me! Yes! There it is!"

She began to enjoy the experience, and by the time they were done, Dora was beginning to think of herself differently. As sexy. As gorgeous. As all the words Ramon used to describe her.

But something else happened during the photo shoot. Her mind wandered to the hospital investigation, and went over the facts, until she had a realization that she knew she had to share with Missy.

That evening, she met Missy at the library as she was getting off work and they drove together to the coffee shop, where they got onto a short line.

"I did that photo shoot for Real Women."

"Oh! How was it?"

"Really fun. I brought home a bunch of clothes you'll be surprised to see me in. Stuff I'd never have worn otherwise."

Missy raised an eyebrow as they arrived at the front of the line and placed their orders.

"I've changed my opinion about fashion for plus-sized girls. I look pretty hot in these clothes."

"You look hotter without them."

They added cream and Splenda to their coffees and found seat at a small, round wooden table. Dora leaned toward Missy and whispered, "Pretty sure Charlie Bernelli's having an affair with Tanya LaRue."

Missy's face fell. "I hope not. Poor Christine."

"Yeah, well. I thought of something else during the photo shoot. From what you read about BSL-4 labs, you'd have to have some serious expertise to handle these diseases, right?"

Missy shrugged. "Unless you didn't care about how you handled them."

Dora shook her head. "If the person wants to carry out their objective, which is to infect people with these diseases, they'd have to do it right, so to speak."

"I guess so," Missy said slowly.

"So you'd have to have expertise, to know how to handle and transmit the disease—even if you don't care about people getting them along the way."

"Yeah. I guess you would."

"Okay. Follow me on this." Dora put a hand on Missy's wrist; Missy turned her hand upward and intertwined her fingers with Dora's. "Take Marilyn Campbell. Would you think she has that kind of knowledge?"

"Well, I don't know. Off the top of my head, I'd say probably not."

"And what about Dr. Yvonne Traxle?"

Missy startled and pulled her hand from Dora's, then slapped Dora's wrist. "You mean the two of them together?"

Dora gave Missy a slow, knowing smile.

This time, Missy slapped the table. "They both have motive. Traxle could be trying to discredit Dr. Babu before he takes over the new infectious disease wing at BCMC."

Dora pressed her lips together. "I think George Campbell's right. These are *not* coincidences."

Missy sipped her coffee. "Well, that's interesting."

"And unless Marilyn Campbell and Traxle, or whoever, is stopped, there's not going to be a gala, much less any new wing at the Beach City Medical Center."

• • •

Shirley Nelson was having difficulty keeping order at the AIC meeting. The loved ones of those who had recently contracted and died of the deadly diseases had descended on the meeting and taken over.

"Come on! You expect me to believe this group is really here to address our concerns?" Albert Chaikin, Suzanne's widower, demanded. "My concern is…my wife is dead. How 'bout you address that!"

Muriel, his mother-in-law and a sturdier version of her daughter, folded her arms across her chest and scowled angrily at Shirley. "And there's been no explanation! My daughter was here, then she was gone." She swiped her hands together several times in a "that's that" gesture. "Other than some noise about how these things happen and how my daughter signed something that acknowledged that, there hasn't been much from you people."

Shirley nodded sadly. What else could she do?

Alison Josephs raised her hand and, when no one noticed, she spoke up. "Yesterday was Marvin's birthday. Know what I did? I went to his grave. Nice, right? We spent his birthday together—at the cemetery! I'm all alone here."

"We deserve better," Margarita Morales insisted.

The others emphatically agreed.

• • •

You drive to the hospital, carrying your friends, your quiet killers. Once there, you can't help but see evidence of the hollow, false accolades. You get a close look at the worst of the hypocrisy and hubris, and it disgusts you. They took credit for miracles and buried the failures, which were everywhere. The whole world was upside down and it would take a herculean, heroic effort to set it right again. You only hope you are up it. You have to be. You try to focus on the scenery, but after a while you give up. There is so much for so many to atone for.

So you get to work.

• • •

A long table had been set up. The government investigators tasked with performing the contact tracings sat on one side and those who believed they may have come into contact with infected individuals lined up on the other. A separate team had been charged with investigating and tracing the movements of the deceased in the days and, in some cases, weeks, prior to their deaths.

The process was arduous and anything but orderly. It was also surprisingly low-tech, with reams of paper and little metal boxes filled with stacks of cards, rather than computer files, for the individuals in question. Many of the investigators were retirees who had been called back into service, whose original jobs predated the use of computers in the work force.

Everyone did the best they could, writing down locations and activities to the degree they could remember, but the human memory is often faulty, and individuals' perceptions about where they'd been and who they'd been with were riddled with holes and inconsistencies.

The result was a general gist of connections, many of which had probably occurred, rather than accurate scientific proof of people's contact with the diseased individuals.

• • •

Dora and Missy walked through the front door of Geller Investigations. Thelma didn't look up from her work, but wisecracked, "Well if it isn't Frick and Frack, Lady Detectives."

Dora stopped a few steps beyond Thelma's desk, turned, and walked back so she was standing directly in front of the office manager, then gave her about ten seconds of the thousand-yard stare.

"Why are you always so pissed off?"

Thelma didn't look up from her work.

Dora frowned, waiting. "We do something to offend you?"

Thelma continued to type. "You're here, ain't ya?"

"Yeah, we're here." Dora planted both fists on Thelma's desk and leaned forward. "*Right*. Here. I repeat: why are you so pissed off? I think we've been pretty courteous, even tolerant, of you."

Missy was tugging at Dora's sleeve. "C'mon, Dor. Let it go."

"Yeah, Dor." Thelma snarked, then looked up. "If you must know, I spend my day—all day, every day—looking at the facts of these divorce cases, which make up most of our business. And most of what I read is all about what the husbands put the wives through. And most of these husbands are dirty, rotten, cheatin', lying, abusive pieces of garbage. So I read all about how the wives put up with their crap until they decided to leave, when some judge—usually a man—cheats 'em all over again. Then, they take whatever few bucks and dignity they have left, and find another patsy bum. That's how I spend my day. With them." She nodded at the computer.

Dora waited, and nodded. "And you take it out on us because you had a husband like that once upon a time?"

Thelma had turned back to her computer, but her eyes flicked up to Dora—briefly filled with tears, Dora noted—then returned to her screen.

Dora took a breath and said, "Look, Thelma. We're about as far from abusive husbands as you're gonna get. So, try not to kill the messenger, 'K?"

Thelma didn't answer.

They sat down at Geller's empty desk, and Missy opened the file she had been working on while Dora sifted through printouts of Missy's case notes.

"Listen to this," Missy said, reading from her screen. "It's from a news report dated about nine months ago. Paraphrasing. George Campbell Jr.—that's Campbell's kid and Marilyn's brother—had a history of anxiety and depression, and died by suicide, after a short stay in BCMC's mental health clinic. The article quotes a roommate, which I read as lover—a guy named Luke—who says that George's constant criticism drove his son to suicide. He wanted to please his father, who was a critical tyrant, but it was an impossible task—so says the roommate."

Dora considered this. "Does the article mention Marilyn?"

"Only in passing. Says he's survived by his sister and father."

"The mother also died by suicide, right?"

"I believe so, but she's not mentioned here at all."

"Maybe we ought to ask George about this situation."

Missy took a breath, let it out slowly. "Look, I know you like to go right at a conflict, but I think it's a bad idea. The man hired us. We'd be overstepping, to say the least."

"Well, if there's smoke, investigating a possible fire isn't overstepping. If he's complicit, even indirectly, it's not overstepping."

"But asking him directly? Yeesh. Anyway, I have something I think we ought to do first. Let's look into Dr. Ramesh Babu. He's the other local infectious disease expert. He has his own lab. He'll be taking over as director of the new infectious disease wing at the hospital, right?"

Dora looked bewildered. "But...why?"

Missy held up a finger and gave Dora an encouraging smile. "Soon-to-be director of new infectious disease wing creates infectious disease crisis so he can sweep in and save the day."

Dora looked intrigued. "Makes sense to a point. But he's already on course to run the place. Why would he need to go to such crazy lengths? I would think that killing people would be just a bit contrary to his ethics."

Missy raised her eyebrows. "You'd think, but who knows? We don't know the guy. We only get to see the tip of the iceberg."

"Can you pull up Babu's lab's website?"

Missy typed Babu Laboratories into a search engine and clicked on the link to the site, which revealed a clean, modern website that advertised a BSL-2 infectious disease laboratory that partnered with multiple medical facilities and physicians' offices in the south Nassau County area. She clicked on Dr. Ramesh Babu's bio through a drop-down link beneath "About Us."

Dora stood behind Missy and bent forward to read the screen, her chin resting lightly on Missy's shoulder. "Second generation from India, parents owned a small store until COVID forced it to close. His sister, Mahira, is an internist." She put a hand on Missy's shoulder. "Let's try to find Mahira. Maybe she'll talk to us."

Missy typed "Dr. Mahira Babu" into a search field and found her practice. "What do you say we call and say we're doing a write-up for the hospital's gala," Missy suggested.

Dora nodded eagerly. "Go for it!"

Missy dialed the number on the contact page of the website, and listened for a moment. "Voicemail." She waited. "Hi, my name is Missy Winters and I'm a contractor working for the Beach City Medical Center, and we're doing a write-up about your brother, Dr. Ramesh Babu, for the hospital gala—the program and the online version—and we were wondering if you could give us a bit more insight—to help the local public better understand the man as well as the doctor." She left her cell number.

"Let's send an email with the same message," Dora suggested, so Missy emailed with an identical query.

Dora sat down in one of the office chairs and went back to the print-outs of the case notes. "So we have Marilyn Campbell, who can't stand her father and hangs out with her infectious disease expert friend. We have Shirley Nelson, who runs a group designed to attract anyone with a gripe against the hospital and who turns out to have a major gripe herself. And now we have this Dr. Babu, who, as far as we can tell, is a paragon of virtue and will be heading the hospital's about-to-be-launched infectious disease wing, and who is also one of the few who might have the expertise to create a crisis like the one we're investigating—as well as to end it."

"These unexplained infections and deaths and Babu's upcoming job all happening at once can't be a coincidence."

Dora nodded and continued scanning her notes. "Agreed."

A computer tone sounded and Missy looked at the screen. "Huh. Well, there you go."

"What?"

"From Dr. Mahira Babu." She clicked the email link and began to read. "Thank you for reaching out. I am confident that my brother will be a fantastic addition to the BCMC family. Following is a bit more insight into the man, and why he is so motivated to save lives by identifying and protecting against infectious diseases."

They scanned the information, which included both typed information and a newspaper article.

"He and his family overcame challenges of misdirected discrimination following 911," Dora read.

"They're Hindu, not Muslim," Missy explained.

"…which were suffered mostly by his mother, Prisha," Dora continued, "who had been a PA at an internist's office in Beach City, and had been let go when a patient made unfounded accusations that she had been rude. She decided to help her husband, Ramesh's father, Kabir, at the store."

Missy read on. "Both parents were sad, but not angry. But both Ramesh and Mahira were furious at the time, which was 2005, particularly that there was no redress."

"As a result," Dora read, "both brother and sister have been focused on delivering the very best quality care equally to people of all backgrounds, colors, religions, ages, and heritages. They both travel to India during their vacations, visiting the poorest villages, where they deliver their care and professional services for free." Dora sat back and turned to Missy.

"Wow," Missy breathed.

"Doesn't sound like our killer," Dora observed.

"At least not on the face of it," Missy agreed. "I say we take a drive to the Babu lab and do a little feeling out."

"Think he can shed any light on Traxle?"

Missy gave her a knowing look. "I'm sure they know each other. Bet they're not BFFs."

"Be you're right. But how do you propose—?"

"Tell you on the way over." Missy looked around until her eyes landed on the stack of 10" by 13" file envelopes Adam used for case files. She took one that was near to bursting with case-related papers and said, "C'mon. Let's go."

She explained her idea in the car, and by the time they parked in the lot behind the lab, Dora had agreed to the plan and knew what to do. Dora pushed the buzzer for Babu Laboratories.

A man's voice answered. "Can I help you?"

Dora stood in full view of the camera that was aimed at the entryway. "I'm from city hall," she said; they had agreed that while this was a distortion of the truth, it was not exactly a full-fledged lie, since Dora had worked out of city hall for years in her garbage collecting days.

"Just leave it at the door," the voice responded.

"Sorry. I need a signature," Dora responded.

The buzzer sounded and they were in.

The lab had no outer office, but instead was a large room around the entirety of which a three-foot-deep counter had been built. On the counter were vials and containers of various shapes, sizes, and colors, tubes with bar-coded labels, and devices that looked to the two newcomers like mini refrigerators.

Classical music—violins and piano—was playing.

A man with a brown beard and handlebar mustache was wearing an N95 mask; he waved a green gloved hand. "I can sign that for you." He retrieved a pen from a container on the counter.

Missy held the file folder out to the man. "Just sign anywhere," she said, and the man signed on the bottom right corner and handed the folder back. He waited for them to leave, but instead, Missy spoke up.

"I'm Missy Winters. We're putting together a brochure for the BCMC gala and we were hoping you might be able to provide a little more information about Dr. Babu."

"I'm Dr. Clay Spontana, Dr. Babu's assistant," the man replied, his voice slightly muffled by the mask. "You should probably get that information directly from Dr. Babu." He walked to the only other door in the room besides the entrance and knocked lightly. A voice responded and Dr. Spontana disappeared for a moment, then emerged, followed by Dr. Babu.

The doctor for whom Babu Laboratories was named was of medium height and weight, with black hair and mahogany-colored skin, a broad smile, and no discernible accent. "Ramesh Babu—friends call me Ram. Sorry if I don't shake hands." He extended an elbow and both women reciprocated. "I haven't much time, but I'll be happy to fill you in with whatever information I can."

"Actually," Dora said. "That's not exactly why we're here."

The doctor appeared taken aback. "No?"

Dora shook her head, "We're private investigators. We're looking into the unexplained infectious disease deaths at BCMC on behalf of the hospital administration."

Dr. Babu's face darkened. He hesitated, then seemed to grow in stature; his features hardened. "So, you're here under false pretenses."

Dora didn't flinch. "We're investigating suspicious deaths on behalf of the hospital. Wouldn't you want to help the hospital bring an end to this crisis?"

Dr. Babu hesitated. "I don't appreciate being lied to. You don't have an appointment and I have no reason to believe you! You need to leave."

"We wanted to ask about Dr. Traxle," Dora said quickly.

The doctor hesitated again, then reasserted himself. "I said get out!" Dr. Babu pointed to the door, then turned and stalked from the room.

Dora and Missy both looked at Dr. Spontana, who gave a sheepish shrug. "It would be better if you left."

## Chapter 19

The informal meeting at Rudy's Bar the night before the union vote was packed and boisterous. Kelvin, who had agreed to play for free, had not shown up. Neither he nor Martine were there, so the house music that played blended with the excited hubbub in anticipation of the following day's union vote.

Keisha Williams was standing and addressing the crowd; she still wore her down parka, as the early December weather had turned chilly. "The good news—settle down, everyone. People!" The talking quickly subsided and Rudy turned off the music. "Thank you. The good news is that we are still at fifty three percent. The challenge is that we can't afford to lose anyone between now and tomorrow. We need all of your votes. And if you can bring in a few more, that would be great. Hakeem?"

Hakeem Woods threaded his way through the crowded to the front of the room. "I don't really have anything to add, except to say to all of you, thank you. You've worked hard and you're going to get a union that works hard for you and gets you the benefits and pay you deserve, and that will make your lives better. Okay?"

"I'd like to say something," a voice said from the back of the room. The same two men who had addressed the crowd weeks earlier in the hospital's lunchroom stepped to the front of the bar. "My name is Darius Winston and my friend is Greg Wright—I just call him Mister Wright." He chuckled at his own joke, but no one else joined him. The bar had gone silent. "We're here to let you know that those of you who vote for this union will be doing yourselves a disservice—one that might just lead to you losing your jobs."

"That would be against the law," said Hakeem, who had not moved from his spot in the center of the front of the room.

"So you say, but when a company feels threatened by an outside influence, sometimes they take matters into their own hands for simple self-protection."

Rudy had come out from behind the bar. He took a few steps toward the men, just as two hefty white men wearing the same light blue shirts and jeans stood up from a table in the center of the room. No one had noticed them because those around them had been partying and enjoying the company of others who were doing the same, while these two men had sat silently through the pre-speaker festivities. Each one was taller than Rudy, and carried more upper body weight. The two men got between Rudy and the two union busters.

"You need to leave," Rudy said to all four men.

"Hey," Darius Winston responded, smiling and holding up a hand. "Freedom of expression."

"This is my place, and I say you need to leave."

"Soon as we have our say," said Wright, and Winston took a breath to speak. Suddenly, he took a step back to make room for another body pushing its way in front of him.

"Man said to leave," Dora said, purposely standing in Winston's space.

Winston's smile broadened. "Look what we got here, a little lady activist. A round, little lady activist. Tom, would you move the little lady so I can say my piece."

One of the union bodyguards placed his hands on Dora's shoulders and began shoving her away from the front of the room.

"Stop assaulting me, sir!" Dora yelled. She stepped to one side at a forty-five-degree angle and windmilled her right arm in a counter clockwise arc, with her thumb extended, sweeping the man's arm out of the way and stabbing her thumb deep into the man's eye. The man screamed and fell to the floor before anyone could react, both hands clutched over his right eye.

"Guy attacked me." Dora shrugged. "You guys saw it," she said. "He grabbed me, then I guess he tripped and fell. Looks like he banged his eye. Maybe someone should call a doctor."

The other bodyguard took a step toward Dora but turned at a sound behind him. Two distinct clicks, which stopped him in his tracks. The sound of a shotgun being cocked.

"You need to leave," Rudy repeated, death in his voice. The room was silent, save for the moaning of the bodyguard on the floor.

Winston, Wright, and the remaining bodyguard helped their companion off the floor and out of the bar.

A phone rang, and moments later, Keisha Williams addressed the room in a shaky voice. "Everybody, I need to have your attention. That was Eunice Paulson. She's been at the hospital with Martine. You probably don't know, but Martine's been really sick and has been in the hospital for the last few days. Well," her voice caught. "Eunice called to say that Martine Franklin just passed."

Kelvin and Martine were widely admired for the love they shared and universally loved by all who knew them. Gasps could be heard around the room, as well as several exclamations of "Oh, my God!" and "No!"

. . .

Elder Reginald Williams, the youngest of Keisha Williams's first cousins, stood at the front of the main viewing room at Trabor's Funeral Home. At nearly six foot nine inches tall, his placid face was easy to see, and more so when he lifted up on his tiptoes whenever he came to particularly meaningful passages in the prayers he was reciting. Elder Reginald claimed he did this in honor of the Jewish practice—the practice of "our predecessors," as he called the Jewish people—who rose up on their toes when they came to the phrase "holy, holy, holy" in their thrice daily prayers.

Keisha Williams had delivered the eulogy, and since Martine Franklin had been beloved by so many members of several different communities, enough time had been made for as many speakers as wanted to speak.

One who did not speak was her husband, Kelvin, who was too devastated to talk to anyone. He always referred to Martine as his rock, and indeed, without her anchoring presence, the normally buoyant, joyous musician was rendered silent and sad. He sat on a bench off to one side and appeared not to notice the proceedings at all.

While the service proper was conducted by Elder Reginald and those who chose to say a few words in Martine's memory, a subtext of fast and furious discussion was conducted around the room in stage whispers.

Martine had died after a ten day stay at BCMC with a rare disease known as Nipah virus, which was said to originate in bats from Asia, and which left those with the disease with symptoms that included fever, nausea, sore throat, and cough—symptoms that might have been attributed to any number of illnesses. Martine's death was also the most recent in a half-dozen unexplained deaths from rare deadly diseases at BCMC, which had eroded public trust in the hospital to the point that many, especially those grieving Martine's passing at Trabor's, were questioning whether the hospital ought to be allowed to operate at all.

• • •

The notice in *The Chronicle* and on BCMC's social media accounts announced a press conference at 3:00 p.m. on Tuesday, which George Campbell had invited Dora and Missy to attend in person.

The protesters numbered in the hundreds on either side—about half protested the mysterious infections and demanded that the hospital close while the opposing protesters demanded that the hospital continue to serve the barrier islands, albeit with appropriate safety protocols. The protests had been moved off of the hospital grounds by police and hospital security, and were now congregated just beyond the gates to the main entrance.

Because New York's mask mandates had recently been lifted by the governor, the protests were now focused solely on the hospital's operation, which was to be the subject of the press conference.

Despite the temperature, which was 43°F, the press conference was held outside the hospital's front entrance and slightly off to one side, so that the facility's signage would be in the picture while the use of the entrance remained unencumbered. News trucks from the major New York news organizations were clustered just outside the patient drop-off and pick-up area, as members of the Beach City Police Department kept the vicinity functioning for patients and their families.

The press conference participants waited just inside the hospital's main double doors and consisted of hospital CEO George Campbell, Senior Medical Director Akira Matsumoto, Bonnie Jansen, BCMC's communications director—a fiftyish, pale, freckled woman with round green eyes and shoulder length blonde hair, and Beach City Mayor Christine Pearsall, who wore a smart reddish brown pants suit. Along with them were two women in blue business attire, both brunette and in their late thirties, who were representatives of the State Department of Health.

At 3:07 p.m. the group stepped outside to a lectern that had been set up for the occasion, and George Campbell tapped the microphone as dozens of cameras focused in on his grim countenance.

"Good afternoon and welcome. Here at Beach City Medical Center we pride ourselves on offering the best care in the state, and yet today we find ourselves faced with a health crisis that must be directly addressed. And so, I am here today to tell you of the actions we have been taking and some new changes that, for the short term, and under the guidance of the Department of Health, we will institute as a temporary safety net. First of all, let me be crystal clear in saying that closing BCMC is not an option. The citizens of Beach City and our barrier island need our hospital."

He paused as a cheer could be heard from beyond the front gate, along with angry exclamations. The press conference was carried live by area news networks and the hospital's social media feeds.

"For the time being," the CEO continued, "we will limit new patient admissions to only those whose lives are in imminent danger, and who, for logistical or health-related reasons, cannot be admitted to other hospitals in the vicinity. The decisions as to who will be admitted to BCMC going forward will be made on a case-by-case basis by Dr. Matsumoto, our senior medical director and patient safety administrator of medical affairs and his team of advisors. Let me assure the Beach City community: we are here for you. We are facing a challenge, but we will overcome this challenge."

Dora and Missy were standing at the edge of the crowd nearest the two health department officials, who were quietly whispering to one another.

"He didn't really address the situation," Dora observed.

Missy looked chagrined. "He didn't exactly *mention* the situation directly, either."

"He's a politician," Dora agreed. "Smoke and mirrors."

"We are therefore," George continued, "temporarily, and I must stress that this is temporary, postponing our gala. Despite the gala's postponement, our new infectious disease wing, which will be headed by renowned specialist and leader in the field, Dr. Ramesh Babu, will continue to move forward. The Anderson Julienne Infectious Disease Center, as the new facility will be known, is moving full steam ahead. Our fundraising continues, with the donations required for the opening of the center already in hand. Rather than hosting a gala, we are tending to the current medical challenge we face, and will continue fundraising virtually. Please visit Beach City Medical dot org and look for the links for the Anderson Julienne Infectious Disease Center, should you wish to donate. Dr. Matsumoto, did you want to say a few words?"

Dr. Matsumoto held up a hand, shook his head, and leaned toward George, who turned to the mayor.

"Mayor Christine Pearsall."

He stepped back and Christine smiled and set an iPad down on the lectern in front of her. "There is nothing more important to me than the health of Beach City's residents. Nothing. And so, while the decision Mr. Campbell, Dr. Matsumoto, and the Health Department have made today is one that is difficult and painful, it is one that I wholeheartedly support as a temporary measure to address the healthcare crisis that faces us today."

At the word "crisis," George Campbell grimaced; the two women from the Department of Health stared at the tops of their shoes.

Christine looked out over those assembled. "We are joining together in support of the health of our community. We are no strangers to healthcare crises. After a two-year battle, we have defeated COVID, and we will transcend the current crisis as well. I wish you all a happy, healthy day, secure in the knowledge that the very best medical staff in the New York metropolitan area is here to address our citizens' healthcare needs. Thank you."

Dora looked at Missy, her tone derisive. "I love the woman, but what did she just say?"

Missy shrugged. "She's addressing fears. It's not what she said, but that she's out front as a calming presence."

"I guess. I wouldn't want to be mayor today."

The women watched as the news anchors took turns interviewing the news conference's participants. Afterward, Sarah Turner did a brief, live interview with George Campbell, and then conducted a longer one with Christine Pearsall.

. . .

You continue to listen as *The Chronicle*'s reporter interviews that nothing, whose answers are gibberish. What is he talking about—going on and on about his infectious disease center? How could anyone publicly support an infectious disease center under the banner of this so-called hospital? Hadn't their credibility been undermined enough? This couldn't be happening, after all that work—the time, the expense, the risks. The world had truly gone mad!

The plan, which had seemed so far-fetched and impossible when you first conceived of it, had been perfectly executed. Your presence in the hospital was barely noticed and never questioned. You had acquired and stored the pathogens, despite lacking the requisite facilities, and had infected the chosen few. You had remained undetected and unsuspected. Beautiful deaths followed, which raised the intended red flags, concerns, and alarms. The illnesses, the causes of death had, despite breathtaking incompetence, been uncovered, their source unknown. Doubt and confusion reigned as to whether such a bizarre collection of exceedingly rare and deadly diseases could somehow have somehow occurred naturally.

All within the scope of the plan. What was not part of the plan was the hospital's intent to not only stay open—which was unimportant; the place could remain open or not—but somehow, the new infectious disease facility remains on course to be completed and unveiled and open to the public, its intended leadership intact. Impossible! Ridiculous! Infuriating!

Unacceptable.

So your work remains. More people would pay with their lives.

## Chapter 20

Dora and Missy had been too tired from the day's events to do much besides going over the case notes, feed the dogs and themselves, and fall into bed together in Missy's apartment.

They awoke to the cacophony of leaf blowers in the yard behind the apartment building. The gardeners had been working later and later into December and beginning their season earlier and earlier in March.

Dora groaned and squinted into the band of sunlight that streamed through the south-facing window. Missy blinked awake, turned her head toward Dora, and took her hand. They laid together, holding hands for a few minutes.

"Poor Martine," Missy said. "I didn't know her well, but she seemed like the sweetest woman."

Dora squeezed her hand. "And poor Kelvin. They were the most in-love couple I know."

Missy turned onto her side so that she was facing Dora, their faces inches apart. "They set a good example." Missy closed her eyes and kissed Dora, who pulled her into a hug, and they held each other for a few minutes.

Dora opened her eyes. "I'm going to say *Kaddish* for Martine."

Missy opened her eyes. "I've heard of that, but what is it?"

"It's a bereavement prayer, but it says nothing about death—only about glorifying God."

Missy thought about this. "How do you believe in God in the face of all the awful things that happen, the awful things people do?"

"I don't know. I just do," Dora replied, looking steadily into Missy's eyes. "Do you want to get married?"

Missy sat up on one elbow. "What?"

"Would you like to get married? Would you marry me?"

A smile broke out on Missy's face. "Are you serious?"

Dora hadn't moved. Now, she nodded imperceptibly. "If you can live with...the way I am."

Missy's expression darkened. "With the violence."

"With the violence," Dora repeated.

"I thought you didn't know what you wanted," Missy reminded her.

"In some ways I don't. But I'd rather be unsure of some things and be with you, than unsure and without you."

Missy sat up and folded her legs beneath her. Comfort milled around her side of the bed until she picked him up and held him in her lap. "I—I do have a hard time with the violence—that part of your personality. You have this...this bloodlust, and it scares me. Why is that?"

"Why does it scare you?"

"Why are you like that?"

Freedom had followed Comfort to the side of the bed and, seeing him in Missy's lap, leaped onto the bed and rested her chin on Dora's thigh, but kept her eyes on Comfort.

"Best I can explain it is this: for the most part, the world, the things that matter, are run by men. Not all, of course, but so, so much. I know so many women who don't get their due, and they get abused—really trashed—for trying. So many men have violence deep in their hearts. I don't just mean tough guys—assholes, criminals. I mean regular guys. So many of them feel so entitled to their positions and possessions—to the detriment of us. And to meet them, to be equal, to beat them, a woman must meet that violence that's hidden in their hearts with her own."

"I don't think I can agree with that."

"Who asked you to agree?"

"But can't you have peace and order and operate out of love? Aren't a lot of people—a lot of men—about that?"

"Maybe you can. Maybe they are. I think people who are truly like that—through and through—are exceedingly rare. I don't think I can operate that way. Not right now—maybe someday."

She smiled and rubbed Missy's arm. "Maybe that can be your project —to get me there." She dropped her hand to the bed. "For now, my actions, my participation in life has to be backed with iron and a willingness to fight—to back up our own entitlement with a violence that's more brutal than theirs."

Missy didn't answer right away. "Sarah looks good. She's starting to show."

"Yeah, to both."

"So…you ever thought about kids?"

Dora looked startled. "What?"

• • •

Dora and Missy had pulled chairs up alongside Adam Geller's desk. Adam was on the phone when they'd come in, but beckoned them over and held up a raised finger, indicating that he would be off the phone momentarily.

"So, what have you got?" He looked at each of them, his hands folded over his stomach.

"We have a severely dysfunctional Campbell family situation," Dora began.

"What does that mean?"

"Everyone has a dysfunctional family situation." Thelma stood in the doorway, her head tipped slightly back, looking like she'd bitten into a lemon.

Dora answered. "His daughter, Marilyn, hates him for contributing to the suicides of her mother—George's wife—and her brother, George Jr."

Adam didn't answer. One of the fingers of his clasped hands began tapping the back of his other hand. "I see."

Thelma scoffed. "If you arrested every girl who hates her father, you'd need a jail the size of New Jersey."

Adam glanced at his office manager, then back at his two investigators. "What else?"

"Marilyn Campbell is a nurse at BCMC, but she used to be a phlebotomist, and she worked at one of the two infectious labs in the area."

"And she's a friend of the owner of that lab," Missy added, her excitement showing. "And has an ax to grind with the hospital."

Adam turned to Missy. "What kind of ax?" He rested his elbows on the arms of his chair and steepled his hands together in front of his mouth. His forefingers tapped together in a repeating 1-2-3 cadence.

Missy glanced at Dora, then continued. "The hospital was planning to announce the successful funding and imminent opening of the Anderson Julienne Infectious Disease Center, which was to be run by Dr.

Ramesh Babu, whose lab is the other infectious disease lab in the vicinity."

Dora continued. "Dr. Babu and Dr. Traxle, whose lab Marilyn Campbell worked at, have the only two facilities that might be able to handle pathogens of the kind that have been killing people at BCMC."

"Technically, even those two labs fall short," Missy said, "but they're the closest to that standard in the area."

"Wasn't the gala canceled?" Thelma asked.

Dora nodded. "It was, but the infectious disease center and its fundraising are going forward."

"The infectious disease specialists, Traxle and Babu, have been rivals for decades, and we think this honor, this position, may have been too much for Traxle," Missy ventured.

Dora agreed. "Whether Marilyn Campbell is the driving force here or Traxle is, we have two people with motive, opportunity, access, and some degree of the special skills necessary to infect patients."

"Huh," Thelma snorted. "But what you don't have is evidence."

Adam looked at Dora, then at Missy, his look questioning.

"No, we don't," Missy agreed. "But we do have ongoing infections that absolutely cannot be happening naturally."

"You're sure of that?"

Dora nodded. "Multiple sources. Though truth be told, nothing is impossible, but this is as close as you could get. This is being done. People are being murdered, and they're being murdered for a reason."

"So, what next?" Adam asked.

"We were hoping you could give us some guidance," Dora answered. "Maybe we bring it to the police?"

"With what?" Adam asked. "We have no evidence of a crime."

"Ya got nothing," Thelma intoned from the doorway.

Adam turned to her. "If you're going to contribute, try to be a little constructive."

"Constructive. Constructive, he says."

"What about surveillance?" Adam continued. "What about seeing if Traxle's been seen in the hospital, and if so, where?"

• • •

For the next three days, Dora camped in her turbo amidst a crowd of parked cars in the lot behind the building that housed Traxle Labs at NYSUNC. She noted Dr. Traxle's comings and goings and followed her as best she could without being spotted. Dr. Traxle entered the building each day just shy of 8:00 a.m., left at 12:30 p.m. and drove to BCMC, returned at 1:20 p.m., and remained in her office until 5:15 p.m., when she exited and returned to her car. Dora followed Traxle to an apartment not far from Christine and Charlie's, along the water, which she assumed was her home.

The fourth day she called George Campbell to try to gain access to the information security had collected from hospital visitors. George directed her to Santiago Alvarez, whose office was on the ground floor, not far from the front desk. Dora explained what she was looking for and Alvarez, a clean-shaven young man in his mid-thirties with a broad face, a heavy jaw, and eager, intelligent eyes, immediately pulled up a computer file with Dr. Yvonne Traxle's information, along with the dates and times of her visits—all of which were during the same one-hour period, in the middle of the day.

"So, those are the only times she's been on the premises?" Dora asked.

"The only times since we installed the system, which is a little over five weeks." He pressed a series of keys on his keyboard and a picture of Dr. Traxle came up on his screen, and then another, and another.

"We take everyone's picture when they come through security, only they don't know it."

"Is that legal?"

Alvarez looked at her. "I have no idea. I'm not a lawyer, but we do have this." He pressed a few more keys and pulled up an image of a sign that stated "This premises is under continuous video surveillance."

"So she's at the front desk, in the cafeteria, at some of the nurses' stations, and…anywhere else?"

Santiago Alverez pressed a few more keys and sat back. "She's been in some of the patient wards. I wonder what she'd be doing there?"

Dora reported back to Missy and they went back to Adam's office.

"Why would an infectious disease doctor be in a patient ward?" Dora posed, once they were situated.

"Good question," Adam said.

"She's a doctor," came Thelma's voice through the wall. "How about to check on a patient with an infectious disease?"

"I don't think that makes sense," Missy observed.

"She's a doctor," Thelma emphasized, "an infectious disease special-ist, and right now, the hospital needs exactly such a person. Maybe she checked on one of the victims. How does that not make sense?"

Adam looked at Dora. "What would you say to having another talk with Dr. Traxle, and while you're there, having a look around?"

Missy looked dubious and anxious, but Dora looked eager. "Sure."

Adam continued. "I think it also makes sense to talk to some of her acquaintances as well."

· · ·

That afternoon, the two dressed in coats, scarves, and gloves and took the dogs for a walk along the beach. They walked along the packed sand into a brisk wind that was whipping the surf into a choppy froth. White gulls circled, hovered, or waddled along the sand and inspected shells and leftover bits of crabs.

The dogs pranced around one another, leaped together until they were nose to nose, then bounded apart again, frolicking joyfully this way and that.

Missy took Dora's hand and they walked into the wind, their backs to the morning sun.

"So we agree," Dora said, "that Marilyn can't be doing this alone—and that her relationship with Dr. Traxle can't be a coincidence."

Missy nodded. "And the hospital's plans for the infectious disease center, directed by the only other infectious disease expert in the area, could certainly be seen as motive."

They were silent for a bit; another couple walked toward them a short ways up the beach, in the looser sand. The woman waved. Missy waved back, and Dora smiled.

"It concerns me that Traxle's lab isn't fit for handling these diseases," Missy said. "And where would she have gotten them? Collecting them in the wild doesn't sound very realistic."

Dora snorted a laugh. "As for her lab not being fit for handling these pathogens—why would she care, other than protecting herself and Marilyn? If she's okay with killing people, you wouldn't necessarily think lab safety would be high on her priorities list."

"I don't know," Missy said. "Scientists are scientists. Even if one is doing something terrible, I'd still think they'd follow the protocols they're used to."

Dora gave sardonic grin. "Now you're a profiler?"

Missy shrugged. "Common sense—food for thought, anyway."

"Well, I agree with Adam. I think we need to circle back to Traxle," Dora said. "Put a little pressure on her and see how she reacts."

"Pressure? How're we going to do that?"

"Talk to her. Reason with her."

Missy stopped walking and Comfort began bounding in the sand, which was as deep as his legs were long. Freedom began running circles around them and Comfort followed, their leashes winding around the two women, who had to spin around to get loose.

"But couldn't that alert her to our suspicions?" Missy wondered.

"At this point," Dora responded, "people are dying. I think we've gotta shake the tree and see what falls out."

## Chapter 21

Dr. Matumoto insisted that he be the point of contact for any discussion of hospital personnel's interaction with Dr. Traxle. Meeting to discuss the subject in person was, he said, not necessary, and while he understood the need for a thorough investigation, his position all along had been that these cases were not part of some conspiracy or murder spree, but simply what they appeared to be—medical cases—an unfortunate spate of diseases that required treatment. Dr. Traxle's interactions with BCMC and its personnel had always been perfectly appropriate, Dr. Matumoto maintained. Her demeanor and behavior had always been professional, and there really wasn't any more to say on the subject.

Missy suggested approaching businesses in the office suites neighboring Traxle Labs. Dora agreed, and they promptly got into Dora's turbo and headed off.

The first office was an insurance brokerage that abutted Traxle Labs on one side and whose gatekeeper, a fiftyish woman with gray hair piled high on her head, was reluctant to "bother" the bosses. When Dora gave the woman her card and explained the reason for their visit, one of the bosses was summoned. Richard Carpenter was a nervous young man with a reddish complexion and darting blue eyes who impatiently explained that he didn't even know who Dr. Yvonne Traxle was. He paid no attention to neighboring businesses, including Traxle Labs.

Across the hall from Traxle Labs was a dental practice—Child's Smiles—that specialized in treating children. The office manager said that she was the one to speak to, since the dentist there dealt with nothing but dentistry—literally, nothing. The manager was a thirty-year-old named Sue, with a round, chubby face, small features, and unruly, thick black hair. She said she ran into Dr. Traxle in the hallway now and then, and found her to be professional but cynical about the medical industry. She also reported that Dr. Traxle felt that care in the medical system nowadays was often mismanaged, and that patients needlessly suffered.

The office on the other side of Traxle Labs was, somewhat ironically, that of a lawyer specializing in medical malpractice. The woman at the front desk—she wore a name tag that said her name was Moira—was sure that Mr. Finch would be glad to help if he could. Jeffery Finch, a fortyish man with black rimmed glasses, curious green eyes, and reddish gray hair, seemed delighted for the interruption.

"Very little that's interesting goes on here other than my cases themselves," he laughed, "so a bit of excitement is always welcome."

"What can you tell us about Dr. Yvonne Traxle?" Dora asked.

"Ah, the bug lady." He grinned. "That's what we call her. She's a bit creepy. There's something about her—I can't put my finger on it. Something hidden—like she's got a secret and it's not a nice one. Oh, and she can't stand the hospital—Beach City Medical Center. She once saw me walking in the hallway with a cane and asked what was wrong. I told her I was going to BCMC for a knee replacement, and she gave me this disgusted look and said she wouldn't bring her cat there."

Next, they pressed Dr. Traxle's buzzer and, once buzzed in, waited behind the wide window that looked into the lab. As on their previous visit, two women were working at opposite ends of the wide white room.

Dora did her best to read the labels on the counter, which were large enough to read from where she stood. Those on the vials and small containers were too minuscule to make out at that distance but one label jumped out at her. On a small, thick, metal refrigerator was a bright red label that red "Danger—Contaminants."

Eventually, one of the women approached them. She was not Dr. Traxle, but a tall woman with frizzy brown hair and a friendly smile. "Can I help you?"

Missy held out a card. "We're private investigators working with the hospital. We've spoken with Dr. Traxle before and were hoping to have a word with her."

"Do you have an appointment?"

"No, but this won't take long."

"Just a minute."

They watched the woman approach Dr. Traxle, who glanced in their direction, nodded, and then walked their way.

"I don't have much time," she said, "but what can I do for you?"

"We're just here for a quick follow-up," Dora explained. "We were wondering what your take is on the Anderson Julienne Infectious Disease Center."

"My take?"

"Are you happy it's in the works?"

Dr. Traxle blinked and nodded. "Why wouldn't I be?" She frowned, as the answer to her question came to her, then smiled slightly. "Oh," she said.

"How do you feel about the center going forward, despite these diseases that are occurring at the hospital?"

Traxle looked irritated. "I'm happy about it. These cases demonstrate need. Now I'm sorry, but I have a deadline. That's all the time I can spare. I hope you understand."

Dora and Missy emerged into the sunlight of the parking lot with Dora in the lead and Missy trailing a few steps behind.

"So, she's a pathological liar *and* a sociopathic murderer," Missy said.

Dora squinted as they headed for her car. "Let's wait in the car. I'd like a private word with the assistant."

They waited just over an hour until Dr. Traxle's assistant exited the building. Dora got out of the car; Missy followed.

"'Scuse me. You're Dr. Traxle's assistant, aren't you? Can we talk for a sec?"

The woman, who had been deep in thought, looked startled, then she recognized them. "You were in a while ago."

"That's right. Do you mind if we talk for a moment?"

"What about?"

"About your boss. Can you tell us a bit about her? We're trying to get a picture of anyone local that's in your field." Dora held out a card. "What's your name?"

"Evelyn. Evelyn O'Neill."

"Thanks for taking a moment, Ms. O'Neill," Missy said. "Or is it Dr. O'Neill?"

Evelyn laughed. "Not yet. Someday. Dr. Traxle…well, she's professional, extremely knowledgeable, and dedicated."

"Okay," Missy said, encouragingly.

"She's also fascinated by the deadliest infectious diseases and often reads up on them in her spare time. I'll tell you this, she's riveted by what's happening at BCMC right now, and says she finds it hard to believe, given how rare these diseases are."

"Interesting," Dora murmured.

"Yes, in fact, Dr. Traxle has been talking about doing more in-depth, hands-on study of these kinds of diseases."

"Really," Dora exclaimed. "Where would she do that?"

"A lab in Texas—Dallas, I think. It's called LeMerre Laboratories, or something like that. They're a BSL-4 laboratory, but you don't hear about them much because all they do is teach. It's essentially a training center overseen by the State Department of Health down there. I think it's kind of hush-hush because they house a range of the most infectious diseases. Anyway, they offer week-long training programs for infectious disease specialists like Dr. Traxle, and they're known to keep these diseases on hand, for teaching purposes. She's mentioned several times that she wants to get down there and participate in that program, but she just hasn't been able to find the time. We're awfully busy, and what with what's going on at BCMC now, we're even busier. The hospital is communicating regularly with us and other labs, trying to track down the source of these incidents and to properly identify and deal with them."

Once back at Geller Investigations, both Missy and Dora got to work on the computers; Dora looked for local news articles that featured infectious diseases, Dr. Traxle, or Dr. Ramesh Babu. Missy attempted to locate the lab Evelyn O'Neill mentioned. The partners circled back after an hour.

"Whatcha got?" Missy asked.

"Four articles with the two doctors in them. Three with Dr. Babu, two of which reference this new infectious disease center. One with Dr. Traxle. They're also mentioned as infectious disease experts in articles about various other things. Nothing's jumping out at me here. You?"

Missy gave a confident smile. "I found a LaMarre Laboratories in Dallas, and it's like Evelyn said. They offer training at a state-of-the-art BSL-4 laboratory for accredited infectious disease doctors whose M.D. degree is in that field."

Dora leaned forward. "So, let's contact them to find out if either of our local doctors has attended their program."

Missy nodded slowly. "They might not be willing to provide us with information without a good reason. At this point, saying we're investigators might put them off. We need to come up with some reason for our call."

Dora considered this. "How 'bout that we work for the hospital, which we sort of do, and we're looking at the possibility of offering positions to infectious disease specialists who claim to have expertise in the field."

"I don't know. That sounds kind of iffy. Wouldn't the specialists just put their expertise on their résumés? So why wouldn't we just ask about these two doctors?"

Dora squinted in concentration. "Kind of a hunch. I think we should do it this way."

"Okay, then." Missy dialed the number on her screen. "Hi, my name is Lola Elanie and I'm calling on behalf of the Beach City Medical Center, in Beach City, New York. Yes, I'll hold."

Dora raised her eyebrows. "Lola Elanie?"

Missy shrugged, then focused as the person on the other end returned to the line. "Yes, we are in the process of vetting applicants for a new infectious disease facility that will soon be a part of our hospital, and we want to be able to double check their qualifications." She paused. "Well, rather than get back to you with each one, might you be able to send a list of your attendees for the past, say, five years?" Her eyes wandered around the room as she listened. "You've been in operation for three? Okay, then. Three." Her eyes widened and she broke into a smile. "You'll look into it? That's all I can ask." She read off her personal Google Mail account and ended the call. "I hope the fact that my email's not a hospital email won't be a red flag."

"Guess we'll see," Dora said, "but nice job!"

• • •

That evening, Dora drove to Vanessa's apartment to watch the boys while Vanessa worked at The Bernelli Group's studio. When Vanessa let her into the apartment, she put a finger to her lips, then led Dora into the living room, where she found the boys watching a live-action TV program featuring singing and dancing fruits and vegetables. On the floor between them sat Kelvin Franklin. He did not look up when they entered, but the boys jumped up, ran to Dora, and hugged her legs.

"Hello, boys!" she responded. "I see you have a guest today."

Drew nodded somberly. "That's Kelvin. Mommy's friend."

Buster gave an exaggerated nod. "He's sad."

"Hey, Kelvin. Good to see you," Dora ventured. Kelvin's eyes flickered in her direction, but he said nothing.

"Come on in the kitchen, Dora," Vanessa said. "I'll show you what to serve for dinner."

Dora followed Vanessa into the kitchen, where she opened the refrigerator to reveal a tray of sliders—burgers and rolls with ketchup and pickles already in place—and a package of pre-cooked French fries. Vanessa leaned close to Dora. "He can't be alone," she said, referring to Kelvin.

Dora pressed her lips together. "I understand," she said.

The boys, Kelvin, and Dora watched TV together for an hour, then the boys and Dora ate dinner. Kelvin, who had already lost quite a bit of weight, did not eat.

After dinner, the boys wanted to listen to music via Vanessa's Spotify account. They knew just what they wanted to hear—songs they could sing along with, and sing they did. They sang nursery rhymes and songs from children's movies and Broadway shows. Eventually, they came to a song that was more than twenty years old. The boys had been begging Kelvin all along to sing with them, but his eyes had a zombie-like vacantness and he had not responded. Until now. After the first few bars of the song, he blinked and looked directly at both boys.

"Sing with us, Kelvin!" Drew cried.

Kelvin's eyes traveled from Drew to Dora and then to Buster.

"Sing!" Buster implored. "Kelvin, sing! Kelvin. Sing with us!"

And very softly at first, Kelvin sang a phrase along with little Buster. And then he sang another. And another.

Exhausted after a single verse, Kelvin closed his eyes, and the boys knew enough to leave him alone.

But Kelvin had sung. It was a start.

## Chapter 22

Dora and Freedom stayed the night at Missy's apartment again. The two dogs had grown close, with little Comfort taking on the role of fierce protector of Freedom. Since Dora's wedding proposal, the women had been spending more and more nights together—their love and intimacy growing by the day.

Missy lay on her back, her dark hair splayed on the sheets around her head, her arms lying half-raised beside her ears. Her face was red and flushed, her breath still coming fast, her chest heaving. Dora had sat up and taken a small, thick, ornately embossed book from her bedside. She had brought the book with her the second night she stayed, which was the first night she knew she would be staying. The book was a Jewish *Siddur* or prayer book.

She read silently, her lips moving.

"Are you praying?" Missy asked, rolling onto her side.

Dora nodded, but continued what she was doing without answering.

"I don't mean to interrupt."

Dora nodded again, and continued her prayer. When she was finished, she lay back down next to Missy and took her hand.

"How does reading prayers help you?" Missy wondered.

Dora thought about the question. "I sometimes get scared and confused."

Missy was astonished. "You?"

"Me? Everyone."

"And reading prayers helps."

"It does."

"Why?"

"I don't know. I tried it years ago, and I found it comforting."

"You believe all that God stuff?"

"Same answer. I tried it years ago, and it helped—made me feel better somehow. Still does. I can't explain it scientifically except to say look at nature—or the night sky, like Einstein said. Then tell me there's no God."

Missy didn't say anything.

"What do you do?" Dora asked.

"I meditate."

"Do you think about something specific?"

"The emptiness of everything."

"Emptiness? I don't understand."

"It's a Buddhist concept. It means that nothing exists in and of itself. Everything is dependent upon other things to exist or to cease to exist. Conditions must be right for a thing to exist. Us, for instance. We don't exist separate from everything else because we're dependent upon our parents, upon air, food, water, and so forth. Meditating on this helps me. Comforts me. I know I'm connected to everything."

"Huh." Dora picked up Missy's tablet, opened an internet page and began to read. "Check this out. Dr. Yvonne Traxle was interviewed by *The Chronicle* and endorses the Anderson Julienne Infectious Disease Center."

Missy sat up and scooted over on the bed so she could read over Dora's shoulder, on which she rested her chin as she read.

"'Dr. Traxle is looking forward to the opening of the facility and endorses its soon-to-be director, Dr. Ramesh Babu. She expects the center to be a boon to the Beach City community and surrounding areas.'"

Dora dropped the tablet on the bed. "But, that *is* what she would say, isn't it?"

"The problem I'm having with this," Missy said, thinking it through as she spoke, "is that Traxle's goal would be to ruin BCMC, its new facility, and Dr. Ramesh, right? So it seems to me that publicly lying about the facility by seeming to support it would take a back seat to doing everything in her power to ruin it—not the least of which would include using her professional stature to disparage it."

Dora digested what her partner was saying, but her only response was "Hmmm."

• • •

The stupid fool. Now she's signed her own death warrant. She should have kept her mouth shut. If she had said nothing, her stature in the medical community would have been raised, simply by keeping her mouth shut. But now, by speaking out, she's guaranteed her own demise —and a horrible demise it will be. She had to take sides. *She had to take sides!* She couldn't mind her own business. This had nothing to do with her, but now...a new plan was required, with new tactics—and new friends.

• • •

Three days later, the two investigators were sitting in front of the computer in Geller's office and Missy was explaining her concerns to Dora.

"I'm having trouble getting past the fact that there are no BSL-4 labs nearby. Wouldn't this killer, who's handling these deadly diseases, want to stay free of infection? Wouldn't they be invested in appropriate handling?"

"We've talked about this," Dora answered. "Maybe so, but who knows what boundaries exist in the mind of a killer. The fact that the killer's a scientist might be relevant, but is he or she a killer first or a scientist first? You're out there killing people. If a few more get infected because of the way you're handling the diseases, so what?"

"Well, but if you have specific targets, it seems to me that you'd want them to get sick, but not others. Would you want to accidentally cast a wide net? Why not just release the pathogens everywhere? But that's not what this person is doing. From what I've read, and from what Adam said, killers are control freaks. They want to control who's going to die, and how, and when."

"And so far," Missy mused, "these diseases do not seem to be contagious among people."

Dora nodded slowly. "You're right. Good point." Missy was looking at her. She could see the wheels turning. "What?"

"Maybe Babu is doing this so that he and his new facility can solve the cases."

Dora shook her head. "I don't see it. I guess it's possible, but that's not much of a motive. The cases are being addressed; at least, the diagnoses are being made. And Babu is already set to head the new facility."

"Maybe Babu is the one making these diagnoses. We don't know who the hospital's infectious disease specialist is. Maybe it's Babu."

"But it's also our understanding that they're working with Traxle," Dora pointed out. "But Babu would be jeopardizing his own involvement at the new facility if he were involved, no?"

"Right. Traxle and Marilyn really seem like a fit—despite Traxle's public support of the new BCMC facility."

"Well, maybe Marilyn still is, and she's doing this some other way."

"That interview had to have been a smokescreen," Missy insisted. "This has gotta be Traxle."

"Agreed," Dora smiled, relieved. "It's just—she's such a smooth liar —for a sociopath."

"Probably a pathological liar."

Dora's cellphone rang. She looked at the caller I.D. "BCMC," she said. "Hello?"

"We've got another one!"

"George?" She looked at Missy and mouthed, "George Campbell."

"We have a case of what looks like H5N1—a deadly strain of avian flu. Something else you need to know. The patient is Dr. Yvonne Traxle."

• • •

Yvonne Traxle was being kept in isolation in one of several suites at BCMC that had been used for victims of the deadly diseases. George warned the investigators prior to scheduling a phone call with Dr. Traxle that she had severe digestive-related symptoms, difficulty breathing, and, occasionally, difficulty thinking. Following a nebulizer breathing treatment, she would be able to speak for a few minutes, but would be monitored by a nurse, who would end the call if talking became too difficult.

The call was set up with the help of the hospital operator as a three-way conversation, which George began by introducing Dora and Missy as investigators working with the hospital.

"I know who they are," Dr. Traxle said, then lapsed into a fit of coughing. After several gasping breaths, she continued. "I didn't know their purpose, but...we've met."

"The hospital is convinced," George explained, "that these rare and deadly diseases are being spread intentionally here at BCMC. Can you think of anyone who might have reason to commit such crimes?"

"No!" She began to cough again and struggled to inhale. When she did, it was with a rasping wheeze. "That's insane." She paused, and they could hear her labored breathing. "But..."

"But...?" George prompted.

"The only people who have the knowledge would be myself and Ramesh Babu, even though—"

"Yes," George prodded. "Even though—"

"Neither of us has a BSL-4 level lab."

Another voice interrupted the conversation. "Hi. This is Dorothy. I'm the nurse with Dr. Traxle. I think that's all she can manage, for now."

"We understand," said Dora.

"And thank you," George said, and ended the connection.

• • •

"I'll tell you who else has the knowledge to do this," Missy posited.

"Who?" Dora asked. They were still in the office of Geller Investigations, using Adam's computer, as Adam was in the field yet again, surveilling a deadbeat husband.

"Evelyn. Traxle's assistant." Missy turned so her body faced Dora. "And who knows, she might have the same motive we ascribed to Traxle."

Dora took a breath. "Well, we could tail her and get into her apartment. At this point, there's nothing actionable for the police, though."

"Right," Missy agreed.

"I'd love to get an hour in Traxle's lab," Dora muttered, crossing her arms.

"You'd think Traxle would be onto her assistant being a part of this, given how closely they have to work together."

"Why?" Dora asked. "We don't know how these labs operate. We don't know if the assistant could hide pathogens somewhere, maybe mislabeling them to keep them away from Traxle. And we don't know motive. With Traxle, you have the rivalry with Babu—ramped up professional jealousy."

Missy didn't answer. They had been reading about the avian flu together on Adam's computer, and now Missy was accessing her email.

"Look at this," she said, clicking on a link in her email. "It's from LaMarre Laboratories in Texas. They sent the list of attendees to their... they call it a training symposium. It's for all three years of their existence. Huh." She sat back with a hint of a satisfied smile. "See any names you recognize?"

Dora scanned the screen. "I wonder if someone could've used a fake name—though I suppose not, since they'd need their degree to...I don't see Traxle, or Babu, or anyone named Evelyn. Wait. Dr. Clay Spontana. Where have I heard that name?"

"He's the assistant to Dr. Ramesh Babu."

"Whoa. When did he attend?"

"Seven months ago, which is the last time the training was held."

Dora considered this. "Still not enough to go to the police. We have a lot of theory that makes sense, but this is circumstantial at best."

"Maybe we should talk to Babu—see if we can gain access to the lab when the assistant isn't there."

"Maybe, but before we do that, I have another idea. Let's call his sister, Mahira Babu. See if she has an impression of Spontana. Contacting Ramesh Babu directly might be cutting a little too close to the bone."

"Meaning what?" Missy asked.

"Meaning whatever Babu's reaction might be could spook Spontana. And calling the sister isn't without risks. It's possible her brother spoke to her about our involvement with the investigation."

"So? Let's call. I won't say a word that isn't true." Missy found Mahira Babu's phone number in the notes and dialed. "It's getting close to dinnertime. Let's hope she's home."

"Hello?"

"Dr. Mahira Babu? This is Missy Winters. I'm a contractor working for the Beach City Medical Center. We communicated by email a while back about your brother's involvement at the Anderson Julienne Infectious Disease Center. You sent me some information for the gala brochure."

"Yes, I remember," Mahira replied. "I'm sorry to hear that the gala is not being held. I understand that the center will be completed though, and is supposed to open on time, early in the year."

"Yes, so far that's the plan."

"Tell me," Mahira continued, "has there been any resolution to the run of diseases at the hospital there?"

"As a matter of fact," Missy answered, "that's why I called. We were wondering what you can tell me about Dr. Clay Spontana."

"My brother's assistant?"

"What can you tell me about him?"

"He's a qualified infectious disease physician. If he wasn't, my brother would not have hired him."

"I understand that," Missy continued, pressing her lips together and trying to think of how to prod Mahira Babu for more information. She forced her voice to sound relaxed—a little bit cavalier. "This is off the record. Nothing to do with a brochure or any material on the website. In fact, this is part of our in-house investigation into the source of these diseases. It's one hundred percent private."

Mahira paused. "This is confidential?"

"Absolutely."

She sighed and paused, as though deciding exactly how much to tell. "Let me tell you a little bit about Dr. Clay Spontana. He is a driven scientist who has devoted his life to the study of infectious diseases, and he's had every reason to. After his grandmother died from a rabies infection believed to have come from raccoons on the family's farm in Kentucky, and after his father, whom he idolized, died at Beach City Medical Center of Creutzfeldt-Jakob disease—"

"Mad cow disease?" Missy interrupted.

"Well—it's a variant of mad cow that comes from eating meat from an infected animal. His mother died of a broken heart soon after his father passed away, and Clay went on to devote his life to studying, containing, and curing infectious diseases, particularly the most deadly and virulent of diseases. He's been honored and lauded and was, for a time, seen as a wunderkind in the field. He personally saved a family from Nipah virus infection with an experimental monoclonal antibody treatment, and was honored with department chairs at two major universities. The father of the family he helped to save was the president of one and was on the board of the other. He was up for three grants, which would have allowed him to set up his own infectious disease lab, which was his lifelong goal—though 'goal' is not a strong enough word for what was really an obsession. Having his own lab, in his name, would have been the culmination of his lifetime body of work, and is something he deeply, deeply believed he deserved."

"What happened?" Missy asked.

"All three of the grants went to my brother."

Missy raised her eyebrows at Dora, who said one word. "Motive."

"It is my clinical opinion—though it's not my area of expertise, of course, that Dr. Spontana is a narcissist. Everything, especially everything in his field of science, is about him. He also happens to be charming and brilliant, and he knows it. He is one of the best in his field. The only problem—my brother is better. I daresay that my brother's name being on this infectious disease center has to have been devastating for Spontana."

"Do you think he's capable of giving people fatal diseases," Dora asked, "so as to destroy the chance of this center opening—to hurt your brother's career?"

Mahira hesitated. "Well, I have a hard time believing anyone is capable of doing something like that. It's what's so bewildering about the situation at BCMC. But if you're telling me that a person caused this, and if you're asking me if that person could have been Clay Spontana, my answer would have to be 'yes.' He's a brilliant yet obsessed scientist, whose perspective has always been lacking. Is he a narcissist? I think so. Is he a sociopath? Perhaps. He's certainly petty and jealous and has a powerful belief in his entitlement and his having been wronged."

"I'm curious," Missy said, "what does your brother think of the possibility that these diseases were spread purposely?"

Mahira answered quickly and confidently. "He thinks the idea is preposterous, but so is every other possibility. His solution is to avoid the subject entirely." She paused. "I do know that he's concerned about anything that might undermine the opening of the Anderson Julienne Center."

They ended the call and Missy pulled up Babu Laboratories' website, which displayed a photo of Dr. Clay Spontana. "I want to memorize his face, as we've never had a really good look at him."

"We should go to the cops," Dora suggested, her mouth set, her eyes resolute. "I wonder if we could get a search warrant, and maybe get a look at his computer."

## Chapter 23

As soon as Dora began explaining to Detective Paul Ganderson the reason for her call, he interrupted and asked that she and Missy meet him and his partner, Detective Gerald Mallard, at the police station downtown.

When they arrived, Lieutenant Gary "Re" Morse, who worked the front desk, recognized Dora and Missy and called for one of the detectives to come to the front to escort the two investigators into the station proper. Mallard appeared in the doorway a few minutes later, wearing a custom tailored, three-piece blue wool suit and a gracious smile. He stood to one side to allow them to pass. "Ladies."

They followed Mallard to the rear of the cavernous room and arrived at the two desks assigned to the detective partners. Seated at one was Detective Paul Ganderson who was the opposite of his partner in nearly every way but gender. While Mallard was gregarious, Ganderson was taciturn and brooding. While Mallard was quick to expound on any one of his manifold theories about a case, Ganderson played his cards close to the vest. Where Mallard was dressed to the nines, Ganderson always wore what appeared to be the same mud brown suit. He was taller than Mallard, and leaner. His black hair was slicked back with a gel; his face displayed the ravages of long-ago acne. Together, the two were referred to as "the Goose and the Gander," in part because of their names, in part because Mallard's theories lent him a reputation as something of a quack.

"Well, well. If it isn't Beach City's twin gifts to law enforcement," Ganderson grumbled, barely looking up from whatever paperwork was in front of him. "Working for Adam Geller, I see. Not sure I would have chosen you to bushwhack into new investigative territory."

"You're just jealous, Ganderson, that I got to Egar and Altamont ahead of you," Dora said, referring to a case she and Missy had broken open six months earlier.

"Let's show the ladies the courtesy of a proper hearing." Mallard suggested. "Er, ah, maybe they're looking for a little help."

Ganderson snorted, scoffing. "'Bout time."

Dora and Missy took turns laying out the facts of the case, and the information that pointed to Dr. Clay Spontana.

Ganderson was first to speak. He shook his head. "Pathetic, Ellison. A long shot, at best." He held out a palm face-up in front of him and flicked his wrist several times. "Even if what you're suggesting were true, we can't make arrests based on 'gee, it looks like this guy might have done x, y, or z.' That's not how law enforcement works. If you'd have stayed at academy a little longer, you might have learned that."

Dora stared at the detective, unblinking. "You're real tough behind a desk, a badge, and a gun. Why not come down to Shay's MMA some-time for a little workout?"

"Come on," Ganderson continued, with cruel half-smile. "I don't know that there's even a crime here. Jealous doctors? You've got sick people in a hospital. Oooh! How bizarre. How mysterious! Come on. We have real cases here to close." He flicked his fingers, dismissing them.

"Er, ah, I'm not so sure," Mallard said. He was still standing, and now clasped the bridge of his nose between thumb and forefinger. "I re-member the case of Dexter Bramley. He was a nurse in the Bronx, I be-lieve, and he was infecting patients. Awfully hard to track and to prove, but it was a judge who agreed to provide the search warrant who turned the case. Who was that judge, again?"

Ganderson shook his head. "There's not enough for a search warrant here."

Mallard squinted and looked from his partner to the two women before him. "Er, I'm not so sure. We just might warrant a warrant." He chuckled. "Let me walk you ladies to the front." He led them to the front of the station as he recalled the judge's name and spoke. "I'm going to reach out to her—Judge Cheryl Rose—and see if we can have a look at some of Dr. Spontana's possessions."

. . .

The next day, Dora received a call from Detective Mallard explaining that they had indeed searched both Spontana's apartment and his possessions at Dr. Babu's lab, and now had in their possession a computer whose contents the police had thus far failed to access.

Missy held out her hand for the phone, which Dora handed to her. "I might be able to help with the computer," she offered.

"You have the skills to unlock a password protected, possibly encrypted computer?" Mallard asked.

"How 'bout we find out?"

"Well, come on down then."

After ending the call, Dora looked at Missy with surprise. "I didn't know you had that kind of IT skill."

Missy grinned. "I don't, but I'm a librarian—a research professional. By the time we get there I will. You drive."

As they drove, Dora received a call. "Sarah? I'm putting you on speaker."

"Hi, Dora. Is Missy with you?"

"Hi, Sarah," Missy said. "How are you feeling?"

"Well, the morning sickness is gone. A few more months and we'll have Olivia."

"How's C3?"

"Nervous. Freaking out—but still sober. Not sure if he can cut being a father, especially to a little girl with special needs. I'm rooting for him big time. I know he *can* do it. *Will* he do it? We'll see, but I know he can."

"Thanks," Sarah responded.

Dora continued, "Anyway, what's up?"

"I received an email. It's a letter, for publication in *The Chronicle*, and it claims to be from Dr. Ramesh Babu. And, listen to this—it takes responsibility for the series of infectious disease deaths we've been seeing at BCMC. I thought it was a scam, a nut, but the server is right—Lemieux says it's coming from Babu's office. And the email address is right as well. So, it does appear to be coming from Dr. Babu."

Dora couldn't hide her excitement; she looked at Missy, who waggled her eyebrows, her eyes bright and expectant.

Sarah continued. "You guys are friends, and you're smart investigators. I thought I'd call you, keeping this confidential, to get your take, before I called the cops."

Missy was working on her computer as they drove, her window lowered so as to avoid carsickness. Dora said, "I can't say anything specifically, since it could undermine an active investigation, but I'll say this. I hear what you're saying, but I'm pretty sure the letter didn't come from Dr. Babu."

"But it did—"

"That's all I'm going to say, Sarah. You've got to trust me. There's an explanation. I also respectfully suggest you don't run the letter, as I believe you'd be doing a disservice to Ramesh Babu. There's another layer to this and I believe we're getting close. Let me leave it at that. Oh, and I think you should give the letter to the police. Call this number and ask for Detective Ganderson or Detective Mallard." She recited the detectives' direct number, ended the call, and exchanged another look with Missy. "This guy's not living in the real world. Did he think she would publish such bullshit?"

"It shows how driven he is to discredit Ramesh Babu," Missy observed. "It shows how sick he is."

They arrived at the police station, were escorted to Mallard's desk. Spontana's laptop computer was open and turned on, but showed only a screen requesting a password. Mallard slid his chair away from the table for Missy to sit. "Have at it."

Missy sat down, with Mallard over one shoulder and Dora over the other. She opened her own computer next to Spontana's.

"So, first, we need access—a password reset. We'll boot from my computer to allow us to use an offline password and registry editor."

She shut down Spontana's PC, plugged it into her own, then booted it up again. The laptop screen appeared, albeit with different information, which reflected a Windows registry.

"Okay. Now we can clear the password associated with the user account, then boot back into Windows and log into the account without a password. Then we simply reset the password of the system's built-in administrator account to gain access."

"If you say so," said Mallard.

Dora was watching with an admiring smile. She glanced at Mallard. "Gotta love librarians!"

"Next, let's take a look at his browser history. Ah. Deleted, as I anticipated."

"So…?" Mallard began.

"Not to worry. We can retrieve it. See, he's already done some of the work for us." Missy grinned at Mallard and Dora. "Not sure this guy cares all that much about getting caught. We to start by logging into the Google account associated with his Chrome browser, which he's already done. See, he cleared his browsing history, but we're still automatically logged into his Google account—so, step one is done. He did it for us. Next, we have to use the DNS cache to recover his browsing history. Just hit Windows, the plus key, and 'R' to open 'run,' then type 'Command' and 'OK' to open the command prompt."

She typed in a code. "From here, we can see the browsing history. But we can do better. We can restore the previous version, which will give us much more leeway. Umm. There." She clicked, typed, and clicked some more. "And, there it is. His browsing history."

Together, Missy, Dora, and Mallard scanned the web addresses, with Missy clicking on some and ignoring others.

"Pretty much what you'd expect from a guy who was researching the world's deadliest diseases," Dora observed. "Finding, keeping, and transmitting. Accessing peer-reviewed articles, no less."

"Along with some pretty out there conspiracy ideas," Mallard added.

Missy said nothing; she just sat back and admired her work and the doors she had helped to open. She sat forward again. "We're not done. This is just browser history. The files he has on the computer are encrypted."

"And...impossible to get to," Dora said, leaving the question open-ended. "...even for a librarian." Missy smirked at her, aware she was teasing, then gave Dora a mock contemptuous glance. "Please. Ye of little faith." She examined what she saw on her screen. "This is an encryption software called LockNet that encrypts everything on your drive so that it's ostensibly impossible to read."

"How do you defeat it?" Mallard wanted to know.

"With decryption software made for exactly that purpose."

"And," Dora added, "I suppose you have an example of just such a piece of software."

"I do. Hey—I'm a librarian. The world's information is at my fingertips."

"Huh," said Dora, who elbowed Mallard. "Girl has serious fingertips."

"Ugh," said Mallard, wincing.

"We just launch DeCryptit, click on the encrypted hard drive, and click 'Go,'" Missy explained. "The software first shows us the files we might want to retrieve, then allows us to click 'recover' to set the process in motion. For security's sake, I'm having the recovered files sent over to my computer, which I'll back up, once I'm back in Adam's office."

"Can we look at them first?" Mallard asked.

"'Course," Missy said, and sat back again so that Mallard could navigate the recovered files.

As the detective read, he nodded slowly. "It's all here—and very organized—in what amounts to a murder spreadsheet. Information about Traxle and Ramesh, about Campbell and the hospital, and about each of the victims—their hospital records, their infection dates, and their responses to infection. And here's information about each of the diseases, notes on proper handling, and modes of transmission."

Missy took the mouse from Mallard, clicked on a directory, then on several files within it, and examined the information within them for several minutes in silence. "He was also obsessed with the classical music composer Antonio Salieri. Links to his music and articles about him."

"Why is that significant?" Mallard wanted to know. Dora looked baffled.

"He was an Italian composer of classical music who was obsessed with Mozart. Salieri was a talented artist, but Mozart was better—the best. Mozart was a genius, and Salieri couldn't handle that."

"So, Babu is Spontana's Mozart?" Dora asked.

"Looks that way." Missy clicked the spreadsheet's last row, which listed "Dr. Ramesh Babu," to the right of which were the words *"necrotizing fasciitis,"* next to the current date.

"That's the technical name for flesh-eating bacteria," Missy said.

## Chapter 24

Mallard called Detective Ganderson who put out a BOLO for Dr. Spontana. Mallard would immediately head to Dr. Babu's lab, while Ganderson went to Spontana's apartment, each with several officers as backup. Another two officers had been dispatched to Babu's home.

Dora suggested they rendezvous with Mallard at Babu Laboratories. "Since Spontana couldn't destroy the infectious disease center, he's going after Ramesh Babu the man."

"I think he was going to kill Babu all along. And I doubt Spontana would be at the lab, because Babu isn't there," Missy said as they got into Dora's car.

"Where is he, and how do you know that?"

"It's on Babu Laboratories' website, under 'News.' I didn't think of it until just this second. Babu is one of the featured speakers today on the advances in the treatment of infectious diseases at the MedSci Pro International Medical Conference."

"He's there now?"

Missy nodded. "It's at the Long Island Hotel and Convention Center, and that's where Spontana's going."

Dora started the car and they raced off in the direction of the main highway that would take them to the bridge off the barrier island. The convention center was fifteen miles north of Beach City, with the latter three miles being suburban streets which were likely to be congested in the late afternoon.

"From what I remember," Missy said, "Babu is giving a series of talks as well as participating in a forum with several other scientists."

"So he'll be easy enough for Spontana to find." Dora glanced at Missy, who was reading from Babu's website on her phone. "Call Mallard and tell him what's going on. The police need to get to that conference."

. . .

"Sarah!" At *The Chronicle's* office, Lemieux was calling from behind his computer. "Looks like something's going down at the Convention Center—something pretty big." He had been scrolling through a live online feed of police incidents in Nassau County.

Sarah had been rewriting an article about the previous night's council meeting. She typed the convention center's information into a browser window. "There's a medical convention there, and—wait—Ramesh Babu is a speaker." She stood up. "Got to be a break in the BCMC disease case." She took a step toward the door, then bent forward in pain and moaned. A pain knifed through her belly, and she reached desperately for the top of her desk and managed to lower herself back into her chair.

"Lemieux," she gasped. "Go to the Convention Center, get the story, write it—and be sure to get some art. Send Esther in here. Ohhh, fuck."

Esther, who had overheard, rushed into Sarah's office.

"Get me to the ER." Sarah's eyes overflowed with tears of desperation and terror. "I think I'm losing Olivia."

"Ambulance?" Esther asked.

Sarah shook her head. "Just help me up, let me lean on you—and get me there fucking fast!"

• • •

The crowd at Rudy's was despondent and silent. It was early evening and the bar was open, and the union crowd took up three tables in the back. Hakeem stood quietly to one side while Keisha addressed the assembled crowd. Craig Balboni watched and listened quietly from one of the tables with some fellow construction union members.

"I'm proud of you all. We really did fight a good fight, but what they did in the end—they bought the vote out from under us. They paid for the union busters to come in and scare the hell out of y'all, and to your credit, most of you voted with us. Most of you did. And for those of you who didn't, I can't blame you. You have your families to think of. Your children, your spouses—even some of your parents."

Hakeem stepped to the center of the room; he looked briefly at the people at the three tables of union organizers. "This," he promised, "is the beginning. They got a few of us—three, to be exact—scared off. But if we keep at it, work hard, and continue to point out the facts, we will get the union in at some point down the road—and soon!"

Hakeem and Keisha embraced, while the rest of the organizers applauded.

Slowly, Craig Balboni rose, walked to the center of the floor at the rear of the bar, and motioned for quiet. "As you know, work is beginning on the new infectious disease wing at the Beach City Medical Center. Who's building it? *My guys.*" His eyes wandered over all of the faces— faces that had been so full of hope so recently, and were now very nearly devoid of hope.

"I so admire what you're doing." He tapped his chest, over his heart. "And so do my people. We've been right here with you, all the way. We've been rooting for you, and when we saw what the hospital's union busters did—well, we decided to see what *we* could do." He paused, looked at Hakeem and Keisha. "So, I asked my guys, and ladies—we have ladies too," he chuckled, "to consider lending our support to your cause, and they want to do it. They voted to do it."

Hakeem looked confused. "What does that mean?"

"What it means is that my guys—the union that is building the new infectious disease wing of the hospital—will strike in solidarity with you people."

"Won't they bring in scabs?" Keisha asked.

Balboni smiled. "They might try. But we'll…convince the scabs that it is not in their interest to cross our picket line and take on our work. But honestly, I already have word that it won't get that far. Lonnie McQuade, our chief negotiator, has already had some preliminary talks with BCMC management, and I can't promise anything, but it looks good. There's a lot of momentum behind this new infectious disease facility—especially with staff shortages, with COVID, with the gala canceled and with the bad press the hospital's getting about these fatalities." He smiled. "I think there's a pretty good chance you're going to get your union."

A moment of stunned silence was followed by raucous cheering and applause that went on for a long time. As the applause died, Hakeem approached a thin man who was sitting at a nearby table and bent to speak to him; the man had removed his glasses and was wiping the tears from his eyes with a closed fist.

"Wilbur. A bunch of us have been talking and we're hoping you'd consider being our union rep."

Wilbur blinked. "What, me?"

Hakeem nodded. "You'd have to be elected, but we need someone who's honest, knows the truth when he or she sees it, and has a good heart."

"You sure you got the right guy?"

"Damn sure."

Wilbur managed a hint of a smile. "Best to answer without cussin'."

Hakeem laughed. "Yes, Wilbur. We've got the right guy."

• • •

The Long Island Hotel and Convention Center was a sprawling complex comprising three buildings—an atrium, a hotel, and a convention hall. The complex was in the center of an enormous series of connected parking lots several miles off the highway exit.

Missy had already called Mallard and informed him of their location as Dora parked in a fire lane and jumped out of the car, and began running toward the main entrance, with Missy not far behind. "Convention hall," Dora called back toward Missy.

She ran right past an easel that held a placard with the conference logo, past sign-up and sign-in tables and security personnel stationed there. "Excuse me!" a woman called after them, and several uniformed security guards shouted "Hey!" and "Stop!" and chased after the two women.

Inside the cavernous hall were row upon row of exhibit booths, each representing a company that offered some science-related product or service. The rows were filled with crowds of attendees, many of whom wore N95 masks, though the state mask restrictions had been lifted only days earlier. As they passed each booth, its representatives smiled and asked if they would like to hear about whatever it was they were selling.

Dora and Missy ignored them, rushing up one aisle and hurrying down the next, dodging visitors and patrons, waving away food samples, and leaving the security guards behind. Dora stopped at the bottom of the return aisle. "We're in the wrong building. They've gotta be the atrium."

They ran back out of the building and into the atrium, which was indeed configured as a conventional auditorium with a stage, audience seating, and lobby.

"Ticket?" a woman wearing blue glasses and an official-looking sticker asked.

"We're part of a police investigation."

A tall, blond man in a blue shirt with a patch identifying him as another member of convention center security, stepped forward. "Identification, please."

Missy handed him a business card. "We're private investigators, working with police, who will be here any minute."

"I need to see a badge," the man insisted.

"Is Dr. Babu speaking?" Dora asked, and the man glanced at her, then back at Missy. "I think so, yes," he said, whereupon Dora pushed past him and into a hallway that ran alongside the auditorium and, presumably, the stage. The security man chased after Dora and Missy took the opportunity to walk up the side aisle within the auditorium, searching for Spontana.

Meanwhile, Dora had found a door marked "Stage Door." Inside was a dark, cramped area that led to the wings of the stage. Wood and canvas sets from other events were stacked against a wall, next to a fire extinguisher, a long metal pole, and an open tool box.

"And who are you?" asked a woman in a uniform.

Dora handed her a card. "I'm working with security and the police. There's an active security threat. We need to get Dr. Babu out of here."

The woman took a walkie-talkie from her belt and spoke quietly into it. "Please come with me," she said, and stepped through the door that Dora entered and back into the hallway. As she held the door for Dora, the woman was jarred sideways as a dark shape hurtled past her and into the backstage area.

"Spontana," Dora called, in a loud whisper.

The man whirled. It was indeed Clay Spontana, though he had shaved his mustache and beard. His eyes were a bottomless black. He did not look angry, only calm and focused.

"Sir!" the security woman protested.

"Apologies," he said, his voice reasonable and friendly. He ignored Dora and focused on the woman in the security uniform. "I'm the next speaker. I'm waiting to go on. I'm…just a little nervous."

The security woman nodded, smiled, and stepped away from the door and into the hallway. The last Dora saw of her, she was bringing her walkie-talkie to her ear.

Dora dropped back into the shadows; she could see Spontana, who had stepped from the lit hallway into the darkened offstage area.

Dora knew that she had to get to him while Babu was still onstage speaking, which was probably the safest place for the scientist at the moment.

"Dr. Spontana," she whispered, loud enough for him to hear.

Spontana was at the side of the stage now, edging toward Babu, who was speaking and using a clicker to advance a PowerPoint presentation.

Dora crept silently up behind him.

"Spontana!" Her whisper was loud now, and he whipped around, and she could see the glass of the syringe in his hand refracting the light from the stage lights. Instantly he lunged toward her, with the syringe arcing toward her neck.

Dora snapped a block to his forearm, hoping to dislodge the syringe, but he somehow managed to hold onto it.

"You're not getting in my way," Spontana growled. "It's his time."

"You're gonna waste Babu's shot on me?" Dora tried to match Spontana's calm tone.

"You think I don't have backups? I have *backups* of backups!"

He jabbed suddenly forward with unbelievable speed, and Dora felt the scrape of the needle against the skin just below her jaw. She prayed he had not had a chance to push its plunger.

Spontana's motion continued to carry him forward so that Dora was able to trap his elbow between her arm and her body and twist, snapping his arm at the elbow. The syringe skittered to the floor.

Babu was still on stage, speaking. He glanced in their direction, but Dora was pretty sure that the light onstage was brighter than that in the wings, so that he could probably not see clearly enough to understand what was going on.

Spontana was lying on his side on the ground, moaning and clutching his arm. He was struggling to crawl to where the syringe lay. As he extended his body, Dora could see he wore some sort of leather utility belt with thin, half-open pockets that held two more syringes.

"You piece of garbage." Dora spat the words out, stepped to the fallen syringe and, as Spontana reached to his belt for another, jabbed the needle into his thigh and pushed the plunger.

Spontana screamed, and at that moment, the stage door opened and the security woman rushed in, followed by Detective Ganderson and Officers Catherine Trask and her partner, Lieutenant Mitchell Weiss. The latter picked up the spent syringe with a handkerchief he took from his pocket, while Lieutenant Trask put a hand on Dora's shoulder.

"You okay, Ellison?"

Dora, who was shuddering with adrenaline, managed to nod.

Detective Ganderson ignored Dora and roughly dragged Spontana to his feet, pulled his arms behind him and slapped cuffs on his wrists.

"You have the right to remain silent," Ganderson began.

"She stuck me! That woman infected me with flesh-eating disease! She's the one you need to arrest!"

"Save it, asshole," Ganderson snarled. "Anything you say can and will be used against you in a court of law. You have a right to an attorney. If you cannot afford an attorney, one will be appointed for you. Now, come on." As he was about to drag Spontana from the room, he glanced at Dora, his face expressionless.

"You're welcome," Dora said.

"Foolish." Ganderson shook his head. "I'll talk to you later."

"Hey Ganderson…" Dora looked back at him. "Don't you have another suit?"

## Epilogue

Once they had finished giving their statements to the two detectives at the police station and speaking with Dr. Babu, who was doing the same, the two investigators returned to Missy's apartment and sat cross-legged, and facing one another on Missy's living room floor.

Each of their dogs was in the other owner's lap. Freedom was with Missy and Comfort with Dora. Both dogs' eyes were slowly closing as the women gently stroked their heads. A half-full bottle of Cabernet Sauvignon stood on the floor between them. Another bottle—empty—was a few feet away.

Dora's phone rang. She glanced at it, then put it on speaker. She mouthed "C3" to Missy. "Hey," she said into the phone.

"You need to come down here ASAP," the young man said.

"What? Where?"

"The hospital. Sarah's here. There's a problem with the baby, and she wants to see you." The call ended.

Dora looked at Missy. "Come on!"

Missy shook her head. "We can't drive."

"Are you kidding?" Dora threw her coat on.

"No," Missy insisted. "You're not driving and neither am I. Use the app."

Within fifteen minutes they were able to book a ride to the hospital with a ride-sharing app. When they arrived, they found C3 in the lobby with his father and Christine.

As they approached, Charlie rushed to Dora and enveloped her in a hug. "Olivia's going to be okay. My granddaughter's going to be okay!"

C3 smiled. "Sarah, too."

Missy took a deep breath. "Oh, thank God."

"You need to go in," C3 said to Dora. "While the baby was in danger, she kept saying she needed to see you."

"Me?" Dora was confused. "But why?"

"She said you're the bravest woman she knows."

. . .

Sarah was sitting up in the bed that was closer to the door. A curtain was drawn down the center of the room, blocking the other side from view. C3 led Dora and Missy to Sarah's bedside, then slipped from the room. His father and Christine had remained in the lobby.

Sarah gave a weak smile. "I'm so glad you came. I kept thinking of you while this was happening, while I wasn't sure whether Olivia—" She drew a quick gasp, stifling a sob. "But she's okay." She smiled. "False alarm."

"We're so glad," said Dora.

"So they caught the guy. C was telling me—*you* caught the guy."

Dora shrugged. "Team effort." She nodded toward Missy. "She figured it out."

"Traxle is going to be okay, we're told," Missy explained. "Apparently she was brought to the hospital in time."

"And we had a chance to talk to Dr. Babu at the police station," Dora continued. "He told us that some years ago, Spontana, who even now Babu says is brilliant if narcissistic, came up with an idea for a process for quickly pinpointing certain pathogens. Something to do with dyes and radiation. Ramesh hired him about that time and enabled him to finalize his research using Ramesh's facility. The credit for the process was shared, but since it was Ramesh's lab, he got primary credit, and the process was named for him. Which apparently drove Spontana over the edge. In a weird twist, after the fact, Babu is asking that the process be renamed for Spontana, though obviously he's heading for a long stay in prison."

"Wow," said Sarah. "Is it true you infected Spontana with a flesh-eating bacteria?"

Dora shook her head. "Absolutely not."

"So how did—" Sarah began.

"Clay stole the pathogens from the BSL-4 training lab," Missy explained, "and possibly collected some from the wild. He then enhanced Babu's lab until it was at a BSL-2+ level and served his needs."

Sarah nodded, then asked, "How are the dogs?"

"They're like a vaudeville act," Missy reported. "Freedom's terrified of Comfort, who's like a tiny general. Except when we're outside, when Freedom is out there aggressively protecting us all."

Sarah smiled beatifically. "Like her owner."

Dora laughed.

"But in the apartment—either of our apartments—Comfort runs around, barking, anytime he hears a noise outside. One of the neighbors comes home from a late night out, slams the car door, and Comfort will go tearing around the place barking like crazy."

"What about you two?" Sarah asked. "Rumor has it you might be tying the knot."

Missy looked surprised. "Rumor?"

Sarah shrugged. "A little bird."

Missy turned to Dora. "Oh, really." Then she looked at Sarah. "We'll get back to you on that. 'K?"

"'K."

"And you?" Dora said, wanting to change the subject. "Will you and C be getting married before Olivia's born?"

"Who knows? I'm just trying to make sure he sticks around. Ooh, got something to show you." Sarah reached for an iPad that was on her tray, tapped the screen a few times, and held it up for her guests to see. "Our new ad for 'Real Women'!"

Dora looked embarrassed. Missy draped an arm around her shoulder. "You look wonderful. A true spokesmodel for women of every shape and size."

"You know who did the artwork at Charlie's agency? Vanessa!"

"She did a great job," Missy breathed, then she gently elbowed Dora. "Hey, supermodel."

Dora winced. "Shut the fuck up," then touched the blanket covering Sarah's thigh. "We'll let you get some rest now." Sarah nodded.

C3 had come into the room, gone around to the other side of the bed, and sat down in a chair there. He took Sarah's hand, looking wrung out and relieved.

Dora and Missy went to the lobby, hugged Charlie and Christine, and walked to Dora's car.

"Dor," Missy said. "I think we need to wait."

Dora glanced at her, but didn't answer.

"To get married, I mean."

"I know what you meant."

Missy went on, "I think we need to give us time."

"Then that's what we'll do." Dora didn't look at her as she got into the car. Her phone rang. "Hello? Thank you. Yes, of course." She listened for a long moment, then ended the call, put away her phone and buckled her seat belt. "That was Geller. He congratulates us, and has paychecks waiting—or, Thelma has them, actually."

"Sounded like more than that."

"He received a call from a man who claims his sister was murdered—murdered and mutilated. The man wants to hire us. Adam sent him an email with our fees and we're a go, if we want it."

"Has he called the police?"

"He has. But he wants to be able to stay on top of the investigation—hence his call to Adam. And, apparently, a similar murder was reported just two weeks earlier—another woman—also murdered and mutilated."

"Jesus. Were these near here?"

"Both within a five-mile radius of Beach City."

"Do they know why these women were targeted?"

Dora looked at Missy. "We're going to find out."

CLICK TO READ **Book 4 in David E. Feldman's**
***Dora Ellison Mystery Series: A Biological Storm.***

**THE END**

*Dear Reader: Thanks so much for reading* A Sickening Storm. *I hope you will join my mailing list to learn more about my next books at:*

https://www.davidefeldman.com/books.shtml

*If you enjoyed this book, I would be grateful if you would post a review online.*

*See you again soon!*

*-DF*

Made in the USA
Monee, IL
16 January 2024